MW01129721

'Candid Shots' is a work of fiction. Names, characters, places, and incidents either are the product of the author's imagination or are used fictitiously. Any resemblance to actual persons, living or dead, events, or locales is entirely coincidental. Contains scenes that may not be suitable for an audience under the age of 18.

2014 eBook Original

Copyright © 2014 by Stacia B. Phillips

ISBN 978-1-312-11719-8

Candid Shots
By
Stacia B. Phillips

Prologue

The commotion in the hall caught my attention and I raised my eyes off my computer screen. Dread filled me. My glassed-in office afforded me no privacy. My office door flew open wide and Dylan stepped in rapidly. Deliberately he squared his shoulders, his curly, mid collar length hair flowing and tousled. The sunlight lit up his auburn highlights in his medium brown colored hair. His appearance was commanding. His stare bore holes into my head. I could see his biceps twitch under his linen shirt. His short-sleeved button down was rolled over the bulging biceps. I remember why now; his shirts were too tight on his upper arms, he had the potential to rip the seams if he didn't roll them up. His muscular chest heaved under his shirt. His waistline was trim and I knew that under that button down shirt sat a washboard abdomen. He narrowed his piercing blue eyes. He was obviously trying to regain his composure, or he'd just run a marathon.

Although I knew why he was really here.

I stood up, instinctively guarding my territory, and crossed my arms across my waist protectively. Trying to give the illusion, I was in control. I walked to the front of my desk to stop his pursuit. I lifted my head and looked him squarely in the eyes, leaned back on the desk front and tried my best to look confident and unruffled. Ashley stepped in right behind Dylan stumbling and stammering.

"I tried, Stacia, he made it past security and up the back stairs before we could stop him. Security's on their way."

As calmly as I could, I said, "Thank You Ashley, security won't be necessary." I waved my hand dismissively. She stood stoically in the doorway, her protective nature was endearing.

"I'll be fine, just make sure security knows to stop running so no one needs CPR." I feigned a smile, my feeble attempt at humor failing miserably. The crack in my voice gave away my rising fear and panic. Ashley's eyes never left mine, as she slowly backed out and closed the door. The click resonated across the room and hit me in my core. I sucked in a huge breath, and tried to hold it. I was shaking. I needed to regain my control.

I could see security personnel flying out of the stairwell door. The look on their faces was like watching a Laurel and Hardy comedy. Eyes darting wildly, heads turning in all directions. Somehow, I knew they never would have stopped him even if they had seen him. I just had not figured his visit would happen so soon after the article appeared in the paper. I could feel my heartbeat in my ears. My face was hot and flushed. My breathing was heavy and rapid; I was prepared for a fight.

"Why didn't you tell me? I would never have let you drive me off if I had known."
He seethed. His voice hissed through his teeth.

"You didn't want to know!" I retorted, "You believed him, I get that, you made your choices, mine were made for me."

Adrenaline surged through my veins. I couldn't peel my eyes off him. My heart beat furiously against my chest and could be seen through my silk shirt. My breathing came in small shallow bursts. And I strained to swallow the lump in my throat.

"I never meant to hurt you." he slowly spit from his mouth. A small muscle on his jaw jumped sideways. His eyes narrowed, and he looked at me through small slits. His anger was visceral and the tension in the air felt as heavy and wet as a London fog.

I gasped for air, my breaths never quite deep enough to keep me from getting dizzy and lightheaded. I stood in front of my desk beginning to feel woozy. I grabbed at the edge of my desk, and looked for better footing before my knees buckled underneath me. My fear glued me in place. I had never seen Dylan this mad before. I had seen a rainbow of personalities, but this type of anger and hurt was deep. It cut me to my core.

Dan and Gary from security waited right outside my glass enclosure shooting pensive looks through the windows. Pacing, waiting for the clue they needed to break down the door and forcibly remove Dylan from my office. Dan held his radio in one hand and a cell phone in the other. Gary's eyes never left me. He watched my every move. The waiting game had begun. Dylan's chest rose and fell rapidly.

"You lied to me!" His shouting brought frightened faces to my glassed enclosure. "Tell me something, how did you think this was going to end? Did you think I'd just walk away? Did you think work was my only goal? Did you need to tear me apart in the process? When did you remember? Because it would kill me to know that you never forgot." A defeated look ran across his face and his eyes looked watery, some of the anger was dissipating but was still a present undercurrent. "Stacia, honey, I never thought I'd fall head over heels, crazy in love with you. Please. I will love you until I take my last breath, until the day God takes me off this earth. I will *never* leave you. *Please*, talk to me; tell me you feel the same. Tell me you love me." I tried to take a deep breath. My knuckles

were blanched white and throbbing under my grasp. I tried to regain my composure.

"No, Dylan, I can't." My response croaked from my throat, my eyes filled with tears, but I refused to let them slide down my face. I shook from my unshed tears. I squared my shoulders, looked through my window, and nodded to Gary. My door opened. Dylan left willingly, but he didn't stop staring at me. Begging me to reconsider with his eyes. The door closed and when the lock clicked; I jumped, feeling I had made the biggest mistake of my life. I never forgot, I will always remember.

Chapter 1

I loved my job. I could hide behind my camera and snap as many pictures as I wanted. I could ask you to pose or just take candid shots anywhere, anytime, of anyone. But, I was hired to shoot baseball games. It's the first place I felt comfortable since leaving home. I would stay here forever.

Mike, my boss, loved that I took the late night ballgames. I loved how night shadows played against the lighted ball diamonds, bathing the players with mist and elongated body shadows. My new digital camera was optimal. I could snap six hundred pictures before changing discs and my telephoto lens was twenty times stronger than my old Canon thirty-five millimeter film camera. Mike had given me the digital to use when the baseball farm league needed magazine and newspaper coverage. I played with the new camera and fell in love with its weight, size and capabilities.

Hiding behind the camera made me feel brave and brash. I could creep up on an unsuspecting family moment from the third baseline, shooting into the stands from the first baseline One hundred twenty seven feet, three inches of total personal intrusion. I could stop cleats in mid step. Stop dirt mid-flight and stop an entire professional baseball team with just a camera and a telephoto lens.

I joined Mike Anderson on our community television station a couple years after I graduated from two years of telecommunications in our local junior college, and after two more years floating from job to job, I landed here. Mike ran the small community paper from inside the local television station. The trials and perks of small town news; one man ran it all with the help of a small staff. All cross-trained to make deadlines and air times.

Mike was an overweight forty some year old burly man with a round belly that he tried to contain with a belt. The belt never did anything to hold back the bulge, which always lumbered over the belt buckle obscuring it. He had a white beard and long mustache peppered with grey. His burly disposition and crass talk was considered by most to be crude. I knew his callused remarks and cat calls were really terms of endearment. He loved fiercely and was always quick with advice. I'd seen him verbally tear apart a guest after the televised morning show when they had intentionally embarrassed our host on live television. He vehemently defended our profession and I was pretty sure if a bar fight ever broke out in the television station, he'd be right in the middle of it. He guided us, advised us and guarded us like a pit bull. Infractions to policy were met with firm guidance and occasionally verbal battering. Rarely did he ever lose his temper, but when it did happen, you could see the pit bull emerge. Many times, I was glad I was not on the receiving end of his verbal tirades. This overprotective persona was probably one of the reasons his past relationships failed, and he was still single. He claimed it was due to being married to the station. And that was a true fact.

My major in communications was sports related. I had spent a lot of time outside prior to getting this job. I thought I'd be happy behind a TV camera. Being cross trained to work the TV station, I was now confined in a small room with no windows. The room was dark, all I could do was look through a lens and listen through headsets. The actors were only slightly entertaining and I had a hard time focusing my attention on them when all I really wanted was to be outside. I would lose track of the job. I would miss clicking on and off camera, synching mics, and cutting action. I was miserable. I missed the movement, the action of being outside. I was eternally distracted. Mike seemed to understand my discontent. One day he decided we should broadcast the weather report from outside the studio. A late season snow storm was slowly shutting down the city. I was in charge of the shoulder camera. I was giddy. I floated around the station for days following the broadcast. My excitement was contagious. I encouraged other employees to step up and out. Challenged some of them to do something out of the ordinary, make waves, and shake the place up. Not all ideas were met with enthusiasm from Mike, but he listened to all of them. His inexhaustible pit bull persona intact.

"Hey trouble!" Mike called to me one day as I passed in front of his office, "I'm sending you out!"

"Out?" I called back. I stopped dead in my tracks and back stepped to his door.

"Yep. Out." His eyes never left his computer screen.

"YES!" I yelled and pumped my fist in the air and ran off whooping down the empty hall. Mike just kept his eyes down, shook his head, and snorted.

I covered my first baseball game that day, with a heavy VHS camera and one hundred twenty five feet of cable I drug behind myself and kept stumbling over for two hours. It was just a local high school game, but I flew higher than any other 'news' reporter for weeks. I would saunter past Mike's door hoping he'd throw me another morsel to cover.

"Oh, darling," he called to me one afternoon, "how are you at stills?"

I stopped and leaned into his door. "Stills?"

"Uh Huh, still pictures."

"Give me a camera, where am I going?" I shot back with enthusiasm invading every syllable.

"Hold on little lady, I asked if you shot stills."

9

"No, but I'm not a slow learner Mike, show me what you want." Mike regarded me skeptically. I stepped in and slid into the oversized leather chair in front of his desk. I reached for the thirty-five millimeter camera perched on the corner of his scarred, abused wooden desk. He leaned back in his chair, steepled his hands, and rubbed his chin with his fingers. His elbows rested on the wooden arms and he swiveled side to side in his chair.

I turned the camera over in my hands feeling its weight, studying the dials and turning the focus with my left hand. I put my eye to the camera lens and said," Smile Mike." His position and facial expression never changed. The flash lit up the room and Mike waited for me to stop admiring the camera.

"You done sweetheart?"
I regarded him with a sideways glance, put the camera back up to my face as he leaned forward to put his elbows on the desk. Amusement flitted across his face. Mike smiled, his eyes crinkled and sparkled. The candid relaxed look on his face was one of my favorite pictures. I framed it. Mike put it proudly on his bookshelf. The camera was mine. God, I loved this job! I took an excessive amount of pictures. I used rolls and rolls of film during the games. All under the ruse of learning the craft of photography.

Mike pulled me into his office one morning. "Have a seat, we need to talk." The sternness in his voice made me shudder. I was afraid I was about to be on the receiving end of a verbal pit bull mulling. Mike demanded the film camera. He had a stern look on his face and with his outstretched hand snatched the camera from my hand. I was crushed.

I sunk broken hearted into the leather chair. I stared wide eyed at Mike, sure my freedom of expression was being squashed, and my time behind a camera was coming to an end.

"I know you liked the paper assignment, but I really can't afford the excessive amount of film and processing we are incurring with you. You're done with this." Mike pointed absently at the camera, as it lay abandoned on his desk. I barely resisted grabbing the camera off his desk and running down the hall to rescue my freedom and the camera. He leaned back in his chair and crossed one leg over the other, scooped up a box, and plopped it in the table.

"You need to start using this."

Inside the box was a Canon EOS SLR digital camera, 85mmf/1.8standard lens, a Canon EF 75-300 mm telephoto lens, three empty digital discs and a computer cable. I squealed with delight. I plunked the batteries in and turned it on, tuning out all of Mike's advice and warnings.

"Don't break the damn thing, it was expensive. Although it will probably be cheaper for the station to have you using the new camera." He paused to scrutinize me. "Good God girl, with all the film you used, this has got to be cheaper." Mike laughed and snorted at my obvious delight.

"Go on, get outta here! Learn to use that thing, I'm gonna have you covering ballgames this summer!"

As I tore out of his office with my new toy, I heard him laughing loudly from his office. In my mind, I could imagine him swiveling back and forth in his chair. Smiling. I knew I'd *never* leave this job.

Chapter 2

I caught on quickly. Within two months, true to his word, Mike had me shooting local high school baseball games and football Spring games. I loved the unexpected action shots. Dirt flying, pinched faces, highflying grabs, and breeze blown hair shots that screamed off the prints. Mike liked to brag to his cronies he taught me everything I knew. He was proud. He started treating me more like one of his kids than an employee. Very fatherly, and protective. One reason I would never think to leave this job, he treated me like family. And I missed family more than anything.

The local minor's baseball team had played their first games out of town, and were coming home for a four game stretch. I covered the Ace's third home game. Mike sent me to shoot some action shots for the next day's paper.

"Watch yourself out there." he warned. "Don't be falling for any of those pretty boy's antics, hear me? You don't want to get involved with one of them. They're leavers, not lovers." I listened to him, but never took the information to heart. I was working, there was no time for any of that nonsense.

If I had any luck, if Dylan got called back up, some of the shots I took that day would be picked up by the Associated Press. It would be good publicity for our small town paper. And I could get credit and name recognition for any picture they used. But someone on the team needed to make it big.

It was a beautiful early spring afternoon. The sun was out, but the wind was still brisk with winters melting snow. I wore my favorite jeans, black heeled boots, and a white vee necked tee shirt with a medium weight jogging jacket. If the sun showed promise, I could shed the jacket and have more free movement of my arms. I liked to get at field level and shoot pictures towards the sky that highlighted the player's physical attributes. It made the players look like they could fly. I studied the internet and other photographers to educate myself about taking the best pictures possible.

I spent a lot of time behind the lens taking pictures, and even more time editing the load of pictures I'd taken. Many times, I'd been caught on the baseline looking through last innings pictures eliminating ones and editing others. Between the innings, I'd sneak to the edge of the dugout and snap candid shots of the team. I quickly became associated with the players. I learned their moods and had pictures of them at their best and worst. I saw them frustrated, angry, cheerful, shouting, backslapping and celebrating. These shots were my favorites. The player's personalities showed through. I could see them as something other than worship material.

They started to notice me too. They saw me at most of their games and since I had a press pass, I was very visible, even if I did have a camera to my face most times.

Sometimes I was not always the most popular person near the dugout. I was an intruder. I captured their good and bad times. I put some of the players on edge. I let the curses and conversations aimed at me roll off my back for the most part. I refused to engage them, ignoring them was my best defense. I stayed behind my camera, where I could peek at them from corner of their lives. I was an annoyance to be dealt with, one who captured some of their most private moments, some moments painful and raw.

The pitcher, Dylan Riley was down on the farm team rehabbing from a torn rotator cuff. When you pitch 162 games in a season, you wear out your arm. He was a good looking, tall man with bouncy, brown hair and glimmering auburn highlights. He had large square shoulders and amazing strength. Those square shoulders led to a chiseled chest and down to a slender waistline. When he returned to the dugout, he'd nod his head and feign a smile. Watching him on the field, I didn't think he'd be down in the minors too long. He spent a lot of his practice time working on his curve ball. Obviously, he was spending his time down here building his strength and perfecting his game.

The catcher, Glen Mather, was a squatty guy who had a loud deep bounding voice. He'd call the count out after the umpire, just to be irritating to the batter. When he returned to the dugout, he was always quick with a smile, and a "Hello." I liked him. He was always dirty and complained about his knees, but he was smart and had a quick arm. He was good at throwing out the second base runners from his kneeling position behind the batters.

The shortstop, Jon Chattham, was tall and lanky, a young fellow who thought he deserved to be moved back to the majors. I believed the only reason he was down on the farm league was his attitude. He'd tear apart his own team members without hesitation. He was quick to anger, and snapped frequently. He was rude to me when he returned to the dugout and I avoided him as much as possible. He'd curse under his breath and used a variety of derogatory nicknames when he addressed me and other players. He had a nasty disposition, and it carried over into his game.

Chris Carpenter, the centerfielder was a nice man. He'd wink and smile when he came in from an inning. He had a childlike attitude and was always playful. I knew he was seeing someone, and she was beautiful. A tall, leggy blonde named Crystal.

The left handed first baseman, Dan Weathers always wore a smile. His vertical leap was at least two and one half feet, an impressive height for a baseball player. He'd whoop and holler with every play and was always good for a show with a lay out, or a spectacularly snagged ball.
He was fun to photograph.

There were other team members like Dale Christiansen. He was the calculating member of the team. Always ready with a statistic to recite. He befriended Brian Robinson, the impressionable high school superstar who needed time to develop a team player mentality. Rob Phillips was the left handed wonder boy. Always quick on his feet and a player you could place anywhere on the field and he'd perform, just not consistently.

I loved the team. I followed their lives in pictures. I wanted to get to know them better. I liked to capture the team's interactions; my camera afforded me the privilege. Some had wives, and families. After some of the games, I captured some of their intimate moments. Wives with their arms wrapped tightly around their husbands waists. Kids being carried on uniformed, dusty shoulders. Girlfriends and acquaintances talking and watching the team until they disappeared into the locker room.

After most games, a group of people gathered outside the locker room waiting for a glimpse of their favorite players. I snapped pictures from a distance. Some shots were intimate and touching. Some were frenzied fan pictures, outstretched hands and endearing looks. Some people thrust pens and paper at their favorite players. Some players smiled, others frowned. Some did their best to ignore their adoring fans. Some like Dylan slipped out the back door, avoiding all fan contact. I wanted to spy on him. Where did he go after the games, whom did he hang out with? What were his secrets?

Chapter 3

Dylan was quietly reserved. I willed him to notice me. I watched him during the games and admired his skill as a pitcher, and admired his beautiful sexual form. I would watch his muscles ripple and wondered how they would feel moving under my hands, or how they would feel holding me flat to the mattress right before he made me scream in ecstasy. After every inning, I would take my eye off the lens when he started back to the dugout praying for acknowledgement. His casual, shy smile and curt nods left a lot to my imagination. But, I continued smiling back. Many times his eyes never met mine. I wanted to get to know him, but his disinterest was obvious. With only a few verbal interactions between us, I could let my mind take me anywhere I wanted with him. I saw us holding hands, walking together on a beach, getting naked, and had images of having his hands roam all over me. Wild imaginings for someone who hadn't even had a conversation with the object of her obsession. My erotic nightly musings only fueled my desires.

What would it take to entice Dylan? I stared into the bathroom mirror one morning. A tall, thin, strawberry blonde looked back. My huge dark brown eyes were wide and round. My father often called them cows' eyes due to their size and the darkness they reflected. High cheekbones and a straight-sloped nose with slightly flared nostrils led to a small cleft centered on my upper lip. Dimples puckered my cheeks when I smiled. I had inherited the best of my English mother, and Cherokee-English father. I was lightly tanned, just kissed by the sun. However, tanning usually led to sunburns, and a vicious cycle of burning and peeling, a gift of my mother's English genetics. A few freckles peppered my nose and shoulders, so when sun did reach those areas, more freckles would be guaranteed.

But, my parents would never know what a striking girl I had grown into. Their lives were cut short in their forties with a collision on a desolate rural road involving farm machinery and an ill placed yield sign. I had sought comfort with my then fiancée, Ryan, who turned into a domineering jerk when the insurance money was finally paid. His control and abusiveness was more than I could handle. And the night he blackened both my eyes and battered my body, I knew I needed out. So I moved half way across the country. I abandoned all my stuff and the comfort I had there, and just left. I missed my parents, but I sure didn't need another one half their age with a strong backhand, and demeaning attitude. I was stronger now, but very lonely. Even though I could financially support myself, I got into relationships with men that always seemed to fail. I gravitated to men with aggressive tendencies. Some found out about the insurance money and tried to use our relationship to get to it. I had endured physical and emotional abuse all because I didn't know what I wanted. I was a failure. I needed to get to know myself. Be in control of just me. As long as I held my tongue and kept myself in check, I could survive a roll in the hay. And right then I wanted to spend time with Dylan. So I thought.

I wondered exactly what it would take to turn Dylan's head. And could he possibly like me? I hadn't really succeeded in any relationship with men. I was leery. I thought I could handle casual sex. I didn't have to get in too emotionally deep. I could keep it superficial. And after my time with Ryan, I wasn't sure if I was over the physically abusive encounters we had had. But, I wanted to take a chance with Dylan.

I started dressing a little more provocatively. On hot days, I wore halter tops, shorts, and strappy sandals. I unbuttoned my shirts a little more and wore tight tank tops that showed off my

18

curves. I started wearing a little more makeup, a deed that did not go unnoticed by my boss, Mike.

"What's up with you baby doll?" he asked one afternoon when I returned to download the pictures to the work computer. His hand waved the air. "What's with the get up?" He leaned back in his chair and eyed me suspiciously. "Don't get attached ladybug, you know they don't stay around long!" he warned. He snickered and shook his head as I walked past his door. I rolled my eyes, and blushed. I knew I had been caught in my efforts to seduce Dylan. It would take an act of God to make Dylan notice me. For all my efforts the only effect I saw I had was to Jon. He was less of an ass to me at the games, but not much.

Then it finally happened. While I was behind the fence one afternoon, with my head buried in the review lens, I heard a crack, and a roar from the crowd. I looked up just quick enough for a foul ball to skim the fence, graze my hand, ricochet off the camera and smacked me in the chin. The blow knocked me on my butt, the camera skidded to a stop inches from my fingers. The Aces dugout emptied. Jon laughed, but stared dumbstruck, making little attempt to hide his humor. Chris' mouth was agape and his eyes were wide in disbelief. Others gathered at the fence to check out the damage. Dylan quickly scaled the fence and helped me up, scooped up the digital camera and handed it back to me. He looked at my chin, and shook his head.

"You Ok?" My face flushed a bright crimson color with embarrassment, and I dropped my eyes. "You can blame that one on Rob, foul tipped it right at you." he stated, as an usher rushed up to me with a baggie of ice. I waved off the usher, wiped off my pants, and quickly started to check out Mike's camera.

"I'm fine, Thanks." was all I could manage. I had waited forever to have Dylan notice me, and all I say is, *I'm fine, thanks?* I couldn't even look at him. I was too humiliated at being caught off guard with my face in the camera lens. My eyes concentrated on the camera. Dylan stared at me for a few seconds. Then he snorted and smiled; a genuine smile that lit up his eyes. I thought I heard him mumble the word, "Damn." before he looked away. I wished I could have caught that smile. That was the Dylan I wanted to get to know. The one who let his guard down.

After the game, Rob came to the fence to apologize and check out my chin. The little mishap brought out the human side of some of the players. Jon just looked away and smiled. Dylan came up after all the other players had gone, as I reviewed pictures.

"Are you really alright?" he asked as he skimmed his eyes over my developing bruise.

"I'm fine." I nodded.

"You took a pretty good hit, should have taken the ice." Dylan said as he pointed with the edge of his glove at my face. He winked, smiled and walked towards the locker room, banging the dirt off his glove on his leg as he walked. He smiled at me again over his shoulder and continued on his way. I melted. A quarter of the way through the season and I had finally gotten his attention. Instead of an act of God, it took an act of Rob.

Chapter 4

Throughout the rest of the next month's home games, Dylan and I shared niceties at the fence. We talked at the baseline after the game, and sometimes even during the game. He smiled more and small talk evolved to some small conversations.

"You had a good game." I started one day.

"Thanks, I need to get better control. I want to move back up."

"You will, I can see improvement already."

"Thanks, that's nice coming from somebody who really doesn't know the game!" he scoffed.

"I know enough. I pay attention." I stopped walking, making him halt. I looked at him with one eye closed against the setting sun, and cocked my head. "I know that when Rob drops his right shoulder he's shooting for the fence. I know when Dan yells from the dugout during Chris' time at bat, he listens. And Dan's .311 average is the highest he's ever achieved. I know that Brian hangs on every word Dale says above the word of any coach; not good for a new recruit. I know, if Glen drops his left knee to the ground before a pitch, you throw to the outside attempting a pitch out. That Jon's a hot head, but dedicated to the game to a fault. I know you're totally unhappy. I know you want out of this league, you miss the majors. And if I ever play a game of baseball, I'd better run really fast on a dropped third strike, because Glen *will* throw me out!"

His eyebrows lifted. Mirth painted his face. "What? Glen drops down on one knee on my pitch out? I need to talk to him about that! He'll never make a play throwing from one knee!

And, if you're batting, I'm looking for a double play and an easy out!" Dylan laughed looking at me incredulously. "Guess you were paying attention, freakishly close attention." The last part of his sentence was barely audible more whispered to himself.

I started walking again, digging my shoe toe in the dirt. My head still cocked to the side, my hands clasped behind my back. "So, am I right?"

"Pretty darn close to perfect."

"So, what was I wrong on?" I asked the leading question to see if he'd take my bait about wanting to leave. I crossed my arms across my chest and jutted my chin in defiance.

"I'm not *totally* unhappy." He snickered and walked away. I smiled even if I had found out he would leave me and break my heart if the opportunity presented itself. So much for just casual sex. I was beginning to really like this guy.

I laughed out loud at his playfulness, but I wanted so much more than our fence talks. I wanted him, even if it would be such a short period of time. But could I let him go without getting hurt? I was falling for the quiet guy with the beautiful arms. I had dreams of him with me in my bed. Nights fraught with sweaty nakedness and blinding orgasms. In my dreams, I had what I wanted, in real life I knew he'd never be able to give it; his time here was temporary just as Mike warned, 'they're leavers not lovers'.

I began walking with him towards the locker room after the games, never crossing the imaginary threshold I set for myself. I never followed as far as the wives and families, but I could dream about being one of them. Someone who held hands after the games and went home with him at night to a soft bed and quiet whisperings. But, I didn't want to push this new fledgling relationship. Could I even call this a relationship? It was barely a friendship, just talks at a baseball fence. But I secretly wished for *so* much more, I could really like this man if I knew more about *him*. He was so closed off.

"So, what do you do in the off season? " I casually asked him one day.

"I have a side job in another town. Then I head to Florida in January 'cuz practice starts."

"Do you have family close to here?" I took smaller steps towards the locker room as we talked. Giving him the time to answer. Dylan paused and looked out over the field.

"Nope, my parents live in Detroit. I don't get there much now. My sister is married and lives in Ohio. Don't see her much either. But I do know they keep up with the team. Dad and I talk on the weekends. He recites my statistics, and keeps me honest." He snickered at the thought of being tamped down by his Dad. "Mom and Dad would come to more games if I were closer." He dropped his gaze and I saw regret and pain in his eyes. "But, until I fix this shoulder, I'll be stuck here." He circled the air with his mitt, indicating exactly where he thought he was imprisoned.

I felt an honest pull on my heart. He had family that loved him. Family he wanted to get back too. Dylan wanted nothing more than to move back up to the majors, go home, and be with his family. He felt trapped here on the farm team. Mike was right; these guys don't hang around long. One season at most, maybe. But it couldn't hurt to try for a relationship, sometimes they lasted longer than what one expected. Could I pursue him without losing my heart, or falling into old relationship patterns?

The team celebrated a two day home game winning streak. I watched with amazement as the team celebrated on the field, and made their way to the locker room. My camera snapped picture after picture of jubilance on the field. It seemed like a good time to insinuate myself into his postgame life, and find out some of his history.

"Where do you go after the games? I asked off handedly.

"Usually home, I ice my arm and get ready for the next game."

"You don't spend any time with anyone?"

"Oh, I go out sometimes. But, no." Dylan wouldn't look at me. He seemed so withdrawn, so introverted. Trapped in his own thoughts. I wanted to know more, I had to find out why he is so distant. So I started spying.

I started to follow team members after the games. I followed Rob and Brian to men's clubs, and used my camera to capture their lives off the field. Dancing and partying with scantily dressed women, and never the same women two days in a row. I followed Glen to night clubs, where he'd meet friends and drink until the bartender would pay a cab to take him home. Dan went out with his girlfriend and their friends after games and I followed them to bowling alleys late at night where the group would giggle, laugh and enjoy each other's company. Dale and his wife, Emily, always went out for pizza with their two little boys and another couple. It was a standing date if the game ended early enough. I followed Jon to a couple shady houses in the seedy part of town, where I wondered what was happening inside. During my after game adventures, I took pictures. I had pictures of drug use, infidelity, spousal abuse, and child endangerment. I had compromising pictures of married and single players. Pictures, that if they fell into the wrong hands would destroy marriages, ruin lives, and end playing careers. Pictures I was not proud of; pictures that I knew I could use to ruin them. I had turned into the worst kind of paparazzi, I liked these guys; what was I doing?

I knew I was wrong, but I kept those pictures to myself, hidden inside a computer file folder with double password protection. Some players knew they were followed, and gave me pictures they waited to see in the tabloids. I never sold the pictures, but some of the players knew I had them; knew I could use them to hurt them if I chose. Just knowing I had the pictures made some players a little edgy. I was not always a popular sight to them as a photographer.

Jon was particularly attentive after he saw my car leaving an apartment complex he had visited after a game. He was with another man, a handsome dark skinned man he picked up at the field after the game. They were only inside the apartment for about thirty minutes, but my curiosity kept my camera trained on the door. They shared a hug and back pat at the apartment door when Jon was leaving, and I took pictures. His attitude towards me changed slightly. He treated me better, tolerated me at the fence and had stopped some his crudeness. It was a strange tense tolerance. Like he was waiting for me to confront him with what I saw the nights I followed him. I never would, and I was actually warming up to him. I thought he might be gay, but I didn't care.

The one person I really wanted to warm up to was Dylan. He would disappear after the games, many times just returning to his house. Occasionally going to a small local bar, Hitter's. Staying such a short period of time, I wondered if he even had time to drink a beer. I didn't see him with many women, and the ones I did see him with acted like relatives or friends. Distant and only friendly touching and gentle banter. I wanted more. I wanted him. I wanted to be the one who cracked him, the one to hear his secrets. I wanted to be the one he spent his time with after the game. Spread eagle underneath him, flattened into the bed bearing his full weight with our bodies sweaty and writhing. Dylan calling my name while he fulfilled my sexual need. Wow, I definitely did not need an active imagination. Alone time during my little surveillances on Dylan and the team after games allowed my ruminations to go into overdrive. My panties were constantly sluiced with juice. I needed to act on my attraction.

Chapter 5

After a Saturday afternoon game win, I walked beside Dylan scuffing my feet in the dirt as we sauntered slowly towards the locker room.

"Where are you headed after tonight's game?" I asked Dylan while he wiped his mitt on his pants, he rubbed and rolled his shoulder in a circle. Obviously, it was bothering him today. My eyes lingered where he rubbed, noticing the size of his bicep, and the movement of his delicious muscles. My hands ached to rub where he just rubbed. Instead, I ran my eyes lazily over his arm and chest. My stomach clenched and my mind wandered to what he'd look like shirtless, naked and me breathless underneath him. Heat flashed through me, and I felt warm all over.

"Had some plans to see a couple guys at Hitter's tonight." Dylan looked at me, smirked and curled his lip up making his eyes sparkle,

"Why? You up for an outing?"

"Maybe." My voice trailed off. My thoughts zeroed in on how he'd look naked. I dropped my eyes so he couldn't see my small smile or my face flush. I tried sneaking a peek at him through my eyelashes. Afraid he could read my thoughts. Dylan tipped his head so he could see my eyes. "You can go with me, it will just be a couple of friends."

My heart skipped and my breath caught in my chest. Our eyes met, humor rimmed his, mine felt like they'd popped out of my head, obscene thoughts filled my mind. I couldn't answer him. Lamely, I nodded.

He turned away completing the distance to the locker room door in record time with a lilt in his step, "OK, see you in the parking lot in thirty minutes." A light inside me started to burn bright. I was making headway. At least he invited me. I hoped I was reading the signs right and he was interested in me. I drove home, changed into a nice skirt and lightweight, sleeveless blouse over a thin camisole. I pulled my hair up leaving small tendrils hanging near my face. Spritzed on some expensive perfume and met Dylan back in the parking lot with time to spare on the clock.

~~ ***~~

Hitter's was a bar frequented by baseball players and sports enthusiasts alike. The patrons were respectful, they let the players unwind and watch the sports televisions and for the most part kept the conversations light and noninvasive.

I followed Dylan into the bar, lurking two steps behind him, my eyes trained on the floor. He reached back and quickly grabbed my hand. I was so shocked, I gasped. Heat flooded my arm and went straight to my groin. He gave my hand a gentle reassuring squeeze, and winked at me over his shoulder. I relaxed a little, but refused to let my guard down. I kept my eyes downcast, staring at our entwined hands. I liked this feeling. I followed Dylan into the dimly light bar. Once inside, my eyes adjusted to the yellow haze and pool table lighting. I looked around quickly assessing the clientele. I exhaled loudly, not realizing I was holding my breath. Dylan's eyes met mine and concern crossed his face.

"Are you alright?" he asked.

I paled and laughed a little too loudly, "Of course, why wouldn't I be?" I pasted a smile on my face; one I was pretty sure looked pinched and fake. Although I wanted it to look relaxed and blissful. Secretively, I was happy I did not recognize anyone in the room. He pulled me up to the bar, but didn't release my hand, and I didn't make any attempt to pull away. His fingers were long, and full. He had broad, strong hands, much like his broad, chiseled shoulders. He was very strong, well-built and physically fit. My mouth watered as I imagined what those shoulders would feel like under my hands. My groin clenched and warmth pooled low in my stomach. This man was lovely. I focused on his back and shoulders as they wiggled under his thin cotton shirt. His sleeves were rolled up, and bulky, thick, sinewy muscles rippled under my gaze when he leaned over to put his elbow on the bar top. Moisture pooled between my legs, my sex tightened, and I shifted uncontrollably. I was wide eyed when Dylan turned around. The look on his face was one of wonder, his eyebrows raised. His mouth was turned up on the edges, and he stared at me with a questioning look.

"What?" I asked, as I pulled myself from my revelry.

"I asked if you'd like a drink?" his soothing tone made me blush. He knew I had been drinking in his physic. I tried to avoid his sparkling blue eyes. They seemed to dance lazily around his face, enjoying my discomfort at being caught. My voice escaped me, and I answered with a high-pitched squeak, "I'll have what you're having." Dylan promptly turned and handed me his drink. I grabbed it with both hands; I needed to distance myself from my overwhelming attraction. The glass jiggled with my excited tremor, the liquid spilled over the edge. I gripped the glass with both hands tighter. Dylan stared at me, his eyes narrowed, attempting to read my face. He smiled. Could he read my thoughts? Did he know how he affected me? I was embarrassed by my wanton, and I didn't want Dylan to see my flushed skin and face. My groin was tight and my crotch was wet. I was shocked by my physical reaction to him.

"Come on." Dylan slipped his arm around me, cupping the small of my back sending jolts of lightning straight to the inside of my thighs. I tingled from the sensation, it was difficult to concentrate. He guided me towards the back of the bar where a door was slightly ajar. He pushed the door wide and stepped aside to allow me to enter. I paled, horrified that the room was filled with over half of the team players. They sat haphazardly around the private room, perched on stools and cross-legged in chairs by lower tables. I was mortified, all the color drained from my face. I wondered how I would be received into the Boys' Baseball Club. I was horribly uncomfortable. I pried into these men's lives. Why did Dylan think this was a good idea? I was viewed as in intruder. My panic solidified when Chris yelled, "Well damn!" and leaned forward on his elbows linking his hands between his spread knees. Eyes peeled away from the televisions and came to rest on me while I tried to back out of the door. I squirmed under the scrutiny. Dylan pushed past me, dragging me in with him. Laughter and camaraderie erupted, and players left their seats to shake hands and clap him on the back. Congratulating each other for a well-played series of games. I turned quickly on one foot trying to make a hasty retreat. But I was stopped short, my arm snapped backwards as Dylan snatched my elbow. My drink swirled close to the rim of my glass.

"Where do you think you're going?' Dylan shielded me from the room full of players, and talked close to the back of my ear. His warm breath tickled against the back of my neck and sent shivers spiraling down my spine. I took a deep breath, unsure if I was trying to calm my nerves from his closeness, or the fear of facing the room of potentially hostile men. I took another deep breath, physically trying to relax. *Ok*, I thought, *I can do this*. I squared my shoulders, lifted my chin and stepped confidently back into the room. Dylan dropped his hand from my elbow, and crossed the room to stand closer to the television. My knees shook uncontrollably. I shifted my drink from one hand to the other, and slipped on to a bar stool at the end of a tall table near the door. I was happy no one joined me, and Dylan didn't force me to interact with the rest of the team, or them to interact with me. I liked that I could sit in the corner and just observe. Even without my camera, I could still hide.

Dylan's easiness with his teammates was evident here off the field. He chortled and threw his head back laughing at a highly energized story Glen was telling with vivid arm animation. He continued to laugh and cohort with the rest of the team. They were a tight group. I was just an observer, hiding in the corner. Although, I caught the gazes and stares of a couple members of the team as I sipped my drink. I was so glad I was not the center of attention. Within minutes, my drink was empty, and there was another on the table. I made a blanket, "Thank You" statement and listened to the stories floating around the room. I began to relax, the liquor loosened me up. I listened to the teams' banter and stories and laughed at the appropriate spots. Careful not to add my own stories or twists to their conversation. I felt like the sun, and all the world and universe just revolved around me; small scenes of interaction erupted everywhere, while I was cemented at the center. Aware I was there, but carefully ignored; the small groups drank, clinked bottles, teased and laughed. It's was good to hear. This group of men were really close, like brothers. Unsure how it happened, I ended up with another drink in my hand. I felt very warm and fuzzy. The camaraderie in the room and the liquor had made me heady and extremely relaxed.

I didn't want to interfere with his boy's night, but I watched Dylan closely. Wow, I loved the way he moved. I watched him finger comb his hair and the way the muscles on his shoulders rolled and tightened, the way his rolled shirt played against his taut, sinewy arm muscles. I imagining them tightening around my back, pulling me close and kissing me senseless. My belly clenched, my clitoris throbbed and moisture pooled below my waist. With my arousal, my eyes brightened and glistened. I was glad I was ignored while I eye raped Dylan. As if on cue, he turned, our eyes locked, and he acknowledged me with a casual nod. I blushed, caught in my fantasy. I kept my eyes locked on him, suddenly brazen and bold. I straightened in my chair, and casually crossed my legs, my skirt shifted higher on my thigh. I continued to eye rape him from top to bottom and ran my eyes softly back to his arms and shoulders. He knew what I was doing and softly chuckled to himself. His gaze lingered a little longer and then he slowly returned to the conversation, giving me a wonderful view of his backside. He continued to steal looks in my direction, glancing over occasionally to lock his eyes on mine, and smile shyly.

After three drinks, I felt bold, and the alcohol took over all my senses. My self-control was slowly slipping away, with my erotic thoughts of the muscular man across the room. I closed my eyes trying to refocus. I tried to listen to the conversation in the room, but quickly lost myself in the music floating in from the poolroom. I swayed softly in my chair, humming along. I started chair dancing, losing myself to the music. I silently thought of myself under Dylan's muscular body, the heat of him, the smell, and the pressure. The last sips of my drink swirled at the bottom of my glass, and the ice clinked softly against the side. My thighs flexed in and out to the music and my pelvis rocked in the chair to the beat of the drum. I allowed myself to become completely absorbed, the alcohol removing any and all of my inhibitions. When the music stopped, I opened my eyes. The room had fallen unusually quiet and twelve pairs of eyes focused on me. Some mouths were gapping, some smirked, and others looked away quickly and tried to hide shy smiles. One pair held my seductive, alcohol induced gaze. Dylan put his drink down without breaking eye contact.

The room filled slowly with hushed murmurs, and soft laughs. Suddenly, I was fully aware of where I was, and who was striding deliberately and quickly towards me. A renewed sexual awareness filled me, I tingled between my thighs, and my blood heated my face and body. I was witnessing a new side of Dylan, one that showed some sultriness and possessiveness. When he reached me, he lifted the empty glass from my hand and spun my chair so he straddled my legs pinning them together. One hand held the chair while the other palmed the tabletop. Dylan's blue eyes glittered in front of my face. He was so close I could see the silver flecks in his eyes dancing around in the dim light. I was hoping he was feeling as sexually charged as I was, this slow seduction was wearing me down.

Dylan took a ragged breath, "Why, Stacia, I never knew a chair could provide so much entertainment!" He blew out his breath, kept his head low and regarded me with half closed lids. When he dared to look up, his blue eyes were darkened to a beautiful grey.

I gave him my most seductive smile. "A little too much alcohol, I imagine." I slurred. I rested my hands lightly on his forearms, and let them slide slowly to the insides of his arms, light enough to tickle and entice his wrists. His smile reached his eyes and he reached out and grabbed my hand tightly, stopping my assault. He pulled me up and out the door towards the poolroom.

"So, dancing is your thing?" he tried to hide a sly smile in his scolding. He pulled me further on the dance floor holding me at arm's length. I looked up at him from under my lashes, the swirl of the music and alcohol swam in my head. I gyrated my hips and moved in to close the distance between us. Dylan stepped back. I raised my hands above my head causing my breasts to peek out of the top of my camisole, and bared a slip of pale skin of my soft belly. Dylan's eyes perused the view in front of him. I knew he was falling under my spell. I stepped in closer, this time he didn't retreat. I rubbed my open palms up his arms, feeling the movement of his muscles as he danced. I slid my hands down to his palms, and rubbed my thumbs in small circles moving our hands to his sides. I tried to circle his waist with our hands, but Dylan stepped back holding me at arm's length. I moved my hands to his ribs, bent my knees, and slid down his body to his thighs, moving my knees in unison until I was rocking side to side on my heels. He responded as I had planned, I could see his erection straining against his zipper, which happened to be eye level right now. Dylan moved back and danced to the music, and feebly attempted to make me stand and remove my hands from his thighs. The music thumped in my head, and I vibrated with the bass and slid myself back up his body. My skin prickled and burned and I continued to dance exclusively for him through the next song. I began to giggle, knowing the effect I was having on him. Dylan's eyes were clouded and dark. When the song stopped, Dylan stopped. He pulled me into his arms trying to keep his hips from touching me, from fitting close enough that I might feel his excitement. I stepped into the open space closing in on the erection I knew was waiting.

"I believe you've had enough." he whispered. "I should probably send you home now. Let me call you a cab." Dylan kept a protective arm around my waist and reached for his cell phone.

Realization fired through me. "*What?* You're sending me home? In a *cab*?" Indignation rung in my voice. *Like hell!* "I think I'll have another drink." I shot back at him. I twisted out of his grip and headed up to the bar. I quickly ordered another drink before he could stop me. How dare he try to send me home in a cab! For God's sake, I was not an insolate teenager. But I was feeling the full effects of the liquor and now, sexual frustration.

Dylan joined me at the bar. I glanced sideways at him. I could see beads of sweat along his sideburn.

"This isn't a good idea", he responded breathlessly. And the double innuendo wasn't lost in my alcoholic haze. I grabbed my glass, took a long sip, and made sure he watched me until I had swallowed completely.

"I can take care of myself. Go back to your friends." I seethed. I took another large gulp of the liquor and exhaled a breath loud and audibly.

"Stacia, this is not a time to be bullheaded. You've had too much alcohol, actually way too much alcohol, and I would never forgive myself if something happened to you. Take a cab home, be safe." he stared directly into my eyes, the blue edges sparkling. He mumbled under his breath, something that sounded like, "Hell, I shouldn't let you go home alone like this." Was he referring to being intoxicated or sexually frustrated? Humor rimmed his eyes. I stared intently, rolled my eyes and took another sip of my drink. I felt slightly foolish. My efforts at seduction were thwarted. Just another failed attempt at a relationship. Maybe I should quit trying. I turned back towards the bar and put both elbows on the glossed wood, my glass steepled between my hands. Dylan turned to the bar mimicking my posture. I glared at him in the bar mirror. His eyes glared back. His blue eyes darkened. As I watched him, it struck me like a hammer to my heart. His sexual need was visible and obvious, but he was pushing me away. Keeping me at a distance to protect himself. Even though we had known each other a couple of months, he had obviously been hurt by a woman before. I wondered if his pain was physical, emotional or both like mine. My heart went out to him. I couldn't force him. I would need to investigate that before I pushed him. This seduction needed more time. Resigned to the fact I would be spending my night alone, I spoke.

"I'll go home. I can catch my own cab." I stood to leave a little too fast, I swooned and my head spun wildly. The alcohol hit me hard. I stumbled and I grabbed at the bar edge to steady myself. Dylan launched himself off the stool and scooped me up under my arms keeping me upright. His touch made my nipples hardened and made my thighs tingle. I looked away and I started to giggle. Dylan smiled and pulled me closer, wrapping his arms around my upper body more in an effort to keep me on my feet than a sign of affection. I quickly tipped up on my toes and kissed him on the cheek.

"Thank You, I'll be going now." Dylan held on to me allowing his hands to roam along my ribs and back in a soft caress.

"Stacia," he sighed, "I'll take you home. You are too intoxicated to be trusted in a cab by yourself." He was warring with his own emotions, his brows furrowed, and I thought I saw regret drift across his beautiful features. He threw a bill on the counter, and twisted me around so my back was pressed against his chest, and swung his arm across my chest from shoulder to shoulder holding me in place and started towards the door. Dylan pushed the door open with his free hand and released me to walk unaided through the door with only his hand on my upper arm for support. Once we were on the street, the cool air tried to sober me quickly. I shivered in the cold. Dylan enveloped me in his arms and rubbed my arm. He pulled me close to his side and pressed me against his side to stop my shudder. I tucked myself under his arm as an involuntary shiver goose bumped my skin. We walked the short distance to the parking lot and he used his key fob to unlock his 2013 Chevy Equinox. Not the over the top car I expected for an accomplished baseball player. I slid as gracefully as I could into the passenger seat, and Dylan closed the door. Dylan slipped easily behind the steering wheel.

"Buckle up." he said when he closed his door and latched his seatbelt. I reached for my belt but had dexterity problems; definitely related to the amount of alcohol I had consumed. Dylan sighed, unlatched himself and leaned over the console and swiftly locked me in. "There that's better." a smile glided across his face as he studied me. He had enjoyed the alcohol floorshow I was trying hard now to suppress. I tried to push the haze from my mind and focus on Dylan, but I struggled. "That was quite a display tonight, Stacia." His right hand rested on the headrest of the passenger seat, while his left was bent at the wrist over the steering wheel, his keys hung between his thumb and forefinger. My head dropped forward and I smiled to myself. I wondered if he knew my intent. My face flushed and my hands knotted in my lap. I wiggled in my seat. Thinking I was cold, he turned on the seat warmers. "Ok, well, let's get you home."

Dylan reached for his keys with his right hand and plugged them into the ignition. I wondered what he was thinking. Was he as aroused as I had been? Did he want this attraction to move forward? Where would tonight lead? I let my head fall back against the headrest, the questions and alcohol clouded all sensibility.

"Before you pass out in my car, remind me, what your address is." I must have taken too long to answer, because Dylan reached over and gently squeezed my hand. "Hey.", he whispered, "Where do you live?" I gave him my home address, my voice slurred, my eyelids heavy. My eyes closed on their own and my head lolled towards Dylan as the alcohol took its toll. He squeezed my hand again, snickered, and drove me home.

~~***~~

"You're home." Dylan softly called my name. "Stacia? Hey, open up your eyes." Dylan ran his fingers down my cheek and cupped my chin with his thumb and forefinger.

"Hum?" I asked incoherently. My body felt heavy and sedated. I tried to shake the feelings and concentrate on Dylan's voice. My eyes floated open and then shut again.

"Do you think you can make it up those stairs?" Dylan nodded at the apartment stairs and waited for an answer. When none came, he tried again. "Stacia? Did you hear me?"

"Hum?" I mumbled, barely stirring in the warm car seat.

"Ok," he snapped, "have it your way." I could hear the grin in his voice. Dylan exited the car, swung the passenger door open wide and heaved me to my feet. I blinked and tried to clear my head. I stumbled, and as my legs gave away, Dylan scooped me up and started carrying me up the stairs. I rested my head on his shoulder and I could feel all his muscles straining and moving under me. I focused on the movement under me; I loved how his arms felt holding me. I wondered how his breathing would sound with the excitement of sex. What color his eyes would be when he finally orgasmed. I was slightly off balance when he stood me back on my feet, but more awake and aroused to beat hell! He leaned with an outstretched arm against the doorframe. Looking scrumptious.

"Wow." he huffed, "I had no idea weight lifting was on the workout schedule for today!" He huffed again and I giggled. Dylan smiled, "Keys?" I fished around in my pockets but found nothing. A look of dismay crossed his face. "Really?" he quipped. I giggled again.

"Turn around." I slurred. When he was facing the stairs, I stared at his beautiful backside. My mouth watered. I liked the view. I reached up above the door jam and the key fell noisily to the floor. I giggled again and Dylan giggled too. He turned around just in time to catch me around the waist before my head bumped the doorjamb as I reached down for the key.

"Lightweight." he grumbled as he reached for the key off the floor and stuck it into the lock and turned it. The door opened wide with flare. I straightened up, took a deep breath and made an obvious attempt to cross the threshold without tripping on my heels. I almost made it. Dylan caught my arm before I propelled myself towards the floor and pulled me into his arms in one fluid movement. He leaned against the doorframe and dipped his head into the crook of my neck to whisper into my ear. "Oh, if only you were sober. There are a few things I'd like to do tonight besides drive you home." his exhaled breath caressed a shiver down to the base of my spine and made my clitoris throb. His voice grew husky and was filled with passion and need. He rubbed the lowest region of my back, just barely skimming the rounded upper area of my buttocks, and then slid his hands up my back. I looked up into his sky blue eyes and smiled sheepishly. He held my gaze and moved his hands to stroke my face with his thumbs.

"You're amazing, Stacia. So strong, independent, kind of wild, and from your pictures, very accomplished. You didn't bat an eye when Rob hit you with that foul ball, the guys fully expected you to fall apart; use it to your advantage. Maybe use

39

it to gain an inside track to the team, but you didn't. And you held your own tonight in a bar full of admirers. Shit, the guys couldn't stop ogling."

I contorted my face. *Admirers? They loathed me! I had pictures that could ruin them!* I must have looked like the liquor had affected every ounce of my comprehension. Dylan's eyes softened and a beautiful smile spread across his face, dimpling his cheeks.

"And from the look on your face I think you doubt the truth." I dropped my eyes, and he used his thumbs to push my head back up and make me look back.

"You're beautiful, Stacia. So fucking beautiful." He leaned as if to inhale me. "One gorgeous woman." His thumbs caressed my chin and color flooded my face. His forehead lightly rubbed mine. I tilted my head, closed my eyes and waited for his mouth take mine. Dylan dipped his head, his lips softly slid across mine from the middle to the corner, where he planted one chaste gentle kiss. I slid my arms up his arms to his neck and twisted my hands in the hair at the nape of his neck, and I placed my lips full on his and kissed him back. Small soft feathery kisses across his lips. Soundless kisses that made me want to deepen the kiss. I nipped at his lip and quickly used my tongue to sooth it. I used my tongue to part his lips and explored the recesses of his lips and mouth. He tasted of beer and a hint of mint. Keeping my lips on him, I stepped into the vee of his body and this time he didn't resist. I nestled my hip against his growing erection.

"Hum." he moaned into my mouth. Even if the rest of the team hated me, I definitely knew Dylan did not. I pulled him further into the apartment and kicked the door shut with my foot, never losing the kiss. I was sensitized, my skin felt prickly, our kiss ignited my belly and liquid heat pooled deep.

Dylan pulled his lips away, I felt the immediate loss. He dropped his head to my neck. His hands skidded along my neck down my back and rested on my waist.

"I could have all this for myself, Oh God." He exhaled loudly against my neck, the air causing a shiver to cascade to my groin. He gave me a quick squeeze and stepped back, using his hands to push my hips away from him putting distance between us. "But, not tonight, not after drinking. I want no regrets." *His regrets or mine?* I was sure he didn't mean mine. He made a grab for the door handle; I stopped him by sliding my back against the door. If this going to be a one night thing, I was going to have to go for it. Now.

"Yes, this could be yours, and I've been trying very hard to make you see that for months now. And now that you're here, you're not leaving." I ran my hands down to the front of my blouse, opening the top buttons as I went. I felt bold, empowered by the alcohol. *I could do this. This could be a new me. Strong and unafraid.* Dylan's eyes dropped to the newly exposed cleavage. I allowed my fingers to caress the cleft between my breasts. His eyes closed and he tried to control himself. I stepped towards him, placed my palms flat on his chest and pushed him into the room. I tipped my head up and took his mouth again planting small wet kisses along his closed lips and down his jaw.

"Umm. This isn't a good idea." he moaned and his head dropped back a little, scanning the room. I wasn't sure if he was trying to gain more self-control, or trying to find an escape. I started a sultry physical assault on his chest and arms. I pulled his shirt from his pants, and allowed free roaming of my hands on his stomach. Using delicate circles on the muscles I found, I traced the groves and felt his wildly increasing pulse. He used his hands to plaster my hands to his ribs in attempt to stop me. I kneaded my fingertips along the defined edges of bone.

"Stacia. Stop. This..." Each word he said was slow and breathless. I didn't let him finish his sentence. I planted another kiss on him and his responding groan indicated a small form of resignation on his part. This time he didn't pull back. His hand traveled back to my neck and tangled my hair at the base of my neck. I plastered my body against him. I felt so in charge, a position I usually let the men in my relationships assume. *This could be me too, strong and in control.* But Dylan was different from my other partners, he seemed chivalrous, scared to proceed with any type of relationship, sexual or otherwise. I wanted to change that. I reached for the buttons on his shirt, my actions clumsied with the residual alcohol. Dylan tried to put an end to my advancement by circling his thumbs into my open palms. I looked up into dark hooded eyes, his breathing rapid and shallow. I pulled my hands away, rubbed my way across his chest, and slipped his shirt off his bulging biceps. The exquisite feel of his corded muscles made my breath catch, and my nipples peak. A small moan escaped him as I flattened my hands and traveled down to his waistband dipping my fingers just inside along the front edge of his jeans.

Dylan moved his hand up under my skirt, pushing it north to my waist, and began a slow sensual kneading of my butt cheeks. He slipped his thumbs under the elastic of my panties aiming for the soft spot of skin between my thighs. I sighed, then groaned, and tipped my head for another kiss. Dylan's lips were moist and swollen. He crashed towards my mouth and took my mouth with an eagerness that caused me to become dizzy. My clit raged with need. My nipples hardened and pressed hard against my satin bra. I craved more intimate physical contact. I wanted him naked with his erection pushed deep inside me, making me scream. I reached for the button of his pants and slowly unzipped his fly, making sure to avoid contact with his skin. He gasped for air and our oral contact was broken. I stared at his beautiful body, knowing he had to be that beautiful all over. I slipped my hand down the front of his jeans and circled his erection. Dylan's eyes closed and his head fell forward, his groan and exhaled breath were the only sign I needed to let me know I was being successful. I slid my hand out of his pants and lead him to my bedroom by the hand. Dylan hesitated at the door and looked around wildly, like an animal about to be put into a cage. I wondered what caused that severe of a reaction. Was he looking for an escape?

"Come with me." I whispered. I kept eye contact with him and slowly licked my lower lip. Dylan's breath quickened and I pressed my body closer. I felt his hardened erection along my hip. I pulled him to the side of my bed and kissed him long and hard. I parted his lips with my tongue and ran my hands down his chest to his crotch, slowly massaging his erection. This was one time I was glad my mattress sat over a drawer set and the mattress was elevated. The mattress hit Dylan at the back of his thighs and he remained standing. I broke the kiss and he groaned loudly,

"You should stop, I need to go. I really shouldn't be doing this. I can't ..." Dylan didn't finish his thought but attempted to push me away. I didn't stop. I kept Dylan's gaze, unzipped my skirt, and slid it seductively down my thighs to pool on the floor. I placed my hands back on his beautiful biceps and worked my way over his shoulders. I kissed across his chest, and rubbed my hands down his back lightly, tickling my way south stopping at the base of his spine. I dropped to my knees in front of him as I kissed my way down his abdomen. I feathered kisses along his stomach and crossed his lower abdomen from hip to hip. His muscles contracted under my touch and, he moaned, "Oh God." under his breath. I hooked my fingers under the edge of his pants and slithered them down his legs to gather at his ankles. His erection popped free from his pants. Dylan rubbed my hair and shoulders; "This is a really bad idea." he choked out, his voice deep and husky. I smiled. My resolve to finish what I started solidified with the gasp he made when I reached out with both hands, circled, and massaged the length of silky skin. I tightened my grip and circled the fleshy tip with my thumb as a small dollop of liquid seeped from the end. I massaged the liquid into the tip causing Dylan's thighs to tighten. His breath hitched in his chest. I slid my hand the length of him gripping the base, and slid back to the tip creaming the second drop of pre cum across the sensitized slit. Dylan's thighs tightened again, and he sucked air hard through his teeth.

"Oh God, Stacia, stop!" he exhaled. At the sound of my name all breathy and stuttered, my own sex clenched and filled my panties with fluid. The control I had was exhilarating. I slowed down and loosened my grip, and Dylan relaxed a little. He closed his eyes and struggled to control himself. With his guard down, I took advantage of him. I closed my mouth around his shaft and ran my tongue over the top of him and down the length, applying a moderate amount of suction on the extraction from my mouth. I glided my tongue around the rim and sucked him back into my mouth gripping the base with my hand.

"Oh, shit." he said breathlessly. His grip in my hair tightened. I sucked harder slithering my tongue along the underside feeling him lengthen and harden under my ministrations. I continued to suck and massaged him.

"Stop." he breathed, "Stop!" he nearly screamed. His breathing was rapid and shallow. I could feel a sheen of sweat on his skin. He tried to pull from my mouth. I grabbed on to his buttocks to hold him into place and sluiced down the full length of him until he touched the back of my throat. I stopped sucking, but refused to remove my mouth. I knew just how far to push him without causing an eruption. I could feel the beat of his heart on his silky shaft as he fought hard to maintain control. Dylan sucked at the air and tried to regain his composure. I swallowed a couple of times until I needed to remove him from my tonsils. I took one more second to tighten the suction and let my teeth skim the underside of his penis as I slid to his tip.

"Oh, Jesus!" he whispered. His legs seized and he pulled away abruptly. "We need to stop, before we can't stop." Dylan reached quickly for his jeans, but I caught his hands. I pushed with all my power to push him on to the bed. He didn't budge. He stood dumbfounded, his mouth gaped. A grin began to creep to his face. I tried again to drop him to the bed. I failed, and a huge smile creased his face, "What is it you're planning to do with me, Stacia?" He smiled wickedly. I didn't respond. I stared at him. I wanted to control this encounter, use his body to satisfy myself, and find out what secrets he was hiding. And keep mine hidden. I narrowed my eyes. I needed to hold my feelings in check; I couldn't let him know how I was falling for him.

"What do *you* want? Talk to me, Stacia. Don't keep it a secret. Tell me." Dylan cradled my face like a child, imploring me to answer him. I was mute. I chewed my lip and stared my hands. Dylan rubbed his thumb over my lower lip soothing the bite mark I had left. I was suddenly sober and acutely aware I was losing every ounce of control I had earlier.

Could he really be interested in me? Could he really want to know what I wanted? He could never find out about my past. He must never find my weakness, how weak I really was. How vulnerable I was. I would take today if it was all I was going to get, but I was beginning to fall hard for Dylan. I wondered how I would heal my heart when he left.

"I want you." I whispered. Now more acutely aware of my own physical need, I pushed him back one more time. This time he sat and pushed himself back onto the bed and toed off his shoes and pants. He locked his eyes on me and I climbed on top straddling his legs. Dylan remained sitting. He took my mouth again, a strong passionate kiss that deepened to erotic tongue fighting. He explored the inside of my lower lip and caressed it with his tongue. I melted into him, losing myself in the sensations. I felt his hands on my buttocks kneading softly and he ran his thumbs under the elastic of my panties and pulled. The elastic snapped loose and my panties shredded beneath me. His fingers grazed my cleft now fully opened for him, and my clitoris throbbed and swelled. Dylan slowly circled my clit with his fingers using my own juices to slicken the folds. I allowed a long moan to escape the sides of my occupied mouth. I pushed against his hand and fingers as he explored my anatomy. I broke our kiss and moaned loudly. My eyes flared with need, and this time when I pushed Dylan to the bed, he went willingly. I climbed the bed straddled his lap and eased his full length into me slowly. Dylan gasped and sucked air into his lungs through his teeth.

"Oh my God." he exhaled through gritted teeth. I began with a slow rhythm, riding him and squeezing along his full length. At the deepest point, I circled my hips to build my own excitement. Dylan kept a close watch on my face, trying to decipher my intent at his sexual torture. I couldn't keep eye contact, I had to look away. If I didn't watch, I could save a small piece of my heart. I rubbed my hands across his chest, and closed my eyes. Without sight, there was no emotional connection, just a physical, sensual sexual encounter. Although I wanted some type of real relationship with Dylan, I didn't think he was willing to go there yet. Maintaining control was pivotal to keeping my emotions in check. I kept up the slow, punishing assault for a few more minutes. Dylan began to push up with his hips on my downward thrusts. He attempted to increase the tempo and I knew he was chasing a release. He grabbed my hips and tried to make me increase the tempo. I didn't want to relinquish any of my control. I stopped his attempt, and slide down sinking him in as deep as he could go. Then I ground my clit into the base of his penis, working on my own pleasure. Dylan could barely breathe; his eyes were glazed and bore into me.

When he spoke, his voice was deep and husky, "I can't take much more of this, Stacia, come on honey tell me what you want." I ignored his request, and kept my eyes closed in my attempt to keep control.

Dylan sat up; the position change was overwhelmingly sensual. Face to face, he pulled me into him and I nearly convulsed. I opened my eyes and gasped for air. "What do you want?" He asked me breathlessly, "Stacia, please. Look. At. Me. Tell me what you want." He planted soft kisses along my neck and continued to pump his hips. I just stared at him and stopped all movement. Now that I was losing control, I couldn't answer him. I couldn't put into words what I wanted from him. I wanted more from this than he did. My mind muddled. Did I want just hot sex with a great looking guy or was I really looking for something long term? I thought I knew, but then I was lost. And I was sure he was talking about the short term scenario, and nothing long term.

"Tell me. Trust me." he whispered breathlessly into my neck. My past failures haunted me. I couldn't talk to him; I wanted something he couldn't give me; wouldn't give me. Fear crashed through me. I began to pale, and I rethought the position I was presently in. Dylan must have seen the fear and regret surfacing and in one fluid movement flipped me onto my back never breaking the intimate connection.

"Don't be afraid, Stacia, tell me now." He covered my neck with kisses, his hot breath caressed along my clavicle and softly licked my rapid pulse point on my neck.

"I want you, just you." I whispered. My voice was so quiet Dylan stilled to make sure he'd heard me. I looked into his eyes and repeated, "Just you."
Dylan started a fast rhythmic assault and my hips automatically pushed up to meet his.

"I just want you." I whispered again as his pace sent me higher and higher until a tingle started to spread across my stomach making a beeline straight to my clitoris. My thighs began to tremble and my soft moan coincided with the clench that started at my core.

"Give it to me, Stacia, let go." His low, husky voice was my undoing and with each repeated thrust, my orgasm spread out. Light filled me, and blinded me to everything but the sensation. I cried out with the release and Dylan dropped his head to the crook of my neck and pumped deeper as he chased his release. He came with a loud moan and a sigh. He continued to move slightly prolonging the sensitive post coital spasms. I could barely breathe. My hands fell loosely above my head as Dylan stilled inside me and laid his full weight on me. Both of us forced the slowing of our breathing; slowly returning to earth.

After a few minutes Dylan propped himself up on his elbows and used his thumbs to caress across my sensitive lips. His smile was genuine.

"You're beautiful." he whispered, "Drunk, but absolutely beautiful and positively amazing. But I have one request." his voice trailed off as he continued to rub his thumbs over my lower lip and cheeks. I pulled my emotions up short. My body stiffened sure this was when he'd tell me this was just a short tryst. One that would end at the end of the season, or maybe tonight. Or he never wanted to see me again. Or worse, that he knew about my past.

"Trust me. I want you to talk to me. I won't hurt you. I *never* want to hurt you." he whispered into my neck. Dylan moved to break the intimate connection and withdraw. I clamped my vagina around his penis and he halted. My legs wrapped around his buttocks and I used them to pull him back inside. Dylan's face lifted from my neck and his eyebrows lifted in shock,

"What do you want?" his sultry voice sending shivers to my spine.

"Just you, Dylan." is all I could say. And I started to kiss him. Using my tongue to explore his mouth and tickle the luscious recesses I found there. Within minutes his body responded, and his cock lengthened and hardened inside me. He began with a slow frictional rub that had us both writhing and had us both flying over the pinnacle together.

Chapter 6

Mike scrolled through the pictures on his computer I had returned with after the last game. Some were great action shots, most were of Dylan. Undaunted, Mike called me into his office.

"Something going on with you? Looks like you're a little preoccupied with one player on that team." he leaned back in his chair and glared at me. "Not a good idea, sweetheart. These guys don't stick around, they move on. I don't want to have to deal with a broken heart when he leaves." He furrowed his eyebrows and steepled his hands together. "Don't do this, Stacia, step back, and just take the pictures because you know he'll walk. If you can't do that, I'll pull you back into the station. Understand?" I had released the pit bull, and it had made a threat I knew it would carry out if I couldn't get my head out of the clouds. I knew Mike was right. He had insight, and I wondered where it originated. Maybe because of his past relationship performances. But I worried I'd lose my freedom so I made every effort to make sure I photographed all the action.

Behind Mike's back, Dylan and I met at the fence after games. We talked only after the games, being careful not to set off alarms with the other players. I had to keep him at a distance or risk losing my job. I downloaded my pictures to the computer and held back the excessive amount of pictures I took of Dylan. I used those in my fantasies. I gazed at the facial grimaces as he released the ball. I marveled at his muscles and movement. Remembering how those muscles twitched and moved under my hands, the look on his face as he came. Remembering the deep satisfaction of him buried to the hilt inside me. I craved that closeness again, I was sure he thought I was remorseful over our first encounter. But I was more afraid Mike would pull me. It was a long week while I sorted through the details of preserving my job, and keeping my distance from Dylan to preserve my heart.

Chapter 7

I was lulled into a sense of wellbeing and security after a couple of weeks of turning in my work to Mike and receiving his praise. The guys on the team began to warm to being around me too. I still took pictures of them off the field, but compromising ones never left my computer. Jon spent more time talking with me. We'd laugh, drink and talk at the tables at the bar. His hard facade faded some, or maybe I loosened up a little. Or he was trying to find out what pictures were floating around about his after game activities. I tolerated his attention, but never wanted the friendship to go anywhere. Not like I wanted it to with Dylan. I was developing deep feelings for him; one's I knew would crush me when he left at the end of the season.

Dale and his wife started coming to the bar after a few games and I got to know Emily and loved that she was so passionate about raising their boys. Chris and Crystal started visiting the bar afterwards too. Crystal was infatuated with Chris. And him with her. They winked and flirted at each other across the room. I was starting to feel comfortable, enjoying the girls company. Wanting what they had. I kept Dylan at arm's length afraid I'd lose my job and my chances with him. I think he thought I had severe regrets after my drunken rape of him. It had been an excruciatingly long two weeks for me.

I regained my boldness one night as we met at Hitter's after the game. After two drinks, I pulled Dylan into the stockroom, pressed myself up against him, and spread my hands longingly across his chest. I slipped my knee between his legs applying pressure to his soft inner thigh. "I need you." I whispered.

Dylan's eyes grew wide and the expression on his face was one of wanton. "I wondered if you remembered what we did the other night, or if you had "alcohol regret". You've been pretty quiet after the games and have acted as if you were separating yourself from me. I wasn't sure why." Dylan rubbed his hands up my back into my hair. "What do you want?" Dylan's voice slid over me like silk, a smooth caress that left me wet and tingling low in my belly.

"I want you." I tiptoed up to whisper into his ear. I slid my hands up his arms and across his muscular chest that tightened at my touch.

"I want to know what else you want, Stacia. Tell me what you want me to do to you. Am I all you want? Are you just going to use my body? And run again when I get close to figuring you out?" He slid his arms around me sending a bolt of desire straight to my core. Heat coiled low and deep, and I clenched involuntarily.

I tipped my head up to gather a kiss from his soft wet lips, but before I could, the door flew open bathing the stockroom with light and Jon leaned against the door jamb looking at the two of us. He made no attempt to avert his eyes. Dylan made no move to drop his arms, silently staking a claim.

Jon glared at Dylan, "I'm leaving, see you at practice." Dylan stuck out his hand and Jon shook it. There was an unspoken message that passed between the two I wasn't privileged to. An odd look on Dylan's face made me shudder. Jon kept a hold of Dylan's hand as if there was an invisible standoff between him and me. I felt Dylan's possessiveness in the way he kept his hand on me. Yep, I could like this. I didn't like Jon's interruption. Jon glared at me and Dylan dropped his arm.

"I'll see you in a minute." Dylan lightly pushed me towards the door.

I stepped from the store room and headed back to the small room at the back of the bar. Allowing the two some time alone. I didn't like that Jon made me feel unworthy of Dylan's attention.

Dylan's team members were guarding him, keeping me away, but why? They must have known what I had planned for tonight. I was suddenly embarrassed that they had figured me out so easily. I tucked my heart away, grabbed my purse and headed towards the door. Suddenly I was feeling weary and a little nauseated. I knew I was headed for trouble. After Jon's display, I would need to convince the whole team I was worthy of Dylan.

Dylan looked behind Jon as I walked away. I could feel his eyes following me to the back room. I wondered if he planned to choose, and follow me out of the bar. I had just enough time to say a few quick goodbyes and make my way out the front door. Deep inside, I knew he'd back his team member, and I ached for him to choose me. Mike was right, his team was his priority, and I needed to save my heart. I began to push my emotions into the floorboards of my car as I drove for home. I felt physically ill. I was hoping it was just my oral alcohol intake. I really couldn't hold liquor well. But I knew it was really my heart breaking in half.

Chapter 8

Dylan showed up at my apartment door forty minutes after I got home. He had chosen to follow me, but the time frame could have led the team to believe he'd chosen to go home. I wanted to sneak a picture of him as proof for later that in some small way I had won against Jon. It wasn't really any kind of a contest. I knew we'd all lose him when the major team called him back. Maybe this was just Dylan's way to have two things he wanted. The teams' respect and my vagina. My mind was foggy, and my face was flushed. I was angry that the alcohol had such a profound effect on me today.

"Are you ok?" I knew Dylan's concern was a lame attempt to placate me. He didn't really want to know. And maybe my feelings were unfounded. I snapped my eyes to his.

"Do you even like me?" I asked tentatively. Dylan's eyebrows shot up and then crossed furrowing into a thick line.

"What's that supposed to mean?" his face fell and I watched as a myriad of emotion flowed across his face.

"I just wanted to make sure I wasn't just a second thought for you tonight. You asked me to tell you what I wanted. I tried at the bar.
Obviously, Jon kept you back to keep you away from me. Why? What's going on between you?"

"Nothing." his response wasn't indignant or angry. Just matter of fact and straight forward.

"You're honestly going to tell me there's nothing else I need to know about you? Because really, I know absolutely nothing. I don't know what you like to eat, what your sister or parent's names are, where you grew up, or if you had a pet growing up!" My anger was so unfounded, so senseless. But once I started, I couldn't filter my mouth.   "Do you like to sleep in on Saturday? Do you watch cartoons? Do you like to hike or ride a bike? What do you want to do with the rest of your life? My voice grew louder, my face flushed further with anger.

Dylan stared at me.

"Wow, well…" He blew out a deep breath he'd been holding and crossed his chest with his arms, linking his elbows with his hands. "I like pizza and Mexican food, My Mom is Doris, my Dad is Ed, my sister is Sara. I grew up in Indiana and had a lab-collie mix named Boots. She died fifteen years ago. Best dog I ever had. I hate cartoons, like to sleep in as long as the other side of my bed is warmed, and I spend most of my time with anything sports related. I want to play baseball as long as I can and in order to do that I have to work hard, and I need to stay focused." He paused and smiled. "Did I miss any questions?"

"Yes, was I a second thought tonight?"

Dylan didn't hesitate; he slipped his hands to my shoulders, looked directly into my eyes, and firmly denied my accusation.

"No, I wanted to come here first, Jon stalled me. I'm sorry if it looked like I wasn't interested. Because, God, I am. I find you amazing. Irresistibly sexy and someone I want to know better. So since we started the twenty questions game let me ask a few."

I stiffened. He'd turned the tables on me. Not willing to give up yet. I stepped back and shouted, "Wait, you missed a question! Do you even like me?"

The corners of Dylan's mouth curled, and a small shy smile crept across his face. His eyes glistened, and the blueness turned into a deep azure glow that radiated from his face.

"I like you, a lot. I can't wait to see you after my games. I can't wait to see your pictures in the paper. I am just thrilled you picked me. With all the other players making their moves, it could have been any one of them. Yet, you picked me. I can't concentrate when I am on the mound and I know you're watching. I think I more than *like* you."

Wow, when he moved to the major's this was going to be harder than I thought. I was going to lose a bigger piece of my heart than I ever imagined. And who did he think was hitting on me? Jon? For God's sake, he was gay! Wasn't he? I had seen him with men before.

And when I had followed him after the games, I had seen him with lots of different types of people, mostly men. I dropped my eyes, my voice was weak and subdued.

"Then don't leave tonight. Please." I slipped my hands around his waist, and buried my face into his chest, inhaling his masculine scent mixed with his cologne. I didn't want the control tonight. I would hide my deepest feelings but, I just wanted to be loved, and cherished. Dylan kissed my forehead, and rubbed his hands up my back. He sighed, a content sound.

Chapter 9

"You feel so nice and warm. Do you still want what you asked for earlier?" he whispered into my hair.

"Yes." I tipped my face up to procure a kiss. Dylan did not disappoint. He took my lips hungrily. Pushing his tongue past my lips with persistence. My hands skimmed his shirt. The rolled sleeves tight against his arms. I traced the lines of muscle on his arms, and tickled my way across his chest to undo the buttons on his shirt. I watched myself unfastening each button. For each button, I gave Dylan a request.

"I want you, Dylan. Naked. Panting. Sweating. Controlling. Licking. Kissing. Satisfying. Me." *Forever*, I whispered in my brain. Eight buttons. There were eight buttons on his shirt. Eight things I wanted him to do to me.
All eight things he could do to me, but hopefully not take my heart with him when he left.

Dylan was quiet while he took in my list. "Hum, I actually think I can do that." He tried to hide the curl of his lips, and tucked his lips together between his teeth to suppress it. I started to squirm. A vision of my ex, Ryan's smirking face flashed before my eyes. The last time I told him what I wanted he had taken, and I witnessed the abusive side of his personality. As soon as the words have left my mouth, I wanted to swallow them again.

I took a step back and dropped my hands off his chest. I just stared at his muscles, afraid to look at his eyes. Had I crossed the line? I thought he really wanted to know. Could he read my mind after all? Embarrassment filled me. Afraid he'd see me for the insecure girl I knew I was. My breath stuttered in my chest. Dylan dipped his head to try and make me look at him.

"Well, I may change the order a little bit, but I like that you told me." He waited for some type of a response. I was too afraid to give him one.

"Are you ok? It looks like you already regret your list."

"It's not the list." I exhaled the words from my mouth releasing the breath I didn't know I had been holding. My intake of breath stuttered as I tried to get oxygen to my brain and wipe away the last image I had of my ex, Ryan.

Dylan tucked his fingers under my chin and forced my head up. He stepped into me, pushed one leg between mine, and cupped my head with both of his hands.

"If it's not the list; and may I say, I think I can accomplish it, what is it?"

I took another deep breath, unable to make eye contact with him even with his hands on my face. I had to think fast, there was no way I was ready to tell him of my past failures.

"I'm afraid you'll leave." My voice cracked, and I swallowed hard. I didn't mean just tonight. I was losing small pieces of my heart, leaving them all over town. On the baseball field, in my pictures, in my foyer, in my bed. Pieces I had already started giving to Dylan without his knowledge.

"Oh, I am *not* planning on leaving. I have a list I have to work through tonight!" he couldn't contain his grin anymore and it glided onto his face and caused the most beautiful dimples to pucker his cheeks. His eyes sparkled, and his lashes trickled down to his cheeks. When he opened his eyes again, the color was a deep grey. He was positively beautiful. The ripple of his chest muscles and the heaving of his chest with his breathing was beautifully breathtaking. I couldn't blink or take my eyes off of him. My face flushed, although it already felt hot. I couldn't breathe. I felt warm all over, but it pooled low in my tummy. My clitoris throbbed with need.

"One. Kissing." Dylan slowly took my mouth, planting soft kisses across my lips. Much softer and slower than earlier. He teased my lips with his teeth and licked a line between my closed lips. I opened. His tongue slid along my teeth and tickled the tender inside edge of my lower lip. His warm wetness slowly invaded and caressed the tip of my tongue so delicately. A soft mewing sound came from deep inside and escaped me. Dylan pulled away and grinned. I took a deep breath, it felt like the first one I had taken all day, and my chest heaved with the effort. He used his thumbs to hold my face and, softly massaged the back of my neck with his fingers. He kissed along my jaw, and moved slowly and sensually down my throat leaving a path of burning skin in his wake. When he reached my carotid he kissed the sensitive area and softly licked and sucked the tender skin. My legs went weak. I held his hands to my face. I was afraid to move. Afraid he'd take his sensual tongue and soft kisses and leave.

"Two. Naked." Dylan pulled me close running his hands up and down my spine sending electricity straight to my thighs. He slowly untucked my shirt and slid his cool hands along my skin. I felt hot, but everywhere Dylan's hands were, my skin blazed. He pulled my shirt up my body and skimmed the edges of my breasts with his thumbs, sliding my shirt towards my head. I automatically raised my arms as he slipped my shirt completely off and threw it onto a chair. He kissed me again, maintaining lip contact, and rubbed his callused fingers over the goose bumped skin along my ribs. Sliding his hands to the swell of my butt, he slowly ran his fingers inside the waistband of my skirt. He deftly unzipped the zipper and let it slide down my thighs to the floor. It pooled at my feet in a beautiful blue puddle. A puddle that was mimicking my emotions right now. I stood exposed in just my bra, panties and high heeled sandals.

Dylan pulled back and looked at my breast. My chest heaved with want.

"Almost there." Dylan noted, as he rubbed his fingers across the lace on the top of the bra cup. He popped the front clasp and my bra fell away releasing them for his view. A low groan escaped him.

"Beautiful." he whispered into my ear as his hand softly cupped my breast and his thumb caressed the pebbled nipple. He used his left hand to push in the small of my back to maintain close contact. He kissed down my neck and again paused at my pulse to softly plant a kiss, suckle the area, and check the increasing rate with his lips.

He continued a slow trail to my right breast and lavished it with his tongue, pulling it to a point. He blew a cool breath across the areola causing it to pucker. My sharp intake of breath let him know he was accomplishing what he's started out to do. Slow torture.

Dylan backed me up to the bed and slowly lowered me to the edge with his hand still on the small of my back, and the other hand cupping my breast. With his mouth he kissed my mouth again and slowly laid me on my back and swung my legs into the bed. He covered me with his body and massaged my breast and circled my nipple with his thumb. He again slowly kissed down my neck and continued to the swell of my breasts. This time his gave each nipple a soft flat tongue lashing and sucked the saliva off each one causing my thighs to tighten and my sex to clench. Continuing south, he kissed across the muscles of my abdomen to each hip and with just his fingertips, plucked the elastic of my panties up away from my over stimulated skin. I was beginning to sweat. Small beads of perspiration formed on my forehead. I needed him, I loved his sweet attention, and I loved the way he was following the list.

Sending me spiraling out of control. He slid my panties off my legs and threw them off the bed.

"Three. Licking." Dylan slid between my legs muscling my thighs apart to fit his shoulders. He slowly kissed my inner thigh sending shots of heated bliss straight to my groin. My clit throbbed and my lips swelled, I felt a gush of fluid reach the entrance to my vagina. I groaned, Dylan smiled. He slipped his hands under my butt and held me in place. He softly kissed the other thigh, and started to touch my thigh with the tip of his tongue. Not full on licking, just the tender circular tip along the sensitive skin. My thighs quaked. He moved up until he kissed and licked the joint of my leg and involuntarily I tried to pull my legs together. A self-preservation move on my part. My legs met with resistance. His shoulders making sure I was unable to retreat. His hands on my buttocks softly kneaded the rounded muscles, but made sure I couldn't pull away. I was under his spell. I would allow this man to do anything he chose today. He used his thumb to spread the swollen tissues and again blew a cool breeze along my cleft. I moaned and pulled towards the top of the bed. Dylan's large hands held me in place. Then the cold was replaced with wet warmth. His tongue delved into my screaming slit. I gasped, I could feel his smile along my thigh as he slowly licked his way to my throbbing clit and circled it with his tongue. I was nearly screaming with need.

"Oh, God, Dylan!" Moisture filled my canal and I squeezed my muscles to try and stop the assault. Dylan continued until my legs quivered and I thought I was blind with ecstasy.

"Four. Panting" Dylan rubbed the sensitive inner lips with his thumbs and continued to circle my clit with small wet warm kisses. He would stop as soon as my channel started to clench, and once the sensation passed, he's start again until I was close to convulsing. I was panting. My breaths came in such short gasps I was getting dizzy from lack of oxygen. He flattened one hand across my stomach and pushed me down towards the bed, holding me still. Another tongue lashing had me writhing under his hand.

"Dylan. Stop. Please." He didn't. He pushed his tongue inside and licked the juices from the folds.

"Five. Sweating." He continued to bring me to the brink of release, and backed off before I could achieve it. The beads of perspiration began to roll down my neck and back. Even my backside was damp, and Dylan knew it with the placement of his hands. I was a quaking, quivering, jellied mess. Dylan looked at my face, and smiled. He was following the list and being very successful.

"Six. Controlling." Dylan stood and with the seductiveness of a stripper, and took his clothes off at the side of the bed. He stood in nothing but his boxers and turned away from me. He sensually slipped them down and bent to slide his feet from the leg openings. I got a wonderful view of finely toned back muscles and a taut butt. I let my gaze slide down his body and as he bent over, a pair of low hanging testicles came into view between his legs. I spasmed and a new flood of liquid pooled between my legs. He looked at me over his shoulder; a small knowing smile crept across his face. I was a wet, hot, panting mess. I shook with want. He slid into the bed and began kissing my lips again. He thumbed my nipples and splayed his hand flat across my stomach, keeping me from taking over this encounter. I couldn't take anymore. Tears formed in the corners of my eyes.

"Dylan, Please. I can't take any more. Take me. Now." I was beyond wound.

"Seven. Satisfied" he whispered into my neck. His breath was wet and steamy on my skin and a shiver cascaded down my spine and settled in my clit. I ached, and small spasms shook my core. He nudged my legs apart with his knee and guided his swollen cock to my opening. I couldn't breathe, my hands were tingling, and I was dizzy. Dylan pushed inside so slowly I cried out. It was torture. My muscles clenched and grabbed at his length as he slowly lowered himself into me. Once seated he stopped. He cupped my face again. "You are so beautiful." He brushed his lips to mine. "Absolutely stunning." He kissed a short path to my neck and nuzzled himself there against my pulse. "Are you ready?"

Beyond ready, tears slipped from my eyes and rolled down my temples. I could only nod. I couldn't bear him not moving. I was so sensitized; I thought I was going to break apart. I was shaking when he started to slide. In. Out, raking his length back across the soft folds of skin so swollen they pounded with my pulse. In, to stop at the depth of him. Out, riding along the soft outer ring. In, to grind against my tender nub of nerves. My orgasm was building up again so quickly. I gasped for air and dug my fingers into Dylan's back. His groan was my response. Out, the pull of his skin along mine felt like sweet tickling. In. he circled his hips and I couldn't get any air into my lungs. Lightning flashes flickered in my eyes, and tears streamed from my eyes. My legs quivered and tightened. A warm heat crawled across my stomach, and coiled deep inside me.

"Now, Dylan, Now." He pulled out and leaned up a little to rake across my clit and he sent me flying. He pushed himself back inside and increased the pace. My stomach clenched and the muscles in my core screamed with their release. Flashes of light flitted behind my eyelids. I cried out and spasms overtook me. Clenching against the hardness buried deep inside me. The orgasm was so strong it was almost painful. Dylan pumped harder and faster. He came with a sharp gasp and hot fluid filled me. He groaned but kept his face buried in my neck. He moved ever so slowly keeping our spasms coming. I was spent. My legs fell out and my hands fell off his back. My hands tingled and my breathing was so erratic I felt like I was drowning. My orgasm was so hard my stomach actually hurt.

Dylan's breathing was just as erratic and uneven. His full weight was on me, his cock still buried to the hilt.

"Eight. Just for you." he exhaled. He wrapped himself around me, pulled the comforter up over us, and sighed. Exhausted I slipped into a blissful sleep.

Chapter 10

I felt feverish, my body felt hot and steamy. After the previous night's activities, I should be sated. We had rolled over during the night and his back was facing me. I watched his ribs rise and fall with each breath. Loving the gentle crest of his soft snore. The sheet was pulled up to his mid chest, his left arm visible and tucked sweetly under the pillow. I touched his shoulder and slowly let my fingers roll over his muscled back. His hair was messed from sleep. He took a deep breath and rolled over in bed. The sheet gravitated towards his waist. His eyes lit up with the knowledge that I had been drinking in his sleeping form. Remnants from our impassioned night were strewn throughout the room, a small sliver of light sneaked in from the blind and glowed across his shoulder illuminating my face. Dylan smiled. Behind him I could see the glint from his belt as it hung from his pants that were haphazardly thrown over the soft leather chair by the window. I prickled. Memories of how Dylan had ministered to me the night before tightened my core. My face flushed. He stared right through me, he knew my inner secrets. He knew what made me tingle.
As we laid there admiring each other his eyes began to twinkle. Reaching over he used his finger to caress my lips.

"How do you feel?" he whispered.

"Fine, why wouldn't I? And you?"

"Well, if you want the truth, still tired, But if you had something else in mind that might wake me up, I could be persuaded."

"I have an idea, but it requires some participation. And no clothes. And I think we've accomplished half of that already." I pulled the sheet back to view his naked body.

He gave me a huge dimpled smile, slipped his hand behind my neck and forcefully held my head still. He rolled on top of me pressing me firmly into the mattress. Heat surged through me and just with his smile he made my thighs tremble. I nervously stroked the muscular form above me. I was still a little nauseated from the previous night's overindulgence of alcohol. Dylan moved closer and continued to slide his thumb pad over my sensitive lips. I parted my lips and he dipped the tip into my soft tissues. My lips felt heated and dry.

"You're so beautiful." Passionately he covered my lips with his fluttering soft kisses. He pushed his tongue past my teeth tangling with mine. I groaned, at the sheer weight of his body covering mine and at the feelings stirring inside me. I wiggled underneath him, uncomfortable with the positioning and pressure on my stomach. His hold on my neck only tightened and he pressed his full weight down on me. I groaned. I couldn't take the pressure and tried to worm out from under him. I was breathless. My hands were still free to roam and I massaged his chiseled biceps. Within minutes Dylan had my hands shackled with his and lifted above my head. He used one hand and pinned my thumbs together in one of his hands rendering my hands useless. With my arms stretched up he had a free unobstructed view of my prickling breasts. He feathered kisses down my neck, to stop short of my breasts and gave me a shy smile. He softly kissed around the edge of each nipple and watched them peak to small little mountains. Small beads of sweat formed between my breasts, as bolts of desire rocketed to my groin. He reached up with his free hand and cupped my breast and sucked my nipple into his mouth. I gasped, and

Dylan moaned a low satisfied growl. He quickly sat up to admire my form. I wiggled beneath his weight. His eyes glowed and a small satisfied smile edged across his face. He held my thumbs tightly so I couldn't escape.

"Damn, you're hot." I smiled, accepting his compliment. "No, I mean, you're really hot! Your skin is so warm."

"I just woke up and now you're working me into lather. What do you expect?"

"So, this is what I do to you? Make you so hot, you burn?"

"I guess so. And before you leave for practice, you'd better finish what you started. Make me explode, set me on fire."

Dylan groaned again and my nipples hardened under his gaze. He reached down with his mouth and took my breast into his warm mouth. I mewed. He tickled my nipple with his tongue and the sensation made my sex clench. My thighs tightened in anticipation, and I wiggled. "Hold still, don't struggle."

My breath caught in my chest. He blew across my wet nipple, sending waves of wetness and need to my groin. He lowered his mouth again. He bit the nipple tip softly letting me know my struggling would not be tolerated. I moaned loudly. The sensation exquisitely painful.
Wetness flooded my channel.

Dylan secured his position over me by straddling my legs and pushing my legs and labia together. *Oh. My.* It was an erotic feeling. I needed to move. I pushed my hips up a little, and groaned.

"Hold still!" With his free hand Dylan pushed his boxers off and gave me the most beautiful view of his cock. I sighed, and strained to see more of him.

"Eyes up here, Gorgeous." He jerked his head up, and gave me a sideways evil grin. I stared into Dylan's beautiful face and watched his eyes cloud over as he held my gaze. I could feel his engorgement resting along my pubic bone. I rolled my hips trying to free my legs so I could let him rest between them, and put his beautiful body closer to mine.

"Stop wiggling." he warned.

He kissed a path to my midsection, and for a split second he released his grip on my thumbs. I slid my hand free to his head and combed his hair with my fingers. His eyes closed and the pure look of satisfaction sent warmth spread through my thighs straight to my clit.

I tried to hold still, but he was just too beautiful. My breaths became shallow and fast. I was becoming dizzy. He nibbled his way across my stomach and dipped his tongue into my navel, making me squirm. He kissed to my hip and bit down on my skin rather hard. The pain was excruciatingly pleasing. I recoiled and pulled away. With lightning speed, Dylan slapped my bare rear. I yelped and jumped. He fixed his eyes on mine.

"Hold still. Wait for me." Dylan slipped his hands deftly between my knees and pushed them apart. A coolness blew across my open slit and I shivered. He settled into the empty space and planted soft tingling kisses along the softness of my thigh. I was beyond aroused. I was shaking with need, and close to hyperventilating. My reflexes kicked in, and I wiggled. I could hear my pulse in my ears and I could feel it pounding behind my eyes. My mouth was dry, but I had nothing to swallow. He blew cool air across my clit again. I groaned and thrust my hips up. I could hardly contain myself. I begged him, "Please, Dylan, please stop." I pulled at his hair, but lost my grip just as he dove into my cleft. His tongue slowly circled my sensitive clit. I cried out, "Please, Dylan."

"Wait for me." he gave me a shy smile and went back to lick the full length of my folds, and stopped to circle my hardened nub again. I was losing control.

I couldn't speak. My voice caught and between my gasping breaths I quivered to my core. Before I could stop myself, I tipped over the top. "Dylan!" I screamed. My orgasm lit me up like fireworks against a blackened sky. I tingled from my belly and thighs straight to my core. My stomach muscles contracted and my sex clenched so tight my stomach muscles hurt.

"You didn't wait. I thought you were going to wait for me." A playful, evil grin developed on his face. "Now I guess I just have to take what I want." He plunged his fingers deep into my vagina, rubbing along the inside wall of my quivering sheath, thumbing my clitoris. I was so sensitive and still quaking from my first orgasm I tried to move away. He slapped the side of my rear hard. The shocked look on my face caught him by surprise. A horrible vision of my ex-fiancée Ryan's face flashed in front of me. Dylan quickly rubbed the stinging skin. He smiled playfully, but held my stare. I was getting scared. I didn't like the spanking. It made me feel humiliated, violated, and vulnerable.

"Don't Dylan, please." I whispered.

"Don't what? Take what I want? I think I deserve it, don't you? You should have waited for me." his playful smile returned, and my eyes widened into something close to being fear. He ignored my expression and shot me a dimpled smile that made me quiver. He continued to plunder my vagina and I felt the wetness seep onto my thighs. I could feel my own climax building again. I closed my eyes, trying to escape where I was, and what my mind thought was happening. Where had this aggressive side come from? Was he seeing the fear in my face? I didn't see the smack coming. When he connected with my bare skin, I squealed. I recoiled in pain and fear. I pulled my legs up as I retreated from him. He pinned me to the bed with his hips. Before I could rise up on my elbows he circled my waist with his massive arm and flipped me onto my stomach. I could feel his erection on the crease of my buttocks. Fear surged through me, I struggled against him, I clawed at the sheets to try and climb from the bed. He slipped his arm around my waist and lifted my butt into the air. He snagged my thumbs with one hand and held them together behind my neck, my face planted firmly in the pillow. He put his thighs against the backs of my bent legs and forced himself inside me. There was a blinding pain. I felt a rip and searing pain deep inside me. He pounded me from behind so rapidly and deeply, I felt nauseated. Tears streamed from my eyes. My screams were muffled by the pillow. I was ragged with fear and pain. He pounded me until he reached his release, pushing so deep that the pain burned my gut and bile roiled my stomach. He released my thumbs when he finally calmed. He leaned over my back and kissed the nape of my neck. He whispered in my ear. "I told you to hold still." He snickered, rubbed my shoulders and kissed down my spine. When he pulled out, I sank to the mattress. Dylan laid down beside me gently kissing me, until he saw my panicked, tear streaked face.

"Oh my God." he muttered more to himself than out loud. "I hurt you. I was…oh my God." His face changed from playful to horrified. He pushed himself up in the bed to look at me. I couldn't look back. I had failed again. When would I learn? All I needed to do was tell him to stop. My past relationships filtered into my mind. Ryan's abusiveness reared its ugly head and I stared off, tears pinching behind my eyes. I felt emotionally numb. I tried to blank my mind. Experience taught me; no reaction was the best reaction.

"Jesus. I was messing around. Why didn't you stop me? Why didn't.... Oh my God! Why would you let me do that, if you... Why the hell wouldn't you tell me to stop?" Dylan's voice raised in a loud, scared tone. He was close enough to my face his hot breath moved a tendril of loose sweaty hair away from my face. I tensed. *Don't react.* My mind raced, trying to put this encounter in some category. It certainly wasn't as violent as my last tryst with Ryan. But I struggled to put it into words for Dylan. Hell, I had a problem labeling it for myself. Fear surged through me. I stared past him at the ceiling, holding back the tears that wanted to fall.

The pain was intense, my side was splitting. My breath was ragged and halted. I winced with the slightest movement. Oh. My. God, what just happened? Fear surged through me. Tears welled in the corners of my eyes again.

"Talk to me, Stacia, please. Please." He continued to stare at me, begging with his eyes for some explanation. He grabbed my chin and tried to force me to look at him. I held my breath and continued to put my emotions into a tight little space in my head. I stared at the corner of the room where the wall met the ceiling. Dylan tried again to gently pull me back to him. I stiffened, using my mind to close the lid on the box I had shoved myself into.

Dylan shot off the bed. The movement made me jump. He fisted his hands in his hair, and snatched his clothes off the floor and chair.

"Stacia, talk to me." Dylan called softly. He had moved into my line of sight, but I stared past him focusing on the corner of the room. He made a move towards me as if to touch me and I turned my face away from him.

"I'm so sorry; I never meant to hurt you. I was playing around; I thought you were playing along." His voice was barely a whisper. He turned away. He looked defeated. His shoulders slumped, his brow furrowed, and he slunk off to the bathroom, alone.

I laid there unable to move, unwilling to give into the pain searing through my abdomen. I curled into a tight ball, facing away from the bathroom door. When the water in the shower started, so did the water works from my eyes. I felt foolish, why was I so afraid to tell him? And what the hell tore inside me? I could still feel the remnants of our sex seeping from my vagina. I closed my eyes still feeling off, uncomfortable. I laid there mortified, and humiliated. How could I let him do that? I thought I'd moved past the victim phase. But this just proved I was still the scared girl I was before I left Ryan. How could I do that to him? He deserved an explanation. I just couldn't give him one, couldn't let him know how vulnerable I felt. I never expected this, to feel so filleted. Dylan had never shown this side of himself before. And I had to admit, at first, he was playful. Hell, at the end he was playful. It was my response to him that was scary. My eyes closed. My body convulsed with my sobs until I fell asleep.

I never heard Dylan leave for practice. But, I knew he was gone when I opened my eyes and the bathroom door was open. The floor was void of all of his clothes. I could barely move. Overcome with nausea, I crawled from the bed, and clawed my way to the bathroom. *Wow, was it hot in here? Did Dylan turn up the furnace, thinking I might be cold when I woke up naked?*

The vomiting came in waves. Sweat poured from my brow. I laid naked on the cool tiled bathroom floor. Not wanting to

move for fear of the pain. What the hell was wrong with me? Could our rough sex have caused some internal damage? I believed my own self-pity and embarrassment were the true reasons for my continued nausea. Maybe the alcohol I drank last night. I made a feeble attempt to rise and get into the shower. I stood in the shower for only a few minutes and let the water flow over me. I started to sweat. I felt shaky and a wave of nausea overtook me again. I sat numbly on the tub edge and tried to reevaluate my misdirection from the morning.
Where did I go wrong? I wanted so badly to please him, I allowed him to take what he wanted. No resistance, no restraint. And I was paying for it now.

Slowly, I rose off the edge of the tub. I was lightheaded and sweating from the warmth in the shower. I was still nauseated and my legs felt like rubber. I returned to the bed. I really needed to call Mike. I didn't think I could cover the field today. My embarrassment was overwhelming, and the pain in my stomach waxed and waned. I picked up the phone, tried to gather my wits and call Mike to send another photographer to the afternoon game today.

"Mike?" I whispered into the phone.

"Yes, darling?" he answered all chipper using another term of endearment. I smiled, even through the pain, he made me smile.

"I think you need to send someone else to the field today to cover the paper, I'm not feeling well." I said.

"Are you alright? You sound like you've been crying." How could he be so perceptive on the phone?

"No, I'm just tired; I think I have the flu." I lied.

"Oh sweetie." he crooned. I could feel his fatherly concern through the phone. "Go back to bed then. I'll cover the game myself. You take care of yourself and call me later. Lots of fluids, stay in bed." I felt his invisible fatherly hug through the phone. I felt bad about my lie. I could place miles between us by lying to him. I hung up quickly just as another wave of nausea hit. I headed to the bathroom, I almost made it.

I vomited so violently, drops dripped down the side of the commode. Oh, my self-loathing and self-pity were doing a number on me! I started to cry again. I knew deep in my heart that Dylan may not get over this. I couldn't talk to him, couldn't tell him he was hurting and scaring me. I had crossed some imaginary line, like the line at the locker room. This time I may not be able to back up, take back what I didn't say. I hugged the tile floor, absorbing its coolness. I wiped my mouth with the hand towel I reached for from the floor. I pushed myself up, and tried to return to the bed. It must've been one hundred degrees in there, it is so damn hot. I was lightheaded and dizzy. I saw black dots floating just inside my field of vision. I tried to stand, I tried to step. Blackness engulfed me and the floor swallowed me. I heard nothing, I saw nothing, and I felt nothing.

Chapter 11

Needles, IV's, CAT scans and X-rays. I was poked and prodded until my arms ached and all I could see were tubes coming out of places I didn't think tubes could be. Somewhere in the middle, I must have fallen asleep. As I woke, I squeezed my legs together and found another tube with warm liquid seeping down inside it. There's something cold underneath me. The oxygen tube in my nose tickled and all I wanted to do was remove it. I tried to move. I hurt, my side burned, but the nausea was gone. I forced myself to open my eyes. Dylan was asleep in a chair across the room. He looked uncomfortable and disheveled. I was confused. What day was this? What the hell happened? Where was I? Another attempt at movement elicited a gasp and a moan. *WOW, did that hurt!* Dylan shot from the chair, and flew to the bedside.

"Don't touch anything." he said. He reached above the bed, flipped a button, and turned on a light. He grabbed my hand a little too tight, and squeezed. "I am so glad you're back." His smile melted my heart. It was genuine and full of emotion.

My voice was hoarse and weak, my head swum with bewilderment.

"Where did I go?" I squeaked out. Dylan laughed out loud, and smiled.

Just then the door opened and a man in light blue hospital scrubs walked in. Dylan straightened up, swiped his hair back and rubbed the back of his neck. The small smile snaked to a thin line on his face with just a small curl edged on his lips. He looked so cute and handsome.

My pensive look at the man, who just walked in, must have been enough to warrant enlightenment. He delved into a lengthy, medical explanation on my ruptured ovarian cyst and the blood that had pooled in my abdomen. My mind was hazy and my comprehension was poor. But a few points burned into my consciousness.

"You have a small tube to drain off the fluid. Your oxygen level is too low, and you need to leave the oxygen running in your nose. You have an IV in your arm for fluids and for antibiotics for three days. If you push this button, you'll get pain medication." He pointed to a machine hooked onto the pole next to my bed. "You have a couple small incisions; it will take a little time to heal. You are one lucky lady that someone found you and we could get this infection under control. You're just going to be weak for a while. But you'll recover quickly."

I looked at Dylan. He looked worn out. A permanent crease on his eyebrow deepened and he expelled a rugged deep sigh. He stared at the doctor, who to me, sounded like a rambling talk show host. Dylan had his hands on his hips, straight backed; stoically absorbing every word being said. Just like a good pitcher, just taking direction from a different coach. After their conversation, Dylan shook the doctor's hand and turned away. I saw him rub his forehead; saw the tired slope of his shoulders. I wanted so badly to hold and comfort him.

Instead, I said, "Go home, you need some sleep, and a shower." He turned stern eyes toward me, and his eyebrows knitted in concern and frustration.

"None of this is your fault, please, go home." I turned my head away from him and closed my eyes. I could feel his eyes on me, hotly burning a small hole into the back of my head. The last thing I wanted was his pity.

"This is not your responsibility. Go home, and get some sleep."

"I'm so sorry. I didn't mean to…."

"Stop. Dylan, just go home." I strengthened my resolve, he'd never know about my past with Ryan. Past experiences with men had always led me to cut and run. It was easier than explaining my past failures. His audible exhale signaled resignation and maybe a little exasperation at me. But I did not want him to feel guilty over something he could not control. I still didn't turn to look at him as he stole from the room. A small amount of relief washed over me that he was willing to go, but I also felt so lonely. It will feel just like this when he gets called back to the major league.

I slept again. The nurses kept waking me up to take my temperature and vital signs. I became acutely aware that I was not alone in my room. I heard breathing. I thought I saw a form fluidly filling a chair in the corner. I was comforted by the fact. In the dim light I wait for any type of movement. I made an attempt to move and look at the chair. The pain shot through my side, I hissed an exhaled, "Oh, my." and grabbed my side and my tubes.

Dylan vaulted from the chair, and stood beside the bed looking helpless. His expression changed from one of concern to anger, before I could even settle back against the pillows. I could see his underlying anger surface behind his beautiful lush lips as they thinned to a tight line.

"Why didn't you tell me I was hurting you? I feel terrible. Not exactly a shining moment for me, and then when I found you on the floor…"

"Don't Dylan. Please don't." I was falling into the same type of relationships I had in the past. I didn't want to repeat the past. Oddly, I couldn't stand to see the pain on his face. I

78

longed to hold him, comfort him and drive that look of despair away. I sheepishly looked away. I lowered my eyes so he couldn't see my shame.

"Look at me!" The force of his voice made me quiver inside. I looked back. I winced unsure if it was from the pain, or from his direct order. He reached for me, I recoiled, and refused to look directly at him. He dropped his hand, and studied my face.

"What happened to you? Why won't you talk to me?" He lifted his hand again, halted long enough to see if I'd pull away, and cupped my face. He softly caressed my cheek. His face was pained, tears pooled on the edge of his eyelid. He inhaled sharply, his voice lowered to a whisper. "I'm so sorry. I never meant to hurt you. I feel so bad, like the worst kind of lover. I really hurt you, and if it happens again, I don't think I could live with that." I dropped my eyes again. His confession hurt, but secretly I was excited by the knowledge that he could have feelings for me, or was this his way of telling me he'd leave? I ached to comfort him. I wanted him. Longed for his touch. I cradled my face in his hand, and he softened further.

"Just talk to me, tell me, all I need is a little trust. I'll treat you right, Stacia." he leaned his forehead against mine. I stiffened again. Did all men ask you for their trust? Because in my experience they were more than willing to destroy it if given a chance.

"I will. I'm sorry." I knew I owed him at least the words. Deep down, I knew this wouldn't last. I knew that once he recovered from his injury, he'd leave and my heart would be severed. He wouldn't stay, and this was just a summer fling for him. The majors were waiting for him, and I would lose him. But I said the words he wanted to hear. Dylan brushed the loose hair away from my face. Just the soft brush of his hand caused a warmth in my belly. I moaned, and without hesitation, Dylan reached over for the pain pump and dispensed a dose of Demerol into my IV.

"No.", I said too late to stop him.

"No, what?" he asked as he smoothed my hair, and rubbed my cheek. He knew exactly what he had done. The drug kicked in, and I started to drift to sleep. Comforted by Dylan's presence and bolstered with the pain medication, I felt like I could tell him, be honest like he asked. As my eyes slowly began to close, Dylan moved back to his chair in the corner.

"I'm afraid I'll lose you." I whispered. My voice was still weak and thready. And my explanation floated away as I fell asleep, falling into the deafness of the room.

My dreams were filled with terrible monsters, an unsatisfied sexual encounter with Dylan, and I screamed just as an anaconda ate him. I woke with a start, sweating, writhing, fretful and moaning. I wasn't sure if I had another temperature, pain or if I was really sexually frustrated, which I doubted. I was afraid he'd leave me. My eyes darted around the room. Dylan sat stoically in the chair his hands clasped together supporting his chin as he stared at me. Only a thin tight line for lips. He exhaled loudly. "Are you ok?"

"Yeah, fine. Why would you ask?"

"Maybe because you've screamed my name twice, kicked all the sheets off the bed, moaned and cried, all in the span of forty minutes. Want to tell me about it?"

I shook my head, and blew air through my pursed lips; tears pricked the corners of my eyes. All I could see was Dylan leaving, either by going back to the majors or getting eaten. I hesitated, and then whispered.

"A snake ate you."

"A snake? Really? What started that?" He was extremely amused. A smile slithered across his face. And I saw his beautiful dimples again.

"We didn't get to....well I didn't....Does this cold thing need to stay on? I'm freezing. And what the hell is this tube for? Why can't they take some of this shit off?"

"We didn't what? Come on, Stacia. We didn't what?"

"Is it hot in here?"

"You just said you were freezing!" Humor edged into his voice. "Is there something else you dreamt about?"

"Not something I want to tell you."

"Why, were there tigers too?" Dylan laughed out loud. "Because, you talk in your sleep you know." He laughed again.

The realization hit me like a mallet, and I was horrified. My eyes rounded, and my eyebrows shot to my forehead.

"I was just seeing if you'd tell me the truth." he continued to smile.

I moaned and swiped my eyes with my hands and rubbed my stomach. More from embarrassment than anything else. He knew. He knew I wanted him, and that I knew he'd just leave me in the end. I couldn't look at him, not acknowledge what he knew.

Dylan stood, kissed me quickly on the forehead, and headed for the door.

"Game this afternoon. Gotta run."

I felt lonely even before he got to the door. Maybe he needed space, or didn't like the idea I couldn't tell him about my dream. But he was leaving. My fears were being realized. One small step at a time. Before he reached the door, he pivoted, headed back to the bed, and hit the pain pump button again.

"You need to sleep, no more nightmares. I'll be back after the game." He kissed me again quickly and with enough force to make me moan. I watched as his frame filled the doorway, light flowed in around him and swallowed him.

Chapter 12

I couldn't move my legs. They were being held down. I flexed my feet and opened my eyes.

"Hello there, beautiful." A small smile tipped my lips. I was so glad he came back.

"How long have you been here?" I asked, my voice still raspy from sleep.

"Long enough. Wow, do you have some wild dreams on drugs!" He flashed me a million watt smile.

"Not fair. All I've been doing is dreaming since yesterday." I quipped.

"Oh, I know what you've dreamed about!" He looked excited. "You forget you talk in your sleep!" His smile was consuming. His dimples were illuminated. An evil grin spreads across his face. "Tell me what you were dreaming." he whispered. I moaned, and tried to keep eye contact with him. This was embarrassing. I loved the fact my dreamy musing would cause him to smile so uninhibitedly. He leaned in and kissed a small trail along my cheek to my ear, and whispered, "I've missed you too."

"Mmm" I blinked my eyes and absorbed his comment.

"And that means, you like this?" He kissed me softly again. Then leaned back and watched my face as he grazed my cheek with his knuckles. My eyes automatically closed savoring the feeling.

"Um huh."

"And you're being reduced to grunts and groans?"

"Um hum."

"I kind of like this." He leaned up again and grazed his lips across mine, "And I'm used to you being speechless."

"We should really talk about the night before last."
My eyes widened and I wanted to avoid the questions I knew would follow. He'd pry into my past and see just how vulnerable and insecure I was. All my past failures would rush out and I couldn't take a chance he'd leave once he heard my tales of woe. I kept my eyes down. Dylan looked up at me from under my lashes. His voice was low and full of remorse.

"I will *never* do that again. I thought you were playing along. Resisting to get a rise out of me. I was so wrong." Dylan looked longingly into my eyes begging me to understand. The honest intensity in his stare was too strong I looked away.

"Tell me, Stacia. What are you thinking?"
That I'm such an idiot. I should tell him what I think, how I feel. But my past failures crept into my skull. If I told him what I wanted, he'd see me as weak, needy and someone who needed to be taken care of, someone he could control. I needed to be strong.

"I treated you horribly, and I don't see a way to repair this, if you don't talk to me."
I was right, he'd be leaving. I took a deep breath and sighed. Shielding myself for the inevitable pain he was going to inflict. What did I have to lose? I should just tell him.

"I've had some relationships I'm not so happy with. Some guys just aren't who they seem to be after a while.' I eyed him suspiciously. "But, I think you're different." The look on his face let me know he knew exactly what I was going to say. He knew what I felt.

"I know, babe. And I am different. I won't hurt you again." He exhaled loudly, leaned his forehead against mine and closed his eyes. His hand softly cupped my chin. I cradled my face in his hand, and he softened even more.

"I will never treat you like Ryan did. I promise." *Ryan? How did he know about Ryan?* I stiffened, barely breathing. I pulled away to look into his eyes. I slowly began to realize how he'd found out. I was shocked. What else had he learned while I slept? Obviously what he heard concerned him, and for that I was grateful, I think. I pushed him back further so I could look harder into his face. I scowled at him.

"You cheated; listening to what someone says in their dreams, I'm pretty sure is cheating."

"At least I found out, I kind of like the use of that truth serum." He tipped his head toward the IV medication. Dylan crept back up the bed and laid soft kisses to my face and lips gingerly avoiding all the tubes and supporting his weight on his arms. I rubbed his muscular arms and shoulders, and kissed him. I parted his lips with my tongue and tantalized the tip of his tongue, and ran a smooth circle on the roof of his palate.

"Ummm." he groaned.

"Have you been reduced to groans and grunts?" I asked as I sucked his lower lip into my mouth and softly suckled it. I slid my hands down his ribs and the vee of his hips, allowed my thumbs to caress the skin that disappeared beneath his waistband.

"Um hum." he groaned and pulled away. "You shouldn't start anything you can't finish."

"I'd really like to though." I shot back at him, as I cocked my head at him.

"Nope, that's not going to work. You started this in a dream." He pushed himself off the bed.

"You were there!" I smiled, doing my best to hold onto him.

"Yeah, but I got eaten by a snake!" Dylan's laughter was a true enjoyment. I did my best not to join him, my stomach muscles a little too sore to participate. But my smile was splitting my face. This was the Dylan I wanted to see on film, the one I wanted for more than a summer.

The one who was starting to get under my ribs, and into my soul.

Chapter 13

"I need a shower!" I announced to anyone in the room who may listen.

"Maybe today, Stac, all depends on what Dr. Palmer has to say today." Dylan snapped the newspaper shut after reading Mike's review of their recent game.

"At least help me sit up. I've gotta get out of this bed. My back is killing me." I pushed up on my elbows and looked into a beautiful set of cobalt eyes. I smiled my sweetest smile.

"It isn't like it will be my first time sitting up. Come on help me out." I pushed myself up in the bed and started to pull the covers back. The snow job would only work if I made it look like this wasn't my first time off the bed. I did my best to fake it. I slipped my feet over the side of the bed and reached out and grabbed his arm. He hoisted me up so I was sitting with my feet dangling off the bed. I felt dizzy and a little lightheaded, but refused to let it show. I stretched out a little, and Dylan stayed plastered to my side. He started to relax, just sitting next to me. My feet dangling inches off the floor. I leaned into him absorbing his heat. We sat quietly for a couple of minutes.

"Come on, help me shower." I whispered. Dylan stiffened. He looked straight into my face and shook his head.

"Absolutely not! I'm pretty sure you're not cleared to do that with all this stuff still attached. No." He shook his head again.

"I won't do anything to hurt myself. Come on. I want to feel normal again, and I can't do that without a little help." I looked at him sheepishly.

"No!" he replied sternly.

"Oh, for God's sake!" I whined, "It will take five minutes, and I need to start moving. I've been here three days." I stole a sideward glance at him and actually saw him thinking about this. I started a convincing campaign. "If I get tired, I'll come right back, promise." I started scooting off the bed before he could object. My feet hit the floor and my knees began to buckle. Dylan caught my arms, and held me upright.

"Back, now." he growled. My head swam, but I was determined to make it to the shower. Instead of heading back as promised, I pushed the IV pole out in front of me. Dylan had no choice but to gather the paraphernalia and follow me. I was wearing nothing but an oversized snap sleeved gown that was open in the back.

"Nice view." Dylan quipped.

"Like that do ya?" I answered in a fake southern accent. Dylan smiled. Four steps away from the bed I could barely keep my balance. I was breathing heavy and starting to sweat.

"Let's go back." He said dryly, as he juggled the tubes, and struggled to keep me upright.

"No!" I hissed. I batted at the back of my gown trying to obscure his view, but had to use both hands on the IV pole to help me propel forward. I reached the bathroom door four steps later. Sweating and breathing heavy, I triumphantly leaned on the door frame.

"Well, there you go. Now, go back." Dylan scorned. I ignored his request, and he mumbled under his breath.

I reached into the shower and started the water. Steam quickly filled the small room. I slid the gown off my shoulders and unsnapped the sleeves to allow it to fall past all the tubes and the IV.

"Um, loving the view now." Dylan said admiringly. His eyebrow raised, and his pants began to peak over his zipper.

The tube in my stomach pulled and pinched, the one in my bladder spasmed. I stepped into the running water. *Heaven!* I stood for a long time and allowed the water to cascade off me. It felt wonderful.

"Are you about done in there?" Dylan's voice implored me to hurry.

"No." My voice was seductive and gravely. I was feeling better already. "Come join me." I waited for a response, but heard nothing. "I need you to help me." He still did not answer. Within seconds Dylan stood behind me. He grabbed the shampoo off the ledge, and massaged it into my hair, with knowing hands. *Exquisite!*

"Mmmm, that's great." The feel of the water, soap, and warmth loosened my muscles.

Dylan leaned into my back, and I could feel his need pressing a line against my butt cheek. He pushed slightly, and I groaned. Unsure if the moan was from pleasure as from the movement.

"You're beautiful. Even in this state; pale and in pain, you're glorious. But I should not be in here."
I turned to face him causing tubes to twist around me. I reached up and pulled his head down, and kissed him deeply. I pushed my tongue past his lips and explored the recesses of his mouth and knotted with his tongue.

"I want this." I grabbed the soap and lathered up my hands. He moaned and leaned in closer as I firmly grabbed the length of his penis. He gasped and slowly relented to the feeling. Oh, my God, I loved this feeling of control. Loved being able to turn him on. I continued to stroke him from the tip to the base, tightening my grip.

The walls seemed a little closer, but I ignored them. Dylan moaned and growled from the back of his throat, I knew he was under my spell. He put his hands on the shower walls to steady himself. I used my thumbs to skate over the end of his glans.

"Oh, God." he moaned. I saw spots entering the sides of my field of vision. My breathing was ragged, I felt hot. I squeezed his shaft, and continued to stroke him. Dylan's head fell back, and his eyes closed. His cock hardened and throbbed in my hand. I kept up the onslaught working the length and massaging his testicles with alternating hands, slipping my fingers under the sack and applying just enough pressure on the underside.

"Oh, shit." he groaned. His legs tightened, as the darkness crept in closer. "Yes, Oh fuck. I'm going to… " His cock pulsed in my hands, hot cum coated my palm.

"Oh fuck! Fuck! Fuuucccckkk!" I heard him shout just as the blackness engulfed me. I didn't feel the thud, I heard it.

Chapter 14

I woke up, my naked body soaking the sheets on the bed. My wet hair stuck to the side of my face like glue. I fluttered my eyes open and looked around for Dylan. He was dressed in his white button down shirt and his black jeans. His hair was damp, but not soaked. I couldn't see him very well but I knew he didn't have his shoes on because I couldn't hear any sound. He paced back and forth running his hands through his hair. His face was pained. I felt a needle stick into my arm, and a familiar beep, beep, beep of my heartbeat. I felt the pull of the tube in my bladder as a nurse picked up the bag. The tube in my side pinched while someone pulled the tape and dressing off the tender skin of my belly.

"Ouch." I rasped.

"Well, was that worth it young lady?" Dr. Palmer frowned down at me while he looked at my incision and drainage tube in my stomach. A nurse wiped blood from my arm, and plopped a bag of ice on my eye, and face.

I looked up at the doctor and slurred, "I believe so, sir." I tried to smile, but it must have looked more like a grimace because he scowled.

"No more of that, understand?" Dr. Palmer's eyebrows furrowed as he turned his attention back to checking my stomach and punishing me for my stupidity by applying more tape than I thought necessary.

"Yes, sir."

A nurse finally pulled a sheet over me, promising to bring back a clean gown. The only sound in the room was the beep of the machine, and the patter of Dylan pacing. Long silent seconds echoed with only his heavy breathing.

"What the hell was that?" Dylan hissed at me after the door closed. His arms fisted on his hips. I was confused, was he really mad? "Why would you do that? That was so foolish!" He mumbled to himself, turned, fisted his hair with both hands and crossed his arms. He whipped around to look at me, "It would have been nice to know that you were going to pass out in the bathroom, for God's sake!"   I stiffened with fear. An incident involving Ryan flashed into my memory, and I tried to push it away. Dylan wasn't Ryan.

"Why are you so mad?" My voice was small, and it was a good thing Dylan didn't approach the bed, as I was sure I would have pulled away.

"Because, I'm mad at myself. I made you a promise and …" He exhaled loudly, "that was just risky. I should never have done that." He paused a second, and ran his hand down to his neck. "And you did that for me?" I didn't answer him. Guilt consumed me. I made him break his own oath one day after he had made his declaration. I couldn't look at him. My inner voice said, '*Break the tension; make it about him.*'

"Did you have fun?"

"Fun? Jesus, Stacia, I was just trying to make sure you didn't smash your skull on the floor! And I did a poor job of it." I took a deep breath and let it out slowly, pushing my fear into the pit of my stomach.

"I wanted to take care of you. Do they know?" I nodded towards the door, and smiled from under the ice bag.

"No.", he smiled back. "They think I went in there to get you." He reached over and moved the ice bag, grazing his fingertips lightly over the swollen area. A small groan escaped his lips and his look of concern focused on my eye. I didn't pull away. I didn't fear him, I didn't flinch. And right now he wasn't leaving. All I could do was smile as I laid naked under the thin sheet listening to the soft beep of my heart. Thinking a little piece of my heart was being torn off each time I heard the sound. I closed my eyes, I was extremely satisfied with myself.

Chapter 15

I woke up with warmth wrapped around me. I was acutely aware there was a warm body spooning me in the bed while I laid on my side. His hand rested softly along the length of my hip; careful not to touch or pull at any of the awful tubes. His forehead was pressed into the back of my neck, his heated breath skittered down my back. His left hand was tucked between his own legs like he needed to restrain it there. I laid there quietly waiting for him to stir. I relished the closeness, not sure if I'd get it again. I wondered if he had practice today, or if he'd already been there. I couldn't shake the feeling I was on borrowed time; this attraction I had to Dylan was short lived and he'd leave me as soon as the league called him. The thought ruminated around in my head. Had I let my hopes for a future with Dylan run too high? I pushed the thought away; sure I'd lose another small piece of my crumbling heart if I dwelled on it. I would just enjoy this moment, right now.

The hospital door opened with a start. Apparently I had closed my eyes and the noise made me jump. Dylan jumped too, and within seconds he stood erect at the side of the bed. The sudden movement made me wince, and cry out unexpectedly.

"The beds are singles for a reason!" the middle aged nurse said as she floated into the room. "Lots of changes today, young lady."

"Can I go home today?"

"Probably tomorrow, but today we are going to remove some of the tubes and feed you real food. But there are rules to today's activities." She stared at the two of us like Dylan needed rules too. "First, you do not get out of this bed without the help of a *nurse*." She shot Dylan a look of disdain, he dropped his eyes as his arms crossed across his bulging chest and heaved a sigh. "Second, we will take out some tubes in a minute. But no shower until Dr. Palmer sees you. Third, the tube in your stomach should come out tomorrow and then maybe home." She continued to talk, as she reached down and pulled the sheet back. Shock registered on my face. She snapped on a pair of gloves and bent my knees. She deflated the balloon that held the catheter in place and quickly pulled the tube. I gasped at the burn and quickly pulled my legs together. I stole a glimpse at Dylan who was obviously getting a lot of enjoyment out of my uncomfortable predicament. His eyebrows raised and I think he smirked. My purpled eye strained to open and glare at him. He should have excused himself; he never should have witnessed something so personal and humiliating. But then again, I didn't ask him to leave and we had already shared some pretty intimate moments, where he'd seen more than the tops of my legs. Dylan planted a quick kiss to my temple and sighed in my ear.

The nurse patted my leg and pulled the sheet back up. She removed my IV tubing, but left just the needle in my arm and put a special cap on the end of it. She put a new dressing on my stomach after she unceremoniously removed all the tape Dr. Palmer had placed planning to punish me with later. The pulling and tugging made me wince once or twice.

"All done." the nurse announced. I thanked her, as she left. Dylan's face was light. His eyebrows elevated, and he flashed me a perplexed smile rimmed by his gleaming dimples.

"Now that was interesting."

"What?" I asked, "Did you enjoy watching my pain?" My purple eye tried to glare at him. But the swelling prevented me from seeing him.

"No, the fact you didn't say a word or tell the nurse you were uncomfortable or it hurt or anything. You just took it, like it's expected of you. Kind of like the other day, and like when you got hit with the baseball. You don't say a word, don't defend yourself. What kind of pain are you hiding, Stacia? What the hell did Ryan do to you? Why don't you protect yourself?" He looked at me like he expected an answer. After a few tense seconds, he sat gingerly on the edge of the bed, and caressed my cheek.

"You can tell me anything you know. Just tell me, I'll take care of you. I'll protect you. No one should treat you like Ryan did. No one ever will again, I won't let it happen." His tone was reverent. Not what I was used too from other men. He shouldn't make a promise he couldn't keep. Because once he left, I was on my own again.

I was embarrassed, then angry. Did he think he could just fix my past with Ryan? I have had a couple years to find a peaceful place, I was still struggling to find a safe place. I could take care of myself! I folded my arm over my face and tried to rub the feeling of humiliation away. I drug my arm over my bruised swollen eye and rubbed it into my sleeve. Dylan snatched my wrist.

"Stop, it will only bruise further!" I bristled. It was a command, not a request. He reached over and gently touched the corner of my eye. Then softly caressed my temple.

"You don't think I feel guilty enough about that without you making it worse? I care about you. What you think, what you want. I just want you to talk to me."
I knew what I wanted, was he willing to give it? Willing to stay here and not go back to the majors? I knew I could never ask him for such a sacrifice. I had expected it from Ryan, and it backfired.

He rubbed his knuckles over my temple and down my face, pinching my chin between his fingers forcing me to look into his eyes.

"What do you want, Stacia, for now, forever?"

"I want you to be happy." I copped out, I would never ask him to stay with me.

"Not what you want for me, what do you want for you."

I didn't answer him, I just blinked. Ok, so he wants to play hard ball. I'll tell him and see how fast he runs. I wanted him, anyway I could get him. I gathered my courage fully prepared to tell him exactly what I wanted. I took a deep breath, looked him directly in the eyes.

"I want…" My thoughts were interrupted when there was a hard knock on my door.

Chapter 16

The hospital door creaked open and I heard a familiar voice, "Hey, baby girl, you awake?" Mike's thundering voice caused the walls to vibrate. If I had been sleeping, his rough voice would have vaulted me awake. Dylan stood quickly, and crossed the room to the chairs.

"Good Lord it's good to see you." He short stepped into the room carrying a huge basket of junk food and cookies. He turned towards the bed and his eyes fell on Dylan. Mike bristled.

"Here, make yourself useful." Mike handed the basket off to Dylan who immediately dropped it onto the bedside stand. Dylan stepped closer to the bed and crossed his arms across his chest. I could see a muscle in his jaw twitch. Mike headed to the opposite side of the bed, and gathered up my hand. "I'm so glad, you're feeling better, sweetie." He leaned into the bed.

"What the hell happened to your face? I don't remember seeing that the night of your surgery!" Mike shot Dylan an accusing look. And if looks could have killed, Dylan would have been flat on the floor.

"How's it going for real?" Mike's dual meaning wasn't lost on me as he glanced at Dylan and back at me. He was terrible at subtlety. I changed his direction and told him it looked like I'd be going home in the morning.

"Good evasive move. " Mike whispered. He continued the conversation with all the work he was doing, the other people at the station, and how he personally took on my vacated position of team photographer. The whole time, Mike fussed around me, tugging the blankets and tucking them under the mattress. He reached to fluff the pillow behind my back.

"Mike, for goodness sake, can you worry and fuss anymore? I don't think the sheets are pulled up tight enough!" My sarcasm dripped off my tongue. I kicked my feet to loosen the bedding and smiled.

"Well, I miss you. The office is too quiet. And I still have not figured out how you can possibly take one thousand pictures at these games, I can barely get three hundred, and none of them the quality I've seen in your work. When do you think they'll let you come back to work?"

"As soon as I go home, I imagine, this isn't very serious Mike. I'll be back next week for sure." I answered offhandedly. Dylan huffed, and mumbled something under his breath. I ignored the blazing look he was giving me.

"Good. I really need you back. Your pictures are much better than anything I've printed."

Mike stayed nearly an hour. We chatted like school girls on a mini vacation. Each laugh stifled with my hand pressed to my side. Mike continued to entertain me even when my eyes began to feel heavy with exhaustion.

"I'll be back on Monday. That's three days away. That ok with you?" I asked Mike. Concerned about keeping my job and putting Mike in a tight spot.

Dylan mumbled again, snatched his bag from behind the chair and quickly announced, "Got practice." He pivoted on his heels and strode out of the room with purpose.

"You know, girly, he doesn't deserve you. You'd be better served to head in opposite directions." Mike scrutinized me from the corner of his eye.

"Oh, Mike, haven't you heard?" I quipped. "Opposites attract."

"Oh, sweetheart," he retorted, "opposites collide!"

I spent a fitful hour analyzing Dylan's response to Mike's visit. If he felt threatened, he was terribly off track. Mike might act like a pit bull, but he was faithful to a fault. The tension between them was obvious, but why? Had they spent time together on the field, talking about me behind my back? I would ask Mike, and hopefully make him see how much Dylan meant to me, and that he didn't need to protect me.

Dylan didn't come back that night. Sleep came in spurts of fitfulness, my dreams wrought with tears as I found myself abandoned and alone looking for love. Looking for Dylan. I started to stretch, and open my eyes, my shiner extended down into my cheek, but the swelling was receding. I could see a small sliver of light, but everything was fuzzy. I caught a glimpse of movement and strained to look into the dark corner. Before I could reach the light to turn it on, a figure filled the doorway and disappeared.

"Dylan?" There was no response, and the door closed encasing the room in darkness again. My heart sank. I knew he was mad earlier with Mike's visit, but now I wasn't sure why he left. These two men needed to get along. I wanted them both in my life. Even if Dylan left soon, I wanted them to love me like I loved both of them. And there it was, I was in love with Dylan.

Chapter 17

Food never tasted so good. After days of ice and clear broth, I got eggs and oatmeal for breakfast. They tasted wonderful and I ate every bite. Dr. Palmer visited around eight thirty in the morning and removed the last of my tubes informing me I could go home after I ate lunch.

"I go back at work on Monday." I added to our discharge conversation.

"Oh, no, Speedy!" he laughed, "Those stitches don't come out until next week. And I will see you in the office to do that."

"I can just work from home then?" The question was posed more like a statement than an actual question. Dr. Palmer leaned down on the bed.

"You seem to be determined to cause more trouble, young lady. No. But we can talk about working next week, *after* I see you."

I opened my mouth to protest, but quickly closed it again. I was happy just to go home. After the doctor left, I picked up the phone to call Dylan. Excited to share my news. But thought better of it after the previous night's disappearing act, and Dylan not calling or stopping prior to practice today.

I ate lunch alone. Not that I wasn't used to it, I just wanted to share my elation with Dylan. Knowing I shouldn't, couldn't. If he wanted to know, he would have stayed or visited. I was pushing him too hard. This is how my heart was going to feel when he left for good. Lonely and sad.

I called Mike, and he came to pick me up.

"Thanks Mike, I just want to go home." I crawled into the car, and gingerly sat on the seat. I held the seatbelt out away from my body, hoping Mike would drive slowly and hit as few bumps as possible.

"Where's your knight now, princess?" I looked down, wrung my hands together, and picked at the Band-Aid that covered my IV site.

"I think you were right Mike, he isn't staying. He didn't call me last night or come by today. What did the two of you talk about at the baseball field?"

"Why? Do you think I did something to send him away? I told you he wouldn't stay, sweets, he has his own game plan, and it isn't sticking around here."

"Mike, I can handle this, I can handle it when he leaves. Trust me, I know what's coming, and I'll be all right. But I like him a lot, and I want to spend some time with him. Even if it hurts when he leaves, I want this time with him. Do you understand?"

"I just don't want to see you hurt, honey. And if what I see is any indication, he's going to hurt you, bad." Mike looked at me out of the corner of his eye; I couldn't look back, because I knew he was right. If it felt bad that he didn't come back to the hospital, and was gone just one day, I'd have no heart left when he left for good. And If Dylan was right; I never protected myself, so this was going to hurt like hell.

Chapter 18

Mike helped me into my apartment. The remnants of my last tryst with Dylan, still visible in the bedroom. I closed the door with a silent promise to clean it all up later. Mike excused himself with a promise to call later. A quick hug and he was gone. The quiet apartment was overwhelming, but I needed to get used to it. Needed to get used to being alone again. So I resisted calling Dylan, and settled on the couch with Mike's junk food basket. I nibbled on a few items in the basket and set it aside. I thought about cleaning up the bedroom, but that would take a lot more energy than I had right now. Instead, I pulled out my computer, opened up my hidden file, and let the pictures of Dylan flit across the screen. I curled up on the couch, to watch. My eyes were heavy and closed on their own, and blissful sleep engulfed me. One where my dreams ended happily with me wrapped in Dylan's arms.

"When did you get home?" Dylan's silky voice caressed me awake. I strained to open my eyes, blinking the sleep slowly from my eyes. I looked at him as his eyes were glued to the pictures playing on the screen.

"What's that on your computer?" Dylan reached over to the coffee table, twisted the computer to face him, and watched the screen as pictures of the team floated from one into another in the slide show.

The computer scrolled through all my candid shots. All of the one's I had sworn to keep hidden. Dylan stared at them, then shot me a very concerned look.

"Where were those taken?" His eyebrows knitted together, as he watched picture after picture of his team in compromising situations. I swallowed hard, trying to make any sound leak from my mouth, hopefully one that sounded intelligent. I couldn't speak. I just looked at him.

"You followed them?" He glared at the screen attempting to comprehend the impact these pictures could have on team members.

I tried to shut the lid, he stopped me. Instead, I touched his arm softly.

"These are candid shots, pictures I plan on getting rid of. I would never release them, never use them." I pushed the lid closed, and the pictures disappeared from view.

"Then why are you looking at them?" He stayed still as I let my hand fall away from his arm.

"I have hundreds of pictures in this file, most of them of you. I missed you, and wanted to see you. I didn't want to call you, so I watched you."

I opened the computer, and restarted the file with all the pictures of Dylan I had hidden from Mike. He watched with raptured interest as pictures floated from one into another. The first thirty pictures were of him. Then there were a few pictures of Jon. He scrutinized them closely before they disappeared off the screen. The next fifteen were him again. Then a few of Rob with a women from a night club. Again he looked closely at the pictures. Another picture of Dylan filled the view. He reached over slowly and closed the lid.

"Why do you have those?" He slowly turned his head, not really taking his eyes off the computer. His hands were clenched together between his knees.

"I took them a long time ago, when I wanted to learn more about the team. I will never release these. I just have so many pictures of you in this file, and I want to save those."

"Never let anyone see those. Those could hurt so many people."

"I would never hurt the team Dylan. That will never happen." I could tell he was mulling over the ramifications of my choices not to delete all the pictures.

"Never, Dylan, never." I reached over and stroked his arm, making him look me in the eye.

"Never." I repeated, making direct eye contact and squeezing his hand. He took a deep breath and let it out. His head dropped forward and he stared at his clasped hands. Tracing mine with his eyes as it softly covered his.

"I hope so, I really hope so."

~~~***~~~

"Are you hungry?"

"A little." I replied.

"You need to eat, I'll cook."

He left the living room and headed to the kitchen. After five days, I wondered just what he might find out there to cook. I soon heard pans clanking, and smelled chicken cooking. Dylan returned with two plates of chicken parmesan, and pasta. It smelled wonderful. My stomach clenched with hunger. Quite a wonderful surprise to find out he could cook too. I ate about a quarter of my plate, my stomach stretched and full. I moved the rest of my meal around my plate. I could hear him chewing and scraping his plate clean. Nice to know, he ate what he cooked. I took one more bite, using every ounce of effort to swallow it.

"Done?" he asked as he reached for my plate. I handed him the plate and he scoffed at the small amount I had consumed.

"Thank You. That was wonderful. I'm just not feeling up to one hundred percent yet. But that tasted great." I offered up my lame excuse with a smile.

"I'm glad you liked it; wish you would have eaten more, just so you'd heal faster." He shook his head and headed off to the kitchen. I heard the dishes clink in the sink. Soft humming drew me to the kitchen. I padded quietly to the archway. Dylan was rinsing the dishes and bending over to place them into the dishwasher. His jeans tightened across his fine buttocks, and I instinctively drew a quick breath.

"What are you doing in here?" his tone was soft and teasing.

I liked this side of him. Double meaning not withheld.

"Admiring the view." I giggled.

Dylan wiggled his butt, then stood and saddled his hands on his hips. His jeans were riding low on his hips, pointing to a perfectly muscled vee that led to a slightly bulged area along his zipper. His broad smile was relaxed and playful. Far from the man who left my hospital room yesterday and didn't return for twenty hours.

"You should be in there, resting." Dylan used his thumb to point me back to the couch.

I slid into the counter bar stool instead. His smile was relaxed and comfortable.

"Carry on." I giggled and waved my hand dismissively, dropping my eyes to the counter like a princess waiting for the jester to entertain her. He seemed comfortable with my admiration. He danced around the kitchen, continuing to load the dishwasher and wash the counter top, wiggling his butt, and striking poses like a body builder. Giving me a full view of his gorgeously toned body. Giggles erupted from me with more frequency as he did his best to entertain me while he cleaned up the kitchen. He rolled his stomach as he reached up to put away the spices. I smiled. He pumped his arms up, tightening his biceps and kissed each one of them gingerly. My groin heated and clenched. My eyebrows lifted in a look of pure enjoyment. I laughed out loud.

Pleased with his performance, Dylan danced around the counter and gingerly squeezed a quick hug to my shoulders. I longed for more. His kitchen antics were a great turn on. I clung to his shirt front.

"You're beautiful you know." I said as I tilted my head and winked.

"Why, thank you. Now you need to rest. Come on, we can watch the game on ESPN." He quickly kissed the top of my head, and slid his arms down my shoulders and gathered my hands up into his warm moist hands. Electricity raced down my spine, and I shuddered, a response that did not go unnoticed. Dylan smiled, and led me into the living room. I folded myself into his side on the couch.

"Dylan?"

"Yes?"

"I just wanted to ask what happened last night."

"What do you mean?"

"Between you and Mike."

"It's not really between Mike and me. It was about…well, it's not really important right now."

"It is important. I'm just trying to make sure there isn't a problem between you two. Mike's my boss, he's important to me. And you're special too, so I can't have you two at odds. He'll always be…"

"It's not him." Dylan sighed.

"So, it's me?" I was met with silence. My unanswered question weighed on my mind. What perturbed him? Was it my blatant selfishness? Did I expect too much from him? Was he aware I wanted him to give up his dreams for mine? And I just couldn't imagine Mike keeping quiet at the fence. He could have said something to Dylan about how I really felt. My blood ran cold. "I'm sorry." I whispered.

"For what? You have absolutely no idea what you're even apologizing for, do you?" He peered at me sideways, using his shoulder to push me away so he could look at me. I refused to look at him. "Why do you do that? Why do you automatically assume the problem is you?"

"Because, I've caused a lot of trouble these last couple of weeks, actually most of my adult life. I put Mike in a tight spot, kept you from practice by getting sick. And pissed off a doctor or two."

"Really? After everything that's happened this week, you're worried about how other people were affected?"

"Yes, and I am sorry. I was being selfish."

"Are you fucking kidding me? Who the hell fucked you up? That Ryan guy? You're not selfish!" I stiffened at his outburst, and recoiled from his side.

"I'm sorry, Dylan. I really am."

"Stop, now." he growled. "It's not you, Stacia. And right now is not a good time to talk about it. Please, let it go. Let's just watch the game." I sat quietly for a minute.

"So, if it's not me, or Mike. What happened Dylan?"

"Not now." He pulled me back in tight, and rubbed my arm. I curled into him, absorbing his warmth, and taking the comfort I wanted to give to him. Who hurt him? Why was he becoming more distant? Was he already getting ready to leave? Why was he not telling me the truth about why he was upset?

"Dylan?"

"Yes?"

"Was it practice?"

"Quiet, the game's on." he snapped.

"I'm sorry." I whispered. Even if I didn't know what I was apologizing for, I was upset that he was upset. I was just sorry for all the pain he had endured.

I leaned into him. I grew quieter. He laid a few soft kisses to my temple, and softly stroked my arm. I tried to concentrate on the game, but I fell asleep sometime during the fifth inning. I felt the comfort of the soft blanket off the back of my couch touch my neck and his hand soothed mine as it laid across his thigh.

I never felt him move out from under me while I slept. I woke up, the couch was empty, and the TV was off. The apartment was silent, and empty. Like the hole in my heart. Dylan was gone.

Chapter 19

I gathered the blanket around my shoulders and headed off to the bedroom. I was filled with dread knowing I still had to clean up the mess. I opened the door and a wonderful sight met me. The bed had fresh linens, the floor that was dotted with clothes and paramedic debris was cleared. The bathroom was cleaned and fresh white towels were hung on the rods. It smelled clean and a slight bleach smell tickled my nose. When could he have possibly had time to clean up this mess? I looked into the bathroom mirror. The bright light illuminated my gaunt, pale face. I looked thin, and my skin was almost iridescent. The purple color around my right eye was now two shades of purple and black. I smiled a little, remembering the encounter that led to the bruise. I examined my face in the mirror and decided I wouldn't have stayed here either with what looked back. Why wouldn't Dylan tell me what was wrong? He was pulling away faster than I thought he would. It would be so wrong to want him to stay, but that was exactly what I wanted from Dylan. I wanted everyday with him. I was selfish. So, he had lied.

I needed a shower. My muscles ached, and all the areas where tubes had been taped were covered with black marred residue, I slid out of my clothes, and looked at my body again in the mirror. It was the first real look at my incisions. The stitches were small, close and evenly spaced. It sure ruined any chances of wearing a bikini, as there were four of them spaced over the right side of my belly. Bruises dotted my arms and stomach. Varied colors of green, blue and purple all in different phases of tenderness and healing. This would heal. I had a different view of the healing of my heart.

I opened the glass stall door, and turned on the water. The sound was comforting, and my skin pricked in anticipation. I reached for a fresh towel, and placed it closer to the shower door. The shower was uncharacteristically empty. My multitude of shampoo bottles, body soaps, and conditioners were gone. I looked behind me, looking for my favorites. I sighed, frustrated beyond hell that he had cleaned up so well. I would have to leave the comfort of the water to retrieve my shampoo. I reached out for my towel, and caught a glimpse of a shadow in the bathroom. Before I could grab the towel, a strong hand encircled my wrist. I gasped and pulled back not positive who was in the room. It was definitely a male hand, he slipped a new bottle of body soap into my hand. Dylan's hand. I sighed with relief. How thoughtful. The smell when I opened it was heavenly.

"Thank You." I breathed. In my mind, I thanked him not only for the body wash, but for returning. I started to wash. I slowly and carefully palmed the body wash in my hand, scrubbing the blackened tape areas to clear them. I sighed loudly. I stood with my hands on the shower wall and absorbed the heat of the water, and steam; letting it loosens my aching muscles.

The glass door opened and a naked muscular form stepped in behind me. "You'll need shampoo." His hand jutted forward and shook the new shampoo bottle. I took it and stepped under the cascading water to soak my hair. Dylan grabbed the shower gel and washed and massaged my back and shoulders.

"That's wonderful." I groaned and let go of a lung full of air. He worked with skill down my back to the small of my back. My sex responded to the seductive massage and the memory of the last shower we shared. I smiled, my palms flat on the shower wall, my hair soaking in the falling water.

He worked his way down to my buttocks, and I exhaled sharply. He continued to massage and wash my thighs and calves. Heated lust coursed through my veins. I moaned out loud.

"If you're trying to heat me up, it is working." I said breathlessly. Wild sensations roared through me. I bent my knees to allow him better access to the area of me that was gathering the most heat. His hands were everywhere, rubbing my shoulders, down my arms and back and slipping around to my breasts. He plucked my nipples with his finger tips, sending raging heat directly to my core. I shivered and groaned. My clitoris throbbed and pulsed. I leaned back into his chest. I could feel his body heat as his hands massaged and soaped my body.

He slipped his hands down my back and pushed me back towards the shower wall. Then he rubbed my thighs and down my calves, gently massaged my sore muscles.

I was hypersensitive. My ragged breathing had my hands tingling but I planted them firmly on the shower wall in front of me. The water continued to skirt down my body.

"Turn around." he ordered. But I hesitated at his command, afraid to relinquish my hold on the shower wall. I didn't want to break the wonderful spell by turning around. I feared a visual reminder of my purpled, pale face would make Dylan stop.

He continued massaging the soap deeply into my thighs, skidding down my legs to my calves and feet. I drew a deep breath, arching my back instinctively.

"Babe, turn around." Dylan's husky voice made me shiver. I slowly turned to find Dylan on his knees on the shower floor. Looking up, he was worshipping my body with his gleaming eyes. He slid his hands up the fronts of my legs, skimming the apex of my thighs making me gasp. His hands rounded to my buttocks and he planted his nose into my cleft. He blew a soft stream of air across my sensitized skin.

"Bend your knees." His grip on my buttocks firmed, and his flat palms massaged deeply. Pulling me closer to his mouth.

I did as I was told, locking my eyes with his. My hands behind my back flattened to the cold shower wall. I gasped, hypersensitive and leaned back against the wall.

"Close your eyes." I couldn't, afraid of what I would miss if I did close them. I fixed my gaze to his face. His eyes were bright and glimmering. Silver flecks floated inside his beautiful blue eyes. Content, he looked content.

"Close them." he whispered. I did, and my head rolled back and thudded against the wall. His tongue slipped up the inside of my right thigh. I quaked. He used his thumbs to separate the soft swollen tissues between my legs.

"Mmmm, beautiful." he hummed along my skin. I was close to hyperventilating. The anticipation was overwhelming. My legs began to quiver. His tongue tickled my engorged, throbbing clitoris. A loud moan escaped my lips, my hands slipping down the wall slightly. I could feel a small smile glide onto Dylan's face.

"You like?" he asked.

"Uh huh."

"This is mine." Dylan slipped his finger up the crevasse raking the rough pad over my bulging nub of nerves. His hand was immediately replaced with the warmth of his tongue as he circled my clit. I slipped down the wall a little more, gasping and crying out.

"And this is mine." he hummed against my lower lips as he plunged his fingers into my vagina circling them and stroking the front wall. I shook with desire. My blood burned in my veins. I couldn't breathe; short gasps of air were hard to pull through the cascading water and the assault on my body. Dylan's words were possessive and powerful. I was affected by his words more than my body's traitorous response.

"And someday, this will be mine." He thumbed the rim of my rectum, and my involuntary clench nearly made me explode. I quivered and shook with need, slipping a little more on the wall. I whimpered, my body sung with the impending orgasm that threatened to tear through me.

"Can you talk to me? Trust me, Stacia?" Dylan whispered as he feathered kisses and soft laps of his tongue across the tip of my clit. I couldn't talk. I barely nodded.

"Oh babe, this is beautiful." He blew a cool breath across me and opened up the soft tissues further with his thumbs. Rubbing the lips spreading my juices with his thumbs while his fingers slowly circled inside me.

"Do you know how beautiful you look right now? In total need, head thrown back, unable to control your breathing? Come for me."

His words were my undoing. I unraveled. His command was met with a violent orgasm that collapsed completely around him, my vagina clutching his fingers and slicking his hand with my juices. I screamed loudly, "Ohhhh" my mouth a perfect circle. I couldn't hold my position anymore, my legs began to wobble. He continued to stroke the orgasm as it rolled into another. I tried to tighten my thighs to hold me into place, but they shook uncontrollably. Dylan rubbed and stroked until I could no longer hold my own weight and I slid down the shower wall to the floor. He gathered me into his lap, my head bobbed as I was totally spent.

"There, there. So beautiful." he cooed. He stroked my wet hair and helped me calm my breathing. He reached between my

114

legs again applying soft pressure to my sensitive nub. My body spasmed. My mind was foggy, my body lax and loose. How did he do that? Reduce me to a bowl of Jell-O? Dylan nuzzled my neck and feathered kisses to my face. My eyes closed as I absorbed him. He used his free hand to rub my thigh and tickle across my stomach until his eyes settled on my incisions. He stiffened, immediately moving back to my thigh.

I moved in his lap, reaching down to find his organ.

"Oh, no. No, no, no. Not tonight. You need sleep." I scrunched my face into a startled gawk, and then a hurt gaze. "I know my limits."

"You, Stacia, do not seem to have any limits. I really don't want to hurt you anymore."

Anymore? What could he possibly mean by anymore? He slid me off his lap onto the cold shower floor, I shivered. He stood and shut off the water. As gently as he could, he scooped me off the floor and wrapped me into a towel, and carried me to the bed. He stayed near the bed, helped me towel my hair, and handed me panties and an oversized tee shirt. I couldn't tear my eyes from him. I kept catching glimpses as he moved around the room picking up items, handing me my hair brush, and cleaning the bathroom.

"Come on Dylan." I crooned as I stared at him. He turned to pick up the towel and brush off the bed, avoiding eye contact and continued to clean up the room. I slipped my feet off the bed and followed him back into the shower.

"Go back to bed." he said sternly.

"No, I won't!" I hissed back.

"Stacia, this is not debatable, go back to bed!" He fisted his hips and my eyes slid down his naked body. "After the events of this week, I think it's better if I just stay away from you."

I was truly wounded. Tears leapt to my eyes and threatened to spill down my cheeks. My thoughts turned to the probability that he'd be leaving, and this was his goodbye.

"What events Dylan?" I skated my eyes to his, and he winced at the unshed tears he saw. "I am fine; none of this is your fault. You didn't hurt me, I am an adult and I make my own decisions. You couldn't stop me even if you wanted to." He turned to walk away. "What's going on Dylan? What aren't you telling me? What happened? Because after the performance in the shower, I can't imagine you weren't affected by any of that." I absently swung my hand and pointed past him to the open shower door.

"Go back to bed!" he hissed through a clenched jaw, and ticking cheek.

I reached for him, he recoiled.

"You don't scare me. I won't run. Even when you leave, I won't be ruined. I make my own decisions!"

"I wonder about your decisions sometimes, Stacia. Are they always what's best for you? Have you even considered that maybe I don't want to stay away, but I don't have a choice?"

"What the hell did Mike say to you?" I yelled, making a mad grab for my side. A move that didn't go unnoticed by Dylan. His eyes stuck to my hand as I covered my incisions and pushed to dissipate the pain. He immediately stepped towards me, gathering me into his arms. I pushed against his chest and stepped back.

"What the hell is going on?" I screeched. Pain seared my sore muscles. I grabbed my side again and folded over with the pain. "Holy Shit!" I murmured. I couldn't ignore the pain, I turned and headed to the commode, sweat began to gloss my face. I screwed my face up and dropped my head to hide my discomfort. I sat down hard, almost missing the seat.

"Jesus, woman!" Dylan's face appeared in front of mine, his hands pulling my shoulders into his chest. "We're just worried about you, that's all. You're pushing yourself too hard. Mike's worried. I'm worried. Hell the team's a little freaked and worried. You will not return to work before Dr. Palmer says it's is ok. You will not be working from home. You will not be going to any games until we make sure you're fine."

"WE? Who the hell is *we*? *I* am fine, *I* am an adult. *I* know what I can and can't do." I tried to pull back, but met resistance. Dylan held me close to his chest. Did he really care? Was he willing to give me what I wanted? At that moment, it felt good. I liked this. Too much. I could feel his chest heaving with his breaths. I was comfortable. He liked me, and he cared. But I knew my time was limited, he'd be leaving soon, and my heart would break in two. I steadied myself and started putting the wall back up around my heart.

"Dylan?" I talked to his chest.

"Hum?"

"When are you leaving?" I wrapped my hands around his back, under his arms.

"Pretty soon, but not tonight, you need someone here."

"No, I'm fine. If you have practice in the morning, I understand. I'll be fine here by myself."

"You want me to leave?" He tipped his head to look at me his eyebrows shot to his forehead. "Not going to happen." He pulled me back in and rubbed my back, keeping me close to his chest.

"Why are you staying?"

"To protect you."

"From what?"

"Yourself."

"Why do you think you have to stay away from me?"

"To protect you."

"From what?"

"Me." He nuzzled into my hair and neck. Breathing in deeply, trying to inhale me.

He cared. Maybe even loved me. Another piece of my heart broke off. When he left, I was going to be crushed.

"Now, do you need help to get back to the bed?"

"Good grief. No." I mumbled as I pushed myself up off the commode. Dylan wrapped himself around me and guided me back to the bed.

"You're going to bed now."

"No, Dylan."

"Where is that medicine the hospital sent home? You need to take it now and go to bed. The antibiotic for sure."

"No."

"Is that the only word you know?"

"No." I screwed my face into a scowl, to try and hide my faint smile.

Dylan started to laugh.

Chapter 20

The apartment was too quiet when I woke up. Dylan was gone, and the coffee he left was cold in the pot. I warmed a cup in the microwave. I had time to flip through the computer at the pictures Mike used for last week's newspaper. They didn't look like mine. One picture was of Brian, playing second base. He'd snatched a ball thrown too high and was sweeping down with his mitt to tag out the runner. Mike had waited too long to snap the picture. There was no dirt flying, no facial grimaces. Nice picture, just no dirt. I would have taken it seconds before that point, as the cleats just starting to cross the base; Brian's face contorted as he came in for the tag.

One feature I loved about the digital camera was the series feature. Five well placed pictures in a row. Mike must not have used it. I looked closely at the newspaper shots and, via remote, accessed Mike's computer to view the other files. I typed him a note to let him know I was fine, sorry I missed his check up call, and apologized for hijacking his computer. I back-doored his picture file. It would take him days to figure out how I had accomplished it, and even longer for him to figure out how to stop me. I secretly smiled to myself. I wasn't really working, just looking.

I looked at all three files Mike had labeled. I highlighted pictures I thought deserved a second look and sipped the coffee Dylan had made earlier. One picture caught my eye. It was either a terrible picture angle or the grainy picture of masculine beauty, was Dylan. I hit the enlarge button trying to place the picture on the field. I scanned the picture from the cleats up to the face. I looked at the background, looked at the fans and the stands. My stomach tightened. Dylan was playing the outfield. Had he lost his position because of this past week due to me? Or was this signaling the end of his career. I resisted my urge to call and demand an explanation. Maybe this was why he had said he couldn't stay. Maybe he was heading home after all. I stared at the picture in disbelief, and when my phone rang, I jumped.

Chapter 21

"Hey." Dylan said softly. "How are you today?" he asked with true concern in his voice. I resisted the urge to ask him about the picture. I willed myself to stay superficial.

"I'm fine, really." I hummed. He quietly sighed on the phone, and a long moment of silence chasmed between us. He drew a ragged breath and my mind thought he'd found a way to tell me about the picture.

"We're out of town this week." he said quietly. "We play in Westerville."

"Oh?" I respond. Truly not remembering the team's schedule.

"Yeah. So…Um…There's something I want you to do while we are gone." Dylan stalled.

"What Dylan?" My tone was clipped.

He inhaled sharply. "Don't come to the games. Stay with Mike or one of your friends. These games are going to be blow outs and we'll be home by Wednesday." he paused.

"And you can't drive, and we think you need to stay home, heal up a little." The lilt and rapid pace in his voice led me to believe he expected an argument. *We?* He'd been talking to Mike. The two conspiring pigs.

"Dr. Palmer hasn't released you yet to take pictures, and there's no need to get into a pissing match with him because I'm not so sure you'd win. But then again…" he let the end of the sentence roll off his tongue.

They were conspiring.

"Ha. Ha." my sarcasm was not wasted on him and he let out a huge belly laugh.

"Really, don't even try it." he was serious. His tone was menacing.

So I evaded the subject.

"I saw the paper. You guys had a great series."

"Thanks."

I gave him every opportunity to talk about the picture I found, but he avoided the conversation. So I changed tactics.

"Maybe Mike will want to drive down and let me take pictures."

"No!" he shot back, "Not this week. You really need time to rest and heal. Take care of yourself, but I'd really prefer if someone came to stay with you."

"For heaven's sake, Dylan, I'm a twenty four year old woman who has taken care of herself for years! I can take care of myself!

"And I'm a twenty eight year old man who wants to make sure you'll do as you're told while I am away!" I could hear escalating anger in his voice.

"Aw, such a chivalrous point of view!" I retorted. "I will not interfere with anyone else's weekend plans! I will take care of myself!" Sarcasm dripped from my voice. I was half tempted to hang up. Who did he think he was? I was perfectly capable to tend to myself!

"Please, just this once. Please?" He sounded so desperate. Like the wind had been knocked out of him. I caved, just as a way to give him an out. I sighed loudly, in a sign of defeat. The back ground noise on his phone changed and I could hear the team filtering into the locker room and surrounding him.

"I've gotta go." he whispered, "Please do as I ask this one time. I'll miss you, but stay home. Please?" And with those words he hung up.

I didn't feel good about this. I wanted to know about the picture. Was it real? Was he losing his position because of my weakness? I couldn't let his dreams fall away. I needed to know how to help him. So I needed to find out what was happening.

Chapter 22

Driving my car was a lot harder than I imagined. I could barely push in the clutch and shift the gears. However, I was determined. I gritted my teeth and drove south to the highway. My backpack had two sets of clothes, clean socks, and toiletries. It was safely tucked behind the passenger seat. My sunglasses slid along the dashboard and nearly out the open passenger window as I accelerated. I cursed under my breath. I would have to retrieve them once I stopped and could walk around the car.

I still needed to stop at the paper and pick up a camera. Hopefully, Mike had taken the time to charge the batteries. I didn't want to be delayed by anything and I wanted to be well on my way by rush hour.

I snuck in through the service entrance door at work. The door to my office was closed, and I slipped into the darkness of the room. I grabbed an empty camera disc out of the top drawer and headed back out to the hallway. Mike's door was closed too. I passed it without knocking and went straight to the secretary's desk.

"Ruth!" I happily chirped. "How's it going?"

"Oh, Stacia!" she cooed. "How are you feeling? Is everything ok? Are you returning to work today? Does Mike know you're here? What are you doing here? It's so good to see you!"

Her litany of questions left me no time to answer any of them. All I could do was take a deep breath, and ask her if my camera was in Mike's office, and ask her if she would retrieve it.

"Oh, I am sure it's there, let me get it for you." Ruth jumped from her wheeled desk chair, and it skittered off the edge of her plastic floor protector. One wheel spun wildly out of control even though the chair had stopped rolling. Ruth strode off down the hall while I watched the wheel spin slowly in circles until it finally stopped. I heard her rap on Mike's door with her knuckles. A muffled grunt responded to her intrusion. I could tell by the continued rumbling of Mike's deep voice that he must have been on the phone. Ruth shut the door to his office and returned with the digital camera in hand. She must have taken it off his desk without explanation because he didn't come out of his office and she handed me the camera without any questions. I sighed in relief.

"Thanks." was all I said as I took the camera from her hands. I had been saved from a confrontation with Mike. I exited out the front door and walked around the building to my car. I plunged my hand into my pocket, and retrieved my car keys, unlocked my doors and slid behind the wheel. I put the camera on the passenger seat, retrieved my sunglasses, and set my sights on my afternoon drive to Westerville.

Chapter 23

It was a two hour drive to Westerville on a good day, but by the time I actually got on the road, highway traffic had started to build. I toyed with the idea of following all those drivers, turning around and going home myself. The sun beat through the window warming me to my core, but I couldn't shake the feeling I was doing something sinister. Something I knew that would either drive Dylan over the edge, or into my arms. The thought of his reception to my arrival gnawed at me. He probably would figure he was very important to me, and I had made the trip to prove how much I cared about him. I snickered to myself. "Yeah, that's exactly what he'll think!" I laughed out loud. He was going to be pissed! After a few short months, funny how I knew how he'd react to my intrusion. I again played with the idea of turning around, it would make Dylan happy, but this trip should answer the question of the picture.

And, this trip was going to take a lot longer than I anticipated. The traffic inched forward then slowed to a stop. I may miss the first inning of the game. We inched forward for fifteen miles until the four lane highway finally opened up and I sailed through the next seventy miles in an hour. I was sore, my muscles ached from downshifting and pushing in the clutch during the stop and go traffic. Yep, this was going to be harder than I thought. Maybe I could just take some Tylenol. I rooted around in my purse, center console, and my glove box to see if maybe I'd find some plain Tylenol. No such luck. I sighed and reached into my purse and pulled out the pain pills, hesitated momentarily, and took one. Hopefully they didn't make me too tired; I was still about a half hour out of Westerville. I also took the antibiotic, I was due to take that two hours earlier.

I buckled down and drove the next thirty miles singing to songs on the radio and looking every part the sunglass clad, teeny bopper. Head thrown back, sun kissed face. Yawning between the songs, fighting to stay awake. Wrong call on the pain pill. I was exhausted by the time I reached the outskirts of Westerville. I really should have just stayed home. I grabbed the camera and used my press pass to get to the field.

The ball game was well underway by the time I reached the field. The Aces were in the lead at the top of the fifth inning. Dylan was right, the game was a blow out. The score was nine to zero. I suddenly regretted my decision to drive down to the game, unsure if I wanted any sort of confrontation with him out here. I scanned the field for Dylan, I didn't see him. Hopefully they were saving his arm for later. I snapped a couple of pictures and was reviewing them when I heard his voice.

"You've got to be kidding me! How did you get here?" Dylan slipped his arm around my waist and whispered, "You were told to stay home. Where's Mike?" He scanned the immediate area looking for Mike.

I leaned back into his body, still perusing the view finder of my camera.

"He's at home." Dylan's body stiffened, his eyebrows shot to the top of his forehead as his face appeared to me over my right shoulder.

He looked at me with disgust on his face.

"Tell me you did not drive down here alone." His voice was low and menacing. His mouth twisted, and I stiffened. His arms dropped away and he stepped directly in front of me. His eyes caught mine, and my blood ran cold.

"What the hell is wrong with you?" His voice was so low, I trembled. He was furious. As I expected, I didn't get the reception I wanted. I anticipated he'd be upset, but he was shaking with fury. "Why are your eyes so glassy?"

"I had to take something for…" Dylan reached out and snatched my elbow, effectively cutting off my sentence. I gasped at the suddenness of his movement. His eyes became huge, large circles. His face burned red.

"Did you drive down here and take pain pills while you drove?" My skin became clammy and pale. His reaction was frightening. So over the top for my presumed crime.

"Do you have any idea how dangerous that was? Oh. My. God, Stacia. It's not just you on the road! What if you had caused a car accident? It might not have been just you that got hurt. What were you thinking?" He glared at me, fury etched his face. I didn't blink or breathe. *No reaction,* my mind screamed. "No. You were not thinking! That was one of the most irresponsible things I have ever heard!" His arms flew wildly around me, finally he settled one on his forehead. He wiped down his face, only to stop and pinch the bridge of his nose. He lowered his voice to a whisper. "I could never forgive you if something happened." He fisted his hands and shook his head, tears forming on his lower lids as the edges began to redden. He turned away from me and looked out over the field. And for the first time since I had arrived, I noticed he was not in uniform.

I stepped back, slid the camera strap over my head and walked into the crowd. I felt physically ill. His tongue lashing was so extreme, and something I could not understand, but it felt familiar. My fear of Ryan returned and was being transferred to Dylan. I had fallen into another failing relationship. I could hear him calling my name as I walked. I saw him struggling to get released by his fans and watched as he became engulfed by the crowd. I turned away from him.

Tears streamed down my face, but I refused to turn back around.

I slipped back to my car, sank into the seat, snapped the door shut, and reached for the car keys, and sobbed. I wiped my sleeve across my face, and leaned back against the seat. I closed my eyes for a few seconds trying to collect my scattered heart. I knew my arrival would make waves, but Dylan's fury was... what? Over the top? Hurtful? Scary?

I shoved the car keys into the ignition when my passenger door handle rattled and swung open. Jon's face popped into view.

"Hey, can I talk to you?" he asked in a voice that sounded almost apologetic. He slid into the seat and stretched his long legs out under the dashboard. Jon didn't hesitate, "We know Dylan hasn't told you a lot. He's quite a private person." He looked sideways at me with a small amount of trepidation on his face. "We know you're wondering why he blew up today." I stared out the windshield and watched the headlamps dance on the concrete wall in front of me, refusing to wipe my tear streaked face.

"He hasn't had an easy time telling you. He's struggling. You seem to be one of the only people who've been able to connect with him. So don't hurt him." My eyes snapped to his face, then narrowed. *Hurt him? Was I yelling at him in public? I don't think so.*
Anger surfaced, but I held my tongue. I decided listening to Jon was a better idea than lashing out. Jon's eyes went to the windshield as he continued.

"Dylan was married once; in college. He had a baby on the way. He was distracted. Busy in school, getting ready to graduate and start a better job. Getting ready for the baby. But moreover ignoring his personal life, driven and self-centered.

Amy went to the grocery store late one night, while Dylan stayed home and studied. He says she never said goodbye, just yelled from the front door that she was stepping out for a few items. She left and…." Jon's voice trailed off. With glassy eyes, he rubbed his forehead and then leaned his chin on his fist. He looked out the passenger window, and sighed deeply.

My eyes rounded into huge circles, waiting for him to finish. A long pained silence passed between us as I watched him compose himself. I tried to swallow past the lump in my throat, afraid to breathe. Jon took a ragged breath and continued.

"The driver was high, he never saw her as she was crossing the parking lot. She didn't die right away, and the baby wasn't big enough to survive. She died too. The driver had taken prescription drugs, ones he bought off the street. I knew the driver, nice enough guy, bad decision. He got a slap on the wrist; thirty days and probation. Dylan hasn't been right since. He didn't finish school, just threw himself into baseball. He excelled until last fall. Torn rotator cuff; he uses pitching as an anger outlet. We just don't want to see him get hurt. He's had enough."

My heart was heavy and shredded into pieces. I didn't blink. I reached forward turned the keys off and threw them to the dash. My hands gripped the steering wheel. I twisted them back and forth trying to think of what to say; my knuckles white with the effort.

"He doesn't want anything to happen to you, too. He really likes you. He's never been this close to any other woman since...well, you know." I couldn't listen to Jon anymore. I swung the car door open and struggled to stand upright. I slammed the door and let the tears fly. My body shook as I held my side and sobbed. My fear of losing Dylan was overshadowed by this new revelation. How had he survived such a horrible event and come out such a caring, compassionate man? One who worried about what I wanted. I was beginning to doubt he was using me to get through the baseball season. If Jon's story was true, then Dylan was like a young child. Putting out feelers, to learn to love again. I continued to sob, my face streaked and red. Jon never moved until I couldn't stand anymore and slid down the side of my car into a heap on the ground.

All his talk about what I wanted, for me to be honest with him; was he really asking me for what he wanted? A relationship to make him whole again. Could I give that to him? Was I too selfish in my needs? I was embarrassed. Wasn't he dishonest by omission? By not telling me his past, was he protecting himself or pushing me away. I felt betrayed and confused. He must have felt he couldn't be honest with me. What a terrible person I was. I wanted to disappear, be swallowed up by the parking lot and covered by the concrete. All this time I knew he was hiding something, I just never imagined it was something so horrible.

Jon stood against the car; arms crossed, staring off into space. He didn't say a word, just waited for me to collect myself. My head dropped back against the door with a thud.

"When?" was all I could manage.

"July first, almost six years ago.' Jon sighed. "The next couple of weeks are going to get rough. He has problems getting through the Fourth of July; the day they buried her." New tears flooded my eyes. I looked at the ground taking time to process this information. Maybe that was the reason he didn't want me to follow this weekend. With the date rapidly approaching, it seemed logical that the picture I saw on Mike's camera was because he was dealing with his own demons.

"Does he know you're here?" I squeaked.

"No, and you won't tell him I told you."

"Where is he?" I croaked.

"With Dale and Glen, at the hotel."

"Is he drinking at the bar?" Why did that idea worry me?

"Maybe, but he's waiting to hear from you."

"I need to go see him."

"Not a good idea right now. He's pretty pissed"

"But, I want to…" My voice trailed off. Jon continued to stare off into the distance.

"I'm sure if you turn on your phone, you'll have at least ten missed calls. When I found you, I called him; told him you were safe. But, I wanted to talk to you first; give you some insight. I wouldn't tell him where you were and the team cornered him so he didn't take off halfcocked. A good thing since he's pretty upset. I don't expect you to understand, I just don't want you to hurt him. He's been hurt enough."

I did this to him. I felt terrible. I made him angry. I made his team rally around him, protect him from me. Why didn't I just stay home like he had asked me? I would give him that now. It was the least I could do. Give both of us some space. But my heart wasn't into leaving. I wanted to be there for him. And now I knew why he was so mad earlier. He wasn't going to hurt me; he was genuinely concerned about me. And I had hurt him. Another failure on my part.

"I need to go home." I sniffed, and mopped my face with my sleeve.

"Come on." Jon offered me a hand, "Get up, I'll take you to the hotel." He never looked at my face, just grabbed my hand and pulled me up. I was exhausted. I took a few minutes to right myself and absently rubbed and held my incisions. I thought about the pain, but it didn't compare to the pain in my heart.

"I'll drive." Jon deposited me into the passenger seat and rounded the car to the driver's side. He slid the keys off the dash and got on his cell phone, as he slid into the seat. I stared out the side window still sniffling, and wiping my eyes. As I did, Jon got on his cell phone.

"Yeah, I got her. No, stay there. No, No. No Problem, just needed time to freshen up I guess. Yeah, girls." Jon laughed into the phone. "In fifteen then."

I glared at Jon. Indignantly he glared back, "What? I'm going to take you to the hotel, you can freshen up there and we'll see how Dylan is handling all of this."

Jon was totally oblivious. I had really hurt Dylan, I wasn't sure I wanted to face him. Jon was a jerk, I wanted to go home. At least he could have used a better lie. His protective character only went as far as his friend. I had half expected some protective nature from him. In truth, I was happy Dylan had such a good friend. Not that I thought he needed a protector, but because I wanted him to have one. Right now, I could use one. My heart was shattered, and it would only be worse when he left. And with what I had done, I knew he would leave. I couldn't protect him and myself.

Chapter 24

Glen and Chris met Jon and I at the hotel door. They talked in hushed voices shooting glances towards the interior of the reception area. I pulled the door latch, and pushed against the door. Chris's hand slowly pushed the door back closed and held it there while the three men talked. Glen opened the back door grabbed my camera and bag from behind my seat. He opened my door and offered me his hand. When I didn't take it, he glared at me. He grabbed my hand and tucked me under his arm, guiding me into the hotel lobby. Chris sidled up on my other side as I tried to peer into the bar. They smashed me between the two of them. I didn't get a clear view inside the bar. I stopped after another few steps as the men pushed me along to a hallway. I sidestepped Glen who wheeled around to reclaim my arm. Chris stopped when I stopped, but continued to push the small of my back urging me forward.

"Stop it!" I snapped.

"Really, now is not a good time, keep moving." Chris gruffed back.

"What the hell! I want to see him!" I had to let him know I truly cared about him. He needed to know how sorry I was that he had endured such pain, and that I had caused him even more. I had to make sure we were still ok; that *he* was ok. I had betrayed him. I felt horrible.

"Not here, not now." Glen hissed as he grabbed me again.

"No! I want to see Dylan. Now!" I was insistent. His friends were overbearing and over protective. I tried to step behind Chris who tightened his grip around my waist. Pain shot through me and I recoiled from his grip. It only served to make me angrier. I wrenched away from Chris and smacked my hands squarely on Glen's chest making him step back and release my arm.

"Stop it, what the hell is going on? I want to know right now!" My voice rang in the empty hall. Slivers of light filled the hall and faces filled the open door frames. I feared I had upset Dylan to the point where he'd didn't want to see me again, and his team mates weren't willing to tell me. I needed to see it for myself, see how much damage I had done to our friendship. Tears sprung to my eyes, threatening to spill down my face. The men stepped back just enough to give me a view of the bar. I stood tall on my tip toes to catch sight of Dylan. His back was to the bar door and he had a pile of empty bottles in front of him. He leaned on the bar top with one elbow talking to Jon. I took in the scene. Once I had successfully ruffled enough feathers to plume a peacock, I stepped back towards Chris, took my bags from Dale and dropped my head.

"Done?" he seethed. "He'll be fine, but right now I don't think you need to be in the middle of that." He cocked his thumb towards the bar. I could hear soft talking and what sounded like sobs, and tones of regret and consoling. I had done this to him, I let the tears slip down my cheeks and relented to walk to a room with Chris.

The hotel room was dark except for a small lamp in the corner. Two chairs faced each other near the window. Both beds were dressed with white comforters trimmed with blue. All the pictures on the walls were flowery and large. A television was hidden inside a large armoire. The gear bag on the floor didn't look familiar. Chris led me in and sat down in one of the chairs.

"What else happened?" I started as I sat on the edge of the bed, crossing my hands in my lap.

"In regards to what?" Chris squinted at me, and dropped his hands between his spread knees.

"Dylan and baseball."

"He takes his anger out on himself. Throws balls so hard and fast. He hurt himself last fall. Didn't rehab slow enough, and pushed himself until he needed a rotator cuff repair. Now he's down here. He hates that he's failing, wants to be back in the majors so badly he's pushing himself too hard. He risks further injury. And if that happens, its career ending. I've been around him three years now. Around this time, he gets a little self-destructive. Coaches pulled him to keep him safe from himself."

"Am I making him worse?" I wrung my hands in my lap, lowered my eyes willing the tears to stay away. Chris only exhaled, and dropped his eyes.

"Wait here until Jon comes to get you. I need to check on Dylan. It was a pretty rough day." He stood, placed a comforting hand on my shoulder and left the room.

I was alone, with only my thoughts. I crawled to the top of the bed and curled up on the pillow. I pulled a tissue from the box next to the bed and wiped my eyes. I slipped my hand under the pillow and a crunching piece of plastic grazed my finger tips. I pinched the plastic and I could feel small round balls. I pulled the plastic baggie out of the pillowcase. It was filled with small white pills. I rolled them between my fingers, making the white powder cover the inside of the bag. *Whose room was this?* I reached over and grabbed my camera. I snapped a picture of the pills and a picture of the gear bag in the room. I pulled another tissue from the box to wipe the camera lens and another small triangled corner of plastic baggie with white powder came out with it. I took a picture of it as I heard the door handle rattle.

I threw the pills back into the pillow case. Stuffed the powder back into the tissue box, and slid down to the end of the bed tossing the camera into one of the chairs. I watched it bounce lecherously close to the chair edge. I laid my hands back into my lap staring at my fingers.

Jon swung the door wide. Chris followed him in.

"Why's she in here?" Jon seemed a little irritated. With what I found in his room, I understood why he was defensive. His eyes darted around surveying the room. I had left a used tissue in the middle of the bed. We both spotted it at the same time. I reached for it, shook it out a little to show there was nothing in it, and wadded it back into my hand.

"Sorry, I needed to wipe my eyes" I looked into Jon's face. "Is Dylan ok?" My voice was small and cracked, tears gathered in the corners of my eyes again. I wrung my hands in my lap, sniffling loudly. I played the distressed woman perfectly, not that I was acting.

"Yeah, he's getting there. Dale's with him now."

"I want to see him." I was no longer the raging woman who walked into the hotel. My voice squeaked from my throat.

"Give us some time, let's see where his head's at in a few minutes." I just nodded at Chris and swallowed the huge lump in my throat.

"I'm so sorry." I whispered between the sniffles. "He'd have been fine if I'd just stayed home. I'm sorry, this puts you guys in a bad spot for tomorrow's game. Having to baby sit me and everything." Jon sighed and fisted his hands on his hips. I couldn't even imagine what he was thinking.

"Dale and Rob are going to take him to his room, we'll see if that goes well, and if it does, you can talk to him then." Jon glared at me. Did he know what I had found? I dropped my eyes, tears pinched at the edges. I reached for another tissue. Jon lurched forward and cupped his hand around the top of the box and pulled out a single tissue and handed it to me.

"Thank You." I wiped the edges of my eyes and kept staring at my hands as they flitted in my lap. "Maybe I should just go home." Tears flowed down my face and I took a ragged breath.

"And you don't think that won't set him off again?" Jon stood between the two beds, his eyes narrowed and burned holes into me. His arms crossed his chest.

"I'm sorry. This has just turned into a terrible mess. And I put you guys in the middle. I just need to leave." I started to stand, my hand snatched my side and I bent at my waist to stop the pinching. Chris exhaled loudly. I pushed past him reaching for my camera and bag.

Chris caught my arm.

"Sit back down. If you leave now, he'll go ballistic. And you shouldn't be driving…anywhere." Chris' eyes scanned over me, and I did my best to drop my hand off my stomach.

"Well, I'm not going to sit here and wait for *you* to tell me when I can see him! I either set things straight with him now, or I'm leaving!" I jerked my arm away from Chris and grabbed my camera. Chris stepped in front of my bag, his arms crossed his chest. "Get out of my way!" My face contorted into an angry pinch, and I flushed deep red. I was furious. "Now!" I yelled and pushed Chris with my arm. He didn't budge. My fists balled at my sides. My breaths raged from my lungs. I hadn't really thought I'd hit him, just wanted to give the illusion I *would* hit him. He raised his eyebrow, a small grin creased his face.

"No."

"I mean it, move, now." I stepped back ready to make a connection with my clenched fist if the standoff continued and if I needed to prove my point; when a pounding came to the door. Jon bolted towards the door. He barely turned the knob, when the door flew open banging the wall.

"Is she in here?" I could hear the pain in Dylan's voice. Rob stood behind him, his eyes darting around the room taking in the scene. I turned around and pushed past Jon.

"I'm here Dylan." I wanted to reach out for him, comfort him in some way, but with the guys watching, I only stepped in front of them and stopped in front of him.

"Why the hell did you come here?" His voice was breathy and deflated.

"To surprise you." My voice was low.

"I told you to stay home. I told you we'd go to the store in the morning. I had to study for finals. Why didn't you just stay home? Just one fucking time, just listen to me? Damn it Amy." He stumbled against the door jamb nearly knocking me off my feet.

His demons were surfacing. Witnessing this was hard, my heart couldn't handle this. His pain was visceral. I watched Rob drop his eyes. Chris rubbed his forehead, and Jon sighed so loudly I thought my ear drums would rupture. I thought of a way out. I'd be Amy.

"I'm here now Dylan. And, I didn't leave. Nothing has happened, and I am still here." I implored him to look up at me. "Dylan? I never left you. Look at me honey. I'm here."

He launched himself into the room, throwing his arms around me knocking me to the ground. Dylan sprawled over me. The air left my lungs in a rush. His body weight crushed me into the floor.

"God Amy, I thought I'd lost you, and the baby too."

"Never, Dylan, never." He passed out on top of me, my arms wrapped tightly around him. My heart shattered into pieces and fell around me like my tears.

Chapter 25

The room was pitch black, and quiet except for the snoring I heard from the other bed. I was aching from head to toe. After our little floor ballet, I was sore as hell. Rob and Dale helped Jon get Dylan to his room, and I sat on the edge of the bed watching him fitfully sleep for hours. His alcoholic ramblings were hard to witness, but his friends had protected him as much as possible, and I guess they had tried to protect me too. They really were brothers.

I needed something for the pain. I wanted a pain pill, but would settle for Tylenol. I slipped from the bed, and headed towards my purse. Dylan snored quietly, his face drawn and tortured in sleep. I stared at his beautiful face, his beard shadowed his dimples, but his eyebrows were drawn in a frown. I wanted to touch him, comfort him, and wake him from his nightmare. But I just looked at him memorizing his muscle structure, absorbing his beautiful biceps and wanting to run my hands over them to feel their sinewy firmness.

Oh, my. I needed to change this thought path. I dug through my purse and looked for any Tylenol. Finding none, I headed to the side table to find the room key. I would just ask the front desk for some, or search my car again. With that thought, I grabbed my car keys.

I slipped from the room clicking the door quietly, so he wouldn't awaken, even though I doubted a tornado could wake him. I padded down the hall to the elevator. Even at three thirty in the morning, I could hear people milling around outside. I rode the lift downstairs and asked the desk clerk if they had any aspirin or Tylenol. She shuffled around under her desk and came up empty handed. Her hands outstretched in a gesture of resignation. I thanked her and headed towards my car. I was digging through my cluttered dash, when I spotted Jon standing at the corner of the building with another man. I watched the verbal exchange, unable to hear anything but mumbling. They weren't very animated, but leaned in closely at times and slapped palms. I watched them as I searched my car for the pain pills. I would need to walk for Tylenol, and I wasn't sure if I could find someplace open at three thirty in the morning. I wish I had my camera, so I could zoom in and see what was happening between the two men. Soon, another man approached Jon, and they slipped into the darkness behind the hotel. I grabbed the pill bottle and left my car heading towards the hotel door. I wanted to slip quietly into the shadows to see what Jon was doing, but after what I had found in his room, I had a pretty good idea. But why? He was successful, why was he selling those drugs? I decided to head back to the room, I could see him through the window upstairs. I quickly headed to the elevator, and rode up to the room. A shiver went down my spine as I feared what I already knew in my heart.

I snuck back into the room, relieved to find Dylan still snoring quietly on his bed. I grabbed my camera and headed to the window, making sure to only open the curtains enough to get a good view of the action below me. I used my telephoto lens and worked the lens into a tight circle around the men's faces and hands. Money was exchanged, and plastic passed between them. I focused on the plastic, and snapped three more pictures. The click of the camera was unsettling, I knew I could ruin him with this, but for some reason, I couldn't take my eyes off the drama behind the hotel. I heard a loud sigh behind me. I dropped the camera to the chair and let the curtain fall silently to the window.

"Hey." Dylan's voice was husky and deep. The alcohol made it heavy, and he cleared his throat and lifted up on his elbow. His eyes were rimmed red and bloodshot.

"Hey, yourself." I slid over to the bed and crawled in beside him. I took a deep breath to stifle the pain in my side. My hand instinctively went to my side.

"Hurting?" Dylan said as he pulled me into his side and rubbed my back and shoulders. His voice was so low and concerned. I could smell the stale alcohol on his breath. I didn't care. I was all too happy he knew who I was and he was back to his quietly reserved self.

"Yeah, a little. Nothing I can't handle though." I lied.

"Did you take anything tonight?" He was truly concerned, looking into my eyes, worry lined his beautiful face. I reached up and caressed his cheek feeling the stubble that had emerged

"No, not since yesterday." My voice trailed off. I wondered if he'd remember any of last night.

"Maybe you need to. You're taking the antibiotic aren't you?"

"Yes, But I'm fine right now." I curled into his chest, keeping my belly from touching him, and him from touching my belly. He started to roll his hands down my shoulders. I stiffened slightly and took a deep breath waiting for him to touch me. He started to run his hands down my ribs. The fire he sent through me was stronger than the pain.

I chanced a glance to his face. His look was serene and comfortable. I grabbed his cheeks and pulled his face into mine. I explored his lips with mine tasting the liquor and felt him soften. I laid soft kisses on his lips from corner to corner. I moved to slither my hands down his sides and slowly rubbed circles on his stomach. I felt his muscles tighten as he let out his breath. I slid my hands up inside his shirt, feeling his muscles contract under my hands. I pushed his shirt up, and he lifted his head so I could slip it over his head.

I shifted to straddle him and began kissing his face and neck. He let his hands roam over my back and let them settle on my butt. I seductively skidded my tee shirt up my abdomen, and pulled my arms inside my shirt, keeping my eyes on him. In one move, I slid my shirt over my head, and sat there across his thighs in just my bra and pants. I gathered his hands and placed them on my chest. He didn't disappoint. He pulled the cups away and used his flat palms to softly knead me, he flicked his thumbs across my nipples until they hardened.

"Ummm. So nice." he groaned.

I could feel his hardness pushing up against my thigh as he closed his eyes and dropped his head back. I rubbed a soft southward path until I tickled the small line of hair that disappeared into his pants. I held his waistband and kissed a path across his naked chest, licking the divots between the muscles. I could feel his thighs contract and relax under my own thighs, and felt the bulge inside his jeans. Kissing him from hip to hip, I unbuttoned his pants and slipped my hand inside.

Dylan gasped as I clamped my hand around his shaft.

"Are you sure?"

"Absolutely." I smiled as seductively as I could, with the amount of discomfort I was in.

I could feel him pulse, and I slid down his legs to tug his pants down.

His cock popped free. He arched up and lifted his butt to allow me to pull his legs out. I sat between his legs watching his face and biting my lower lip. I rubbed my hands up his thighs and

Dylan sucked in a huge breath. I avoided direct contact with his veined pulsing organ as I slipped my hand down and cupped his testicles. I softly massaged his sac and balls and felt them tighten and contract. Dylan groaned his satisfaction. I licked my lips watching his face turn from satisfied to relaxed, almost comfortable. I put his entire prick into my mouth. Dylan's legs stiffened and he tried to retreat, but the bed prevented him from wiggling away. I used my hand to massage his testicles and pumped him into my mouth; sucking slowly with a feather light touch. My other hand pumped his base. He cried out softly and took a gasping breath. I slipped my finger behind his balls to the small seam of skin leading to his butt hole. He tightened everything and recoiled from my touch. I increased the suction and returned to massaging and rolling his balls in my hand. Small ridges of skin formed under my ministrations, and his sac tightened, as his dick hardened and lengthened in my mouth.

"Oh my god." he hissed looking down to watch me. I smiled, slid all the way to the tip and used the point of my tongue to explore the small slit on the top. I lapped around the rim, keeping a grip on his base. With hard suction I slid all the way to the base. Dylan shuddered, and groaned loudly. "Oh shit." he whispered, all breathy.

I stopped, released the suction, stopped the pressure, sat up and looked at him. He was in ecstasy. His eyes were hooded and such a deep steel blue. I released his testicles and started kissing his inner thigh. Dylan shivered, the cool air I blew across him torturous. He reached for me, I avoided his grasp.

"I'm not ready yet." I knew he couldn't tolerate much more.

"Come on honey, come up here." Dylan's eyes were imploring, begging me to meet him at the top of the bed. I stayed between his legs, preventing him from reaching me.

I licked my lips again and smiled at Dylan from under my lashes. I dropped my head again, and took the whole of him into my velvety soft mouth and sucked hard.

"Shit." he groaned loudly. His knees tried to stiffen, but I held my position. His hips surged forward. I placed my palm back on his balls and rolled the two walnuts around in my hand and gave a gentle squeeze. His sac wrinkled and grew taunt in my hand, harder this time. I slipped my other hand back to the base and slowly milked him as I sucked the length of him into my mouth. His testicles were tight in my hand and I skated one finger up to apply a little pressure to his puckered butt hole. He cried out loudly and bucked furiously against my mouth. I sucked hard, fisted his base and ran my tongue up the underside of his cock. The next time I took his length, I rolled the sac, applied the pressure and he came in a fury, bucking against my face. He pulsed and gyrated under my hands. I swallowed as much as I could tolerate, running my hands up his inner thighs. I flicked my tongue over the sensitive mushroomed head until he exhaled and jerked under me.

"Holy Shit." he let out a ragged breath and looked into my face. "That was fantastic." He laid there gaining his strength as I curled up next to his ribs. He slowly rubbed my back in small circles. "Thank You." he managed after a few minutes.

"Um Hum." was all I could manage before I fell into a deep, fitfully painful sleep.

Chapter 26

I really couldn't move, I hurt so badly, tears were blinding me. I woke up alone in the hotel room. A note laid where Dylan's head had been earlier.

"Our game is at twelve-thirty. We will be heading home after tomorrow's game. DO NOT leave this room. I have a plan to get you home." When I looked at the clock it was already three in the afternoon. I had slept the day away, and missed my antibiotic and birth control. *Damn it.* I pulled myself from the bed and headed to the bathroom. I would just have to take both pills tonight. *Better late than never.* I let the shower run hot and crawled into the shower. I stood in there allowing the steam to rise to the ceiling. Dylan could be back any minute. These games usually lasted only three hours. I was beyond sore, I let my tears flow while I stood under the pounding water.

I never heard the door open. Never heard him call my name. I stood in the stall and sobbed. The stress of the last two days was overwhelming. The first inclination I had that I had company was when the steam sucked from the bathroom and was replaced by a cool breeze.

I was past the point of stopping my sob crying. I hiccupped and stuttered as Dylan crawled into the shower behind me.

"Babe, I'm sorry." he wrapped his arms around me. I pulled away in pain.

"Please stop." I hiccupped.

"Babe, Jon told me what happened last night. I'm so sorry. I never meant to hurt you."

"Please let me get out of here." I sobbed.

"I can't let you go." he whispered into my hair. He circled my shoulders with his right arm, and planted the other one on the shower wall. I cried harder trying to shrink away from him. I wasn't able to support myself anymore, totally spent from sobbing, and the pain. I grabbed his arm and leaned back into him and gave him my weight.

Dylan gathered me into him and started kissing my neck.

"I can't Dylan, I can't…" I choked on my sob. "I hurt so badly, please..." Another sob escaped along with a deep moan that brought on a new onslaught of tears. The hot shower was doing nothing to tame the searing burn in my side.

"Please, Stacia. I won't let you go. I am so sorry." He buried his face into my neck and tightened his hold. He guided his left hand to my breast.

"I…I…" I needed to tell him, I knew we weren't in the same conversation.

When he slid his hand down to my stomach, to pull me to his chest, I screamed and collapsed against him.

"Jesus Christ! Are you all right?" Dylan gathered me to him and I tried to pull away. He stared into my eyes searching for his answer. I continued to sob, my head falling into his chest, my hand grabbing at my stomach. Dylan picked me up and carried me to the bed. I rolled into a ball. He stroked my hair and back, trying to soothe me. I continued to sob and rolled tighter. "What can I do, sweetheart?" Concern infiltrated his voice. He sounded ready to cry himself.

"Dylan, I can't stand it, I need something for this pain." I stammered, sobbed and tightened further into my ball.

"Don't you have anything from the hospital?" He continued to make a feeble attempt to comfort me. Smoothing my hair, rubbing his hands down my back, and wiping away water at the same time.

"I didn't take it, not after last night, I just couldn't do that to you."

"You're kidding, right? Oh my God. Why would you do that? What happened…?" Dylan's eyes grew wide and wild. His voice grew quiet and low. "Oh no. No. You know." He dropped his hands. "Son of a bitch. What else happened last night?"

I continued to sob and cry, trying to roll into a tighter ball. Dylan pushed off the bed in a hurry. I screamed again as the pain tore through me.

"I'm sorry, I'm sorry, I am so sorry." His mantra really did nothing to stop the burning, nauseating discomfort. I was going to vomit, my stomach roiled. I tasted the salt in my mouth, but couldn't move fast enough before my stomach started to empty. I clawed for the trash, and dry heaved until I could no longer hold my own head and it lolled over the side of the bed. Yes, I knew. My heart's pieces shattered into pieces.

Chapter 27

"Do you think you can move?"

"No."

Dylan had moved up behind me cradling my head in his lap. I was covered in sweat, my breathing too heavy, waiting for the next wave.

"You need to take a pain pill." Even laying across his lap naked, I refused to move. I could feel the tension in his legs and the way he pressed too hard into my back trying to provide some comfort.

"No."

"Stacia." His exasperated tone made me edgy. "You really can't continue this. Maybe I should call our team physician, he's right…"

"No."

"Honey, this is out of control. The pain is out of control and making you…"

"No."

He exhaled loudly. Rubbed my back harder, and I could feel his thigh tightening in anger.

"You have to try…"

"No!" I gagged again.

"I'm going to call Ray."

"No, absolutely n..." The wave rose up my throat and flew from my mouth, the new sheen of sweat glazed my skin. I doubled over in pain.

Tears sprung to my eyes and rolled down my cheeks.

"That's enough!" Dylan leaned over my body and grabbed his phone from the stand, and punched in a number.

"Ray? It's Dylan Riley. I...ah...got a girl in my room. Yeah, I know, but we need some help. Medical help." There was a pause. "I know, I wouldn't, but she drove down here to see me after having surgery last week. Doc, she's sick, really sick. Puking, and all sweaty. No nothing's coming out, but she says it hurts really badly." He listened to Ray on the phone. "When's the last time you took something for the pain?"

"Yesterday." I answered unwilling to unwind myself from Dylan's lap.

"Yesterday? Really?" He shot me a shocked look.

"Yesterday.", he related into the receiver. I won't, just let yourself in."

"Just let yourself in?" I said incredulously. "I've gotta get some clothes on." I pushed myself up, as I rode out another wave of dry heaving. Dylan grabbed one of his tee shirts and helped me slide into my panties. The heaving subsided, as Dylan laid me back into the bed, stroking my hair. This was going to be embarrassing.

"Dylan?"

"Hum?"

"Am I getting you in trouble?"

"Not really." He continued to smooth my hair.

"*Not really?*" The realization that I was indeed getting Dylan into big trouble made me shudder.

"This is wrong then. Call him back, tell him I left. Don't let him in here."

"Either Ray sees you, or I take you to an E.R."

"Call him, hurry. I'm better now."

"No." he reached over and kissed my cheek.

"Dylan? You can't get into trouble because of me. I just need to leave." I made an attempt to move from the bed. The

151

pain grabbed me, and the bile rose up and I wretched, just as the door to the room opened.

I could only imagine what I sounded like to the team physician. With my head hung off the bed, the sound echoed around the room. Dylan held my hair back as I coughed and sputtered.

"What's going on here?" Ray's voice rumbled through the room. He walked around the bed as another dry heave wracked my body. He laid his hand on my back, it felt cool through Dylan's tee shirt, and I was extremely glad I had gotten dressed. When the retching subsided, I laid back on the bed. My face was flushed and sweat poured off my forehead.

"She had an infected ovarian cyst removed last Saturday, got home on Wednesday, and followed us down here to take pictures for The Herald yesterday. I came in from the game and she was crying in pain and then started vomiting." Dylan relayed the facts to Ray.

"So, less than one week after having surgery you drove two hours away for *pictures*? When did you start getting sick?" Ray cocked an eye at me incredulously.

"Yesterday." I answered. Dylan looked at me, another look of shock raced across his face. I shrugged my shoulders.

"Let's just take a look, ok with you?"

I shook my head and let Ray stick a thermometer in my mouth and take my blood pressure. He placed his fingers on the inside of my wrist and looked at his watch. I looked at Dylan, his face was etched with concern. Ray grabbed a stethoscope and held it to my heart as I gave Dylan a look of disdain. This was all so unnecessary, and could cost him his playing time.

Ray slid the stethoscope down to my stomach. With the slightest of pressure, he started to listen. I moaned. The pain made me retreat from the pressure, and the salty taste returned to my mouth. I pulled the thermometer from my mouth, and headed back over the edge of the bed reaching for the trash again.

"I think we need to stop the nausea, and then get the pain under control, and I think she'll be ok." Ray said confidently. He dug around in his bag, and pulled out a small locked box. After lining up the numbers on the side of the box, it opened to reveal several syringes full of liquid. My eyes widened and rounded with a small amount of fear.

Ray picked up one syringe, pulled the top off the needle and leveled it with his eye. He pushed the plunger and I heard a small hiss of air. I offered my arm, I figured I wasn't going to avoid this with Dylan hovering nearby.

"No, this one goes 'South-of-the-Border'." I looked at Dylan with a look of repugnance.

Ray reached under the tee shirt and tugged the top of my panties down over one hip. He swabbed my skin with alcohol and jabbed the needle unceremoniously into my hip. I jumped. Dylan put his hand on my shoulder almost to hold me into place. The medicine burned as Ray injected it. He snapped my panties back up and grabbed another syringe from his arsenal. I looked at Dylan indigently and shook my head.

"Other side, Stac." Ray pulled the other side of my panties down and repeated the procedure; pushing the cool liquid into my muscle.

"When did you eat last?" Ray's question unnerved me. I hadn't had anything yesterday, and wasn't sure if I'd even had more than sips of water. *Crap.* If I had to tell the truth, it had been two days, or maybe since coffee the morning Dylan left for this series. So maybe two and a half at most. I played it safe.

"I'm not sure." The medicine Ray had given me started working. I was getting groggy and the nausea was starting to wane.

"We'll wait a bit and try some water." The two men stayed in the room. Dylan watching me, Ray making small talk.

I closed my eyes, giving into the lull of their voices, and the side effects of the medication. After about twenty minutes, I felt my shirt being lifted and cool hands on my stomach. I opened my eyes expecting to see Dylan. Ray's face smiled back.

"Better now?"

"Yes, Thank You. Thank you very much."

"You ready for some water?"

"Yes, please."

I was tired as hell. All I wanted was to close my eyes and wake up in the morning next to Dylan.

"Stacia, sip this." Dylan held a glass to my lips, and I gladly took a small sip.

"That's wonderful. Thank You." I said gratefully.

"Call me if you need me." Ray stood, packing his bag to leave.

"Ray?" I stopped him before he could leave. "This isn't Dylan's fault, I came down here on my own. Don't let this be a reflection on him, and please don't tell the coaches."

Ray shot a glance at Dylan, who looked at him, imploring him for his silence.

"Please?" I begged.

"I won't, you got my word." Ray's resignation was a small smile that crossed his lips, and the soft huff of air he aimed at Dylan.

I was comfortable. The pain was nearly gone. My breathing had slowed. I laid so still on the bed, afraid to move fearing the pain would return. My eyelids heavy from the medicine. Dylan pressed the cup of water to my lips, and I swallowed.

"Dylan?"

"Yes?" His voice was so soft and almost sad.

"Tell me about Amy." Dylan took a deep breath, and sighed. I waited a few seconds while he scowled at me. My eyelids were heavy and closed on their own.

"I can only imagine she was beautiful." I started, hoping he'd take the lead.

"Ah, yes, she was." I could hear his smile as he remembered her. "She was so beautiful, long dark hair, green eyes. A smile that could stop a train. Soft curves, and she loved me." I could hear the love in his voice as he remembered.

"Umm." I hummed, waiting for him to go on. I opened my eyes to look at his softened features, he looked at a spot off the bed his memories filling his head.

"She was my saving grace my freshman year. She made sure I finished my Humanities classes. And even helped me study my Criminal Law." I heard the small smile come back. He put the cup to my lips again and I took another sip of water.

"What was she like?" My eyes flitted closed. Dylan talked about Amy, his voice so low and heavy. When he grew quiet, I'd ask another question prompting him to continue. I laid very still and smiled as he chuckled about some of their escapades while dating and through their brief marriage. He talked about his college years, and how he'd been too egotistical to worry about anything but graduation and baseball.

Every so often he'd push the cup to my lips and make me drink. The gesture was so caring and compassionate.

His voice lowered, and I fluttered my eyes open and saw tears forming in the corners of his eyes. I closed my eyes, so he wouldn't know I had stolen a glance. I stayed immobile as he told me about the night Amy died. His guilt, his anger, and the rage he took out on himself. He stopped talking. I kept my eyes closed allowing him the time to ruminate. The room was stifling.

"Dylan?" My voice was small and quiet.

"Hum?" he responded, holding the cup suspended above me.

"I'm glad you had her. She sounds wonderful. I would have loved her." I couldn't open my eyes again, and within seconds, I was asleep.

Chapter 28

I woke up in the middle of the night, I was starving. Dylan was wrapped around me, his head buried in my neck, his hand draped over my chest, his full masculine scent invading my nose. I tried to slide out of the bed and out from under his arm. He tightened his grip, and snuggled into me further.

"Dylan, I've gotta get up." I whispered into his hair.

"No you don't." His voice was heavy with sleep and throaty.

"I'm thirsty and hungry."

"You'd have to go out to get food. There's no room service here." He rubbed his hand through his hair, making it stand up at crazy angles then raked it down his face trying to wipe the sleep from his eyes.

"I'll go out and get you something." He yawned, and stretched like a cat waking after laying in the afternoon sun.

"No, you can't go out, league rules. If you get caught, it's a possible team suspension. I'm not chancing it." I looked into his eyes sternly.

"If I get caught with you in my room, I'll get suspended too." He quirked a smile at me.

"I'll just get some water then." I started to push off the bed when a huge arm came down to pin me to the bed. I giggled. He was so playful.

"I'll get your damn water, woman." He grumbled as he threw back the covers, left the bed and flipped on the bathroom light flooding the room in bright light. "God, I'm blind!" I heard him grouse. I giggled again. The light went off and Dylan wound his way back to the bed tapping the small lamp at his side of the bed making it illuminate a small patch of the bed and ceiling. "So you're feeling better?" he asked as he flopped down on the bed, and handed me the glass of water.

"Yes, Thank You." I gulped the water down, handed him back the glass and gave it a shake. I raised my eyebrows in question asking for a refill. He stumbled from the bed, filled the glass in the relative darkness and came back. I sipped the second glass. I smiled into his beautiful eyes as he laid down on his side facing me. He sighed, sounding almost content.

"Are you tired?" *What a dumb question to ask,* I thought as I peered over his shoulder at the clock. It was four fifty in the morning.

"What time is it?" He closed one eye against the lamp, and looked at me sideways.

"Ten minutes to five." I waited for him to respond, he sighed loudly and batted his eyes. His lashes arched beautifully across his cheeks. I reached out and rubbed my hands down his naked chest, and feathered my hands down to his waist to the tie of his sleep pants. His sleepy eyes darkened and the corners of his mouth tipped up.

"I assume you're not tired anymore." He closed his eyes to shut me out.

"You're right, I'm not tired anymore." I leaned in and kissed his chest. I lightly licked along his sternum eliciting a low growl.

"And I can only guess what you have in mind since you can't sleep." He opened up one eye and raised his eyebrow to look at me. I kissed a wet path to his nipple and sucked it into my mouth.

"I'd only keep you up if I had something really fun in mind. Besides, I have to kill some time before breakfast." I continued my wet path heading south, licking along the edges of his beautiful stomach muscles.

"Hum, I guess your entertainment includes me." He let his eyes close.

"Unless you'd like me to leave the room, and look for some other type of entertainment." I let the words click off my tongue, and gave him a wicked smile.

"Well, I guess sleep is overrated." Dylan grabbed my hands so fast, I squeaked. Within seconds he had me whipped onto my back with my hands pinioned above my head. I giggled. He had absolutely no plans to go back to sleep now. I wiggled and tried to get away. My resistance spurring him on. Dylan groped me and kissed my neck fiercely. I feigned irritation. But this time I was not afraid. I knew he'd never act like Ryan again. He used his free hand to strip off his pants as I struggled underneath him, still smiling and giggling. He reached his free hand between my legs, pressing the wet spot that had formed on my panties, and stroked a trail upward.

"These have to go." Dylan's voice was low and throaty. I wiggled so he held me by only my hands and one hip as I almost securing my freedom. I giggled again, when he clamped his leg firmly over my thigh. Instead of trying to salvage my fragile lace, he grabbed the crotch and pulled, until they gave way and he held only a small scrap of fabric.

"Ta-Dah!" He held the rag up for me to see, a huge smile plastered on his face. His eyes filled with humor, his dimples deepened and puckered on his face. He was beautiful.

He pushed his knee between my thighs and worked to settle himself between my legs. His beautiful dick pressed against my entrance. His eyes met mine, sparkling with jollity.

"Ready for *your* wakeup call?" His eyes were the deepest color of blue and danced with excitement. As he dropped his head to my mouth, he pushed forward and slipped in with one push. He was passionate and slow, lifting me up to levels I hadn't achieved with any other man. Working us both until our orgasms overtook us causing us to clutch each other holding onto the crest of the wave. I was falling hard for this man. It was going to take me years to recover from the shattering when he left.

Chapter 29

I snuck from the bed at six thirty leaving Dylan snoozing, naked; laying on his stomach with his hair flowing softly across his forehead and tousled on the back of his head. The bed sheet was pulled so low the top roundness of his naked buttocks peaked out. The pale, untanned skin there begged to be touched. But, I needed food. I was starving. And he needed sleep, he had a game.

My quest for food would need to be done stealthfully. I dressed quietly in the corner of the room, in shorts and a tank top. I slipped my shoes on, and grabbed a room key I found next to the television, and slipped out the door allowing it to click closed quietly.

I looked down the hallway and was relieved to see the hall empty. I started off towards the entrance keeping my head down, and altering my step a little so I didn't look like myself. Suddenly a door opened, and I slowed to see who was exiting their room. If it was a coach, I needed to think up a great excuse to explain my presence, and it needed to be quick. I was hardly dressed like a photographer, and I didn't even have my press pass or camera. *Crap!* I dropped my eyes and looked through my lashes, hoping to avoid detection. I faced a strong broad back, a black tee shirt stretched across it. I breathed easier. After following the team for so long and taking their pictures. Seeing Jon in the hallway was a relief. He let his door click shut and turned to meet my gaze.

"Hello." He ran his eyes over me, maybe trying to decide if I was worth talking to.

"Hello. Where's a girl gotta go to get breakfast?" I smiled, hoping to keep our rocky friendship on level ground. I knew I

161

wasn't his favorite person, and coming down here and interrupting their baseball series put me in a worse standing with him.

"Come on, I'll take you." Jon's smile was genuine. We headed off to the hotel lobby where a small al a carte breakfast area sat. It had fresh fruit, toast, waffles, eggs, bacon, sausage, and a variety of warm breakfast breads and rolls.

"You're here taking pictures, nothing else." Jon whispered as we started down the breakfast line. Other players were already sitting around eating. Jon headed to a table where Chris was already sitting and pulled out a chair. I wasn't sure if I was to join them, or sit by myself. I stood at the end of the line adding salt to my plate and balancing a cup of juice and a plate on one arm and my hand. I waited for acknowledgement from Jon, but it never came. I headed to an empty table hidden in a back corner. I looked around the room smiling at a few of the players, avoiding coaches, and ate my food feeling so alone. These guys really didn't like me. A large rumbling voice broke into my thoughts. Doc came up and slid a chair out and joined me.

"I see you're better today." he stated rather loudly. A few heads turned to see who he was talking to.

"Yes, thank you, so much better. I really appreciate what you did last night. I just feel horrible that I put you in that position. I am sorry." I whispered.

"No problem at all, Stac, I was glad Dylan thought to call me."

"What could happen if the coaches' find out I stayed here last night?" I wanted to find out if Dylan was in danger of being suspended, and if Doc was planning on tattling.

"Dylan's safe. Let it go." He smiled, reached over and patted my hand.

"Thank You, for everything."

"Again, you are welcome, besides if Dylan hadn't called me I wouldn't have gotten to see any lace on this trip." He laughed, grabbed his plate and moved off towards a table filled with laughing coaches and staff. My face flushed.

Chapter 30

I opened the hotel room door with a plate piled high with breakfast foods. The light was still off and I closed the door as quietly as I could thinking Dylan was still sleeping.

"Where did you go?" Dylan's voice resonated through the room and I jumped. The plate see sawed in my hand, and I dropped his cup of coffee. I juggled the plate a couple of more seconds before righting it in my hands. The apple I had tucked under my arm fell, bounced and rolled into the room. Coffee splashed up my legs and pooled in a dark circle on the carpet.

"Shit!" I yelled, as I jumped away from the hot coffee. I headed towards the small side table and set the plate down. I grabbed the apple off the floor and tossed it across the room at Dylan; who seemed to watch my clown act as if it had great comedic value. It landed two feet from his hand and bounced wildly on the bed.

"When did you wake up?" I asked as I wiped the coffee off and crossed one leg under me taking up residence on the end of the bed.

"About ten minutes ago." He stretched and reached above his head giving me a fabulous view of his muscle ripped abdomen. I bit my lower lip, really wanting to sink my teeth into something else.

"I brought you some food." I said in a rushed breathy tone.

"You did? Where did you find food?"

"Continental breakfast buffet, compliments of the hotel staff. Are you hungry?"

"Are you eating?"

"I ate once, but I could be persuaded to eat a little more. No coffee though, it seems the carpet wanted it more than you did." I reached over to the table and grabbed the plate, and moved up to the head of the bed. Dylan pushed up to the headboard and leaned against it looking at the plate. The bed sheet slipped further down his hip exposing the small trail of hair that I knew led to a very beefy manhood.

"Here, I'll feed you." My offer came out all breathy and low. I took the fork, and gathered a bite of egg, and fed it to him. He chewed it, staring into my face. I stabbed a piece of melon and held it close to his lips. He pushed it back towards me, and I ate it off the fork and closed my eyes as the juice rolled down my throat. I scooped up another fork full and waited for him to open his mouth. When he opened his, I opened mine, like a mother bird mimicking her baby. I watched him chew, and swallow. I watched him closely, my eyes began to glisten. My thighs clenched automatically. I followed his egg with a bite of toast I had folded in half and placed within reach of his mouth. Dylan took a bite of the toast. Before I could pull my hand back, he circled my wrist with his large hand and held it tight. He sucked my finger into his mouth and suckled the tip. I sucked in a large breath. My eyes widened, and I made a soft mew with the air in my lungs.

"Butter." He said in the flattest tone I had ever heard. I put the toast back on the plate, and stabbed a sausage with the fork. I twirled the fork in my hand while waiting for him to swallow. His eyes were getting dark, the edges of them turning a shadowed grey. I tipped the fork and bit one end of the sausage with more vigor than I intended. Dylan's butt clenched, and his hand went immediately to cover his crotch... *Ew, a little too visual.*

I lifted the other end of the sausage up to him. He sucked it into his mouth, and right off the fork. My eyes were rounded in arousal. I tried to rip my eyes off his mouth. I moved the fork back to the plate, and scooped another bite of egg. Dylan reached up and grabbed my forearm, circling his thumb on the soft skin inside my wrist. The fork shook in my hand, and the egg dropped onto my bent leg. Dylan stared at me, I kept looking into Dylan's eyes; they grew heavy and sedated as he sat forward and sucked the egg off my leg, and ran his tongue up my short clad thigh. I gasped.

"Egg." he whispered as he laid back again, smiling, waiting for another bite of food. The sheet had fallen past his hips and covered just his manhood. I couldn't look anywhere else. My mouth made a silent 'oh' as I watched his cock jump under the sheet. I had trouble getting another bite of food onto the fork, mostly because I couldn't stop sneaking peeks at Dylan's privates.

"Are we done eating?" he asked, when I couldn't get any more food on the fork, and couldn't take my eyes off the bulge that was exposing itself under the sheet.

"Yep." I managed to utter, while my crotch clenched and throbbed waiting for him to take the lead.

"I'm glad." He reached up and rubbed his fingers down my face to splay against my neck and took my mouth in the sweetest, sensual kiss I had ever had. He laid me down, stripped me naked and made slow passionate love to me.

Chapter 31

I napped while Dylan went to his game. When he left, I had orders not to leave the room. And promises, that he'd explain his plan to get me home without me driving when he returned. I was willing to let him take control since I was tired of losing most disagreements we had. Mostly due to not using any of my own common sense. I stretched upon waking and wanted to go see the game, knowing I really shouldn't. But waiting for him to return was excruciating.

I changed into my clothes, and grabbed my camera. I headed out the door. I was stopped short outside the door when I ran into the solid chest of a man. My eyes looked up at his chest and I could tell at a glance it wasn't Dylan. My eyes scanned up the solidness into a set of chocolate eyes laced with anger.

"Back inside before somebody sees you!"

"What?" I said indignantly.

"Back. Inside. Now!" he growled.

"Did Dylan make you stay out here?"

"What part of 'Back inside', didn't you understand? Back inside now!" He reached up and grasped my upper arm lightly, and pushed against my shoulder to push me back into the room.

"Excuse me, who are you?" I narrowed my eyes.

"A friend of Dylan's and until we are ready to get you out of here, stay inside the room!" His voice was soft but menacing.

"I don't need a babysitter!" I retorted.

"From your history of shenanigans, I would say you need one. Back Inside."

I tore my arm from his grasp, and shot him a look of pure disgust.

"I was headed to the game to take pictures."

"Not today. Back inside, and if you don't move now, I will have to physically move you. Now, Go!" He pointed towards the door, then crossed his arms across his huge expanse of chest.

I turned on my heel and stalked back into Dylan's room. Stomping my feet once the door started to close.

"Asshole." I muttered under my breath, not sure if I was calling the man outside the door the name or if it was aimed at Dylan.

"Watch it, I'm your ride." I heard him laugh out loud, as the door closed behind me.

I stomped around the room, waiting for Dylan to return. When he entered, he looked at me sheepishly.

"And just what the hell is that all about?" I thumbed my finger over my shoulder with my arms crossed defensively as the man from outside let the door close in his face.

"Insurance."

"Are you fucking kidding me? You kept me captive in this room for three and a half hours, guarded by a Neanderthal, while you were out playing baseball!" I was infuriated. My lips were pinched into a thin line.

"I didn't play today, even though I was ready to."

"I don't give a flying rat's ass wha….what? You didn't play today?" My fear was evident in my tone.

"No." Dylan lowered his eyes and plunged his hands into the pockets of his jeans. I wanted to cry. I could only imagine the coaches had caught wind of my visit and punished him for my indiscretion. I shook my head.

"I'm sorry Dylan."

He slipped his arms around my waist and squeezed me burying his face into my neck. Nuzzling me and kissing up my neck.

"You're not going to tell me, are you?" I asked.

"No. But just so you know, if you hadn't been here, I wouldn't have been ready to play at all. But, I was, and I'm thankful for that." I latched my hands behind his neck and gave him the only thing I could, my unconditional love and acceptance.

"Take me home, Dylan." I whispered into his ear.

Chapter 32

"Wesley Hernandez, meet Stacia." Dylan made proper introductions after he invited Wesley into the room. "Stacia meet Wesley, your ride home."
I sized up Wesley. He was a big man, six foot four, and about two hundred and thirty pounds of pure muscle. I scowled at him, more for how he followed Dylan's orders, than for the man himself.

"And you know each other…how?" I pointed my question at Wesley, ignoring Dylan's attempt to intercede my standoff with Wes.

"Baseball."

"And…?"

"Friends from baseball."

"And….?"

"I play for The Astros." I turned slowly and eyed Dylan with a look of confusion and shock. He had called in a favor from a major leaguer to make sure I got home safely. If he couldn't see to it himself, he called for someone he could totally trust.

"I could have driven home myself." I mumbled, and pushed past Dylan to gather up my bag and camera.

"I don't think she's impressed." Wesley whispered. An amused look crossed Dylan's face and was reflected in Wesley's. The two men both turned simultaneously with raised eyebrows and looked at me as I gathered the toiletries I left in the bathroom. I shook my head, and slammed the bathroom door, muttering "Jack-asses" under my breath. The two men snickered, and continued to talk, occasionally laughing out loud with each other. I was angry, I expected to take myself home.

There was no reason I couldn't. There was a knock on the door, and Dylan pushed the door open.

"You need to take these, he held the antibiotic and a pain pill in his hand. He reached past me and turned on the tap and filled a glass.

"Here." He dumped the pills into my hand, and waited for me to put them in my mouth.

"No, I'm only taking the antibiotic." I tried to hand back the pain pill.

"It's a long ride, and you'll need the pain pill for the bumps and ruts on the way home." He looked at my reflection in the mirror. I cocked my eyebrow at him.

"I think I over reacted. You know, at the game." He pursed his lips and dropped his gaze. "I'm sorry." He pushed the pill back at me.

"You're not sorry, and I don't need a babysitter." I popped the two pills into my mouth and swallowed them both in one gulp, keeping my eyes locked on his reflection.

"I can't let you drive."

"Well, now I can't, can I?" I slammed the glass back to the counter. The sound reverberated against the wall. I shot him a look of total disgust. The sarcasm in my voice dripped off my tongue.

"It's better this way."

"Elaborate!" I stared at him in the mirror.

"Wes is my best friend. He'll make sure this exchange is smooth and drama free."

"Drama free, huh?"

"I'm not trying to offend you, just keep you safe."

"Safe? From what?" I started glaring at him in the mirror, my anger raising, struggling to keep my tone monotone.

"From yourself." He dropped his eyes and made one quick look through his lashes.

"God damn it, Dylan! I'm a grown woman. I've been taking care of myself for years! I don't have anybody else to rely on. I can do this myself."

"I've heard that from you before. And it's exactly why I called Wesley." He stepped back towards the door, hesitating for just a second. "Oh, Ray wants to see you before you leave, just to check up on y…" I threw him a look that would melt an iceberg.

"Pushing it?" he asked sheepishly.

"Past! Now out!" I heard a muffled laugh from the bedroom. Apparently I was entertaining to Wesley. I slammed the bathroom door in Dylan's face.

"She's pissed!" Wesley pointed out to Dylan, and the two men roared into fits of laughter.

"Yep, she is at that." Dylan laughed again. I was not winning this at all. "So much like Amy it's scary." I heard a gasp from Wes, and the room fell silent.

"Dude." Wesley's voice was low and his words drawn out. "Shit. You love her." His last words were barely above a whisper as they filtered through the door. My chest bloomed, he loved me!

Chapter 33

Ok, I must admit the ride home would have been hellish without the pain pill, but I stayed awake by constantly reminding Wesley how to drive my car. His grumbling, and his smile belie his humor and satisfaction that he was helping his friend. By the time we hit town, I was tired and just wanted to head home. Wesley turned down the back street entrance to the stadium.

"Wes?" I looked out the windshield at the road in front of me.

"Just picking up some stuff." He smiled.

"I'm not going home am I?" I said more like a statement than a question.

"Not until he can take you."

"Freaking Neanderthals!" I whispered through my pursed lips.

"Did you just make that a plural?" He scowled at me, but the smile on his face told another story. One of pure elation that he had been put in the same class as Dylan, and gotten under my skin.

"Yep. And you've added yourself to the group." I exhaled my disgust loudly, and threw myself back on the seat.

"Dylan will be back here in a few minutes. I want to go say 'hi' to a few guys, ok?"

He had a huge smile on his face when he turned in the seat to look at me.

"Can I trust you to stay put until he gets off the bus?" I plopped my head back against the seat, and nodded slightly. My driver's door swung open and he ran off towards the stadium. I grabbed my camera and pulled myself from the car.

Even tired, I wanted to review my pictures and I needed to stretch my aching muscles. I headed across the street towards the locker rooms back entrance. When I looked up from the view finder, I spotted Jon darting around the building walking with another man. Camera in hand, I snuck around to see what was transpiring. Lord, I knew this was wrong. I needed to stop my peeking. I tiptoed around the building and saw a door just beginning to close. I hurried to stick my foot into the crack before it closed. I could hear raised voices. I was looking into an unfamiliar room. A waist high padded table was visible on my right, and the rest of the room was dark.

The voices were beyond another door that stood open.

"What do you mean you're missing five thousand dollars of product?"

The other man's voice rung loudly above Jon's quiet question. "The supplier got stopped on his northern journey." The accented voice responded. Stress infiltrated his high pitched response.

"Damn it! What's left?" The voices had lowered to whispers again, and I strained to hear the conversation. I couldn't see anything, so I snapped off the flash on the camera and silenced the sound. I stuck the camera into the room and snapped a few pictures.

Ever the photographer, I started to review the pictures in the first room.

A few fuzzy images came into my viewfinder.

The man with the accent held a square plastic wrapped package. I stuck the camera back into the room again and snapped more pictures as the two men exchanged packages and curses. I pulled the camera back again and viewed the pictures. I was still in paparazzi mode and without thinking or listening to the room, it become completely quiet. I stuck the camera back into the room. The soft click was even loud in my ears. *Shit!*

"What the fuck?" Jon's voice was loud and angry.

I scrambled to my feet, and headed to the cracked door. I didn't make it. Jon grabbed my hair and pulled me back into the room. He kicked the outside door closed, and pushed me up against the wall, his palm firmly around my throat. Pure anger was painted on his face, and made his body shake.

"What the fuck, Stacia? What the hell are you doing here? What the fuck did you hear?"

I struggled against his hand, unable to talk due to the pressure he used on my throat to hold me in place. Fear creased my face and made me gasp for air, that I knew wasn't coming. Struggling made his grip tighter, so I relaxed as bolts of light infiltrated my eyes and I felt my hands start to tingle. I gripped my camera tighter, as I was losing my battle to get air. He loosened his grip and I sucked a huge breath of air.

"Jon." My voice was pinched and strained.

"What did you hear? His anger was visceral and he spit his question into my face.

"Nothing."

"Bullshit!"

"Jon, what are you doing?" My voice was strained, I pleaded with him to gain reason.

"This does not concern you."

"It does if people are getting hurt. You haven't hurt anyone yet, let's not start today."

Jon's face pinched and his eyes narrowed. There was a long silent pause as the conversation from my car came rolling back. It tumbled into my memory and slammed into my consciousness. He said he knew the driver, and that the driver had been high. The news hound in me kicked up a notch, and pieces of the puzzle fell into place.

"Oh my God. You've already hurt someone. You sold those drugs to the driver! You hurt Amy. You bastard!"

I realized my mistake as soon as the words left my mouth. Jon's face was furious, he lashed out with the intent to back hand me.

"Jon, look." I pulled my camera up offering him the only evidence I had gathered.

"Take it, it's all here, only here." I was trembling, but Jon didn't take my camera. He made a fist, cocked it back near his shoulder, and came at my face full force.
I threw my left hand up to defend myself. The camera still clutched in my right hand.

His blow didn't connect, but with profound quickness he snatched my wrist. He twisted my arm up behind my back, spinning me around to face the flat physical therapy table.

"I'll never tell Jon, You know I won't. I've never let anything leak before. I swear."

The table hit me, mid abdomen level. I lost every ounce of air in my lungs in one loud *Umphf.* I gasped for another breath. With his free hand he pushed hard between my shoulder blades. My face slammed into the table top with a sickening crunch.

"I know you'll never tell, I'll make sure of it." His fist connected with my cheek as I tried to turn my head.

"Jon, please stop!" I screamed. He pushed my arm up higher on my back, and pain shot through my elbow and shoulder. I didn't scream out loud, although my brain was screaming in agony. I tried reason.

"You can't do this Jon, it will kill Dylan. You've got the pictures, it would be your word against mine. And he has no reason to believe me."

"You fucking bitch! He better never find out!" he screamed. Spittle splattered on my cheek. I winced and closed my eyes. His fist connected with my face, again, my vision blurred and lightning bolts shot through my eye socket. He pulled my arm tighter. I tried to climb up on top of the table to relieve the pressure on my elbow. At my squirming, he reached up and pulled my hair so he could look into my face. I yelped. I let go of my camera and reached at his offending hand. I clawed and scratched at him. I tried to twist my body over so I could use my feet to kick. Infuriated he used his hips to pin me to the table, and slammed my face down again using my hair for leverage. This time I could taste blood in my mouth.

Panic rose in my chest choking off my air supply. He twisted my left arm harder and a loud cracking sound rented the air. I screamed, unable to contain myself. Pain shot through my elbow instantly and I lost all the strength in my arm. My fingers were numb, but it didn't stop me from struggling and attempting to kick free. Tears streamed down my face, my voice pitched into a screech.

"You can't do this Jon! I will never tell Dylan! I would never hurt him like that!" I wailed. With a wild sweep of his arm, he sent my camera careening into the wall.

"You *never* will bitch, I'll fucking kill you first!" His hand and arm slammed into my face again, and my nose veered off toward the side of my cheek. Blood poured from my nose. Pain shot through my head. Nausea rolled my stomach, and I screamed in agony. The panic rose again as I wondered if he truly planned to follow through on his threat to kill me. Jon pushed down hard on my arm as he released me. The blinding pain was unbelievable. My breathing was harsh and cut with screams of pain, and sobs of panic.

My left arm laid loosely on the table. I tried to pull it out in front of me, but my hand was numb, and my arm wouldn't move. The pain was unbearable.

"Remember this bitch, if one word of this gets out, I will hunt you down and fucking kill you! You aren't safe anywhere, understand? And as for Dylan? I will cut him down too. 'Keep your friends close, your enemies closer.' You'll do good to remember now why I am so close to Dylan." With those words he gave me one last smash to my face, and pushed down hard on my shoulder, just to hear the crunching. He sent lightning bolts of pain cursing through me.

I barely registered the scraping of my camera off the floor as Jon pulled the memory card out, pocketed it and threw the camera against the wall. I saw pieces fly in several directions. I couldn't move, I was devastated and my heart was broken.

"I would never hurt Dylan, never." I whispered in my sob. My sentence was one I thought I said in my head.

"You already have, just by being here, you already have." His snide remark had a sob rip from my throat. I knew he was right. I had already hurt him.

Someone yelled his name from behind a wall and pounded on the door, drawing his attention. The muffled voice informed Jon, they needed to move the product quickly before it was found. He started to leave and slapped the inner door open with vigor.

"I'll be back to deal with you in a minute. He will never believe you, remember that." His voice was menacing.

"I know he never will. He never will." I whispered as I cried into the table top.

The door slammed shut, making me jump. I laid on the table gathering my scattered thoughts. Tears of fear streamed down my face. Sobs wracked my chest. Pain circuited my body. Blood mixed with my tears was spread across the table top. Where was Dylan? Surely by now he would have come to collect me. I knew in my heart he would return to 'deal' with me. Humiliated, confused, and in pain I could only think about getting out.

Cold air goose bumped my skin. I could see nothing out of my right eye, and the bulge of tissue I could see from my left, I could only assume was my nose. My face and head pulsed with pain to every one of my rapid heartbeats. I needed to think. My breaths were rapid and erratic. I needed to get out. I slid my body to the edge of the table. My toes touched the floor, if I could stand. I needed to escape. I tried to ease my left arm to the edge, it didn't move. I pushed my chest up with my right arm. My left arm crunched and hung limply to my side. I screamed, the pain blinding me. My knees buckled, but I refused to let the pain take over me. I took several deep breaths staving off the dizziness and nausea. Blood dripped off my face, staining the floor in front of me. *Get out, find Dylan. Find Dylan.* I repeated the mantra as I forced myself to stand. Dizziness threatened to consume me. I had to move.

My right eye was blurred with blood and swollen, but I could see my camera on the floor. I had to have it. There could be evidence on the internal memory I could show Dylan, something, anything. I felt like I was going to pass out. I grabbed the table edge and gripped it with all of my strength. I had to make my legs move. They wouldn't, until I thought just how much Jon could hurt Dylan. How much I had hurt him already. I had to save him.

I pushed myself forward, the blood from my nose stained my blouse.

My breathing was labored and I exhaled heavily. *Find Dylan, Damn it move!* I screamed at myself inside my throbbing head. I stooped and grabbed the camera strap. I screamed and started sobbing again as my left arm swung wildly at my side. Crunching and grinding sounds echoed in my head. The pain threatened to overtake me. *Find Dylan, fucking move!* I headed to the door and pulled it open as the camera banged on the door frame. I could only hope I still had an ounce of evidence I needed to put an end to Jon's little business.

Night had started to fall and the streetlights illuminated the sidewalk in small round circles. I leaned against the outside wall of the locker room gathering every ounce of energy I could muster. The cool night air gave me some strength as I looked down the street for any help. The street was empty. I let my head roll back against the cool brick, waiting to gain some control of my respirations. That's when I saw him. I saw a single shadowy figure walking down the sidewalk on the opposite side of the street. I would have recognized those shoulders anywhere.

Dylan. Thank God!

With the camera strap clutched in my hand I headed towards the figure. The silhouette seemed so far away, but I pushed myself. He was here, he was safe. I needed to get to him. I stepped off the curb heading towards Dylan. I heard the blare of the horn and saw the headlamps too late to stop. The trucks impact threw me thirty feet into the street. The camera skittered on the asphalt. My head bounced into the ground with a sickening thud. I saw the silhouette running towards me just before the darkness took me.

Chapter 34

I felt like I was drowning. I couldn't breathe, I had pain everywhere. Suddenly, a burst of sound reached my ears, and air was forced into my lungs. I couldn't move, couldn't open my eyes, but I could hear. A strange voice.

"She has a shattered arm, closed head injury with a blood clot on her brain, broken ribs, fractured leg, and her face must have taken the full impact of the street. She may never…." I floated away taken back by the water. The sounds of machines lulling me to sleep. I may never what? The question rolled around in my head. I slipped into sleep, totally unaware of time.

"Not looking good right now."

"The blood clot in her brain may have…"

"She may never wake up."

"….may not make it."

Snippets of conversations. I slipped back under the water.

"Dylan, go home. I'll wait for a while." Mike's voice reached through. He sounded all fatherly. I wanted to open my eyes, move, do anything to let him know I was there. But I couldn't. The machine forced me to take another breath. One I couldn't take on my own. There was only darkness. I slid away and allowed the water to absorb me.

"Jesus, dude. You look like shit." I know that voice.

"Crystal and I have got this for a while." I feel a warm hand leave mine, and a warm path across my stomach cools, where his arm had laid. Why was he laid across me? Had he been asleep on the edge of the bed? How long had he been here? Was he checking to make sure I was breathing? Soft machine sounds and back to swimming. The darkness was comforting. Such a strange feeling.

"They're going to fix her hip today. Just a couple pins and a plate. Dylan are you hearing me?" Mike's voice is soft and fatherly. "Son, take off for a couple of hours, I'll wait. You've been here for days." I heard Dylan sigh, and he brushed his knuckles on my cheek. A soft beep, beep, beep and I slept. Sinking back into the water, slowly drowning.

"She's not going to be okay, is she? What if she doesn't wake…?" I heard Rob whispering. His comment a statement, not a question. I wanted to scream, '*I can hear you!*' But I couldn't move, couldn't breathe, and couldn't talk. So I listened for sounds, waiting for someone to wake me up.

'*I'm in pain. My head, my arm, my leg, my ribs. Oh God.*' A tear formed in my eye. I could hear and I could feel. '*Someone, please help me.*' The tear rolled down my cheek, and a soft thumb wiped it away.

"I don't know if you can hear me, but I'm here Stacia. You need to fight from wherever you are. Come back. I want you back here. Honey, please wake up. I can't be left alone again. Wake up, please." He spoke so slowly and softly, truly concerned, the whole time stroking my arm, head, and face. Using every trick in his arsenal to reach me.

'*I hear you Dylan, I'm trying. But if I come back, he'll hurt you and I can't let that happen.*' Another tear fell down my cheek, only that time it wasn't mine. The water is a safe place to be, just floating and sinking. So I let it take me.

"It's been almost three weeks Mike. When the fuck is she going to wake up? I can't take this! I can't sleep, I can't eat, I can't even remember what fucking day it is anymore. These God damn doctors don't say shit; just that it will take time. There's not a place on her that isn't fucking broken, bruised, cut or fucked up. Damn it Mike, she's suffering. I'm afraid to touch her, anytime I do, she cries. She is suffering, and here I sit like a fucking log. I feel helpless Mike, I never told her just how much she means to me. I love her, and now she may never know."

"She knows, son, she knows."

The machine pushed another breath into my chest, but with the swelling of my heart at Dylan's words. I'm not sure there's room for it.

Time slipped away. I couldn't tell if it was day or night. I couldn't tell if one day or two had passed. All I knew was I had to fight this sleepiness. I wanted to wake up. I wanted to see Dylan.

"Anything new?" Wesley's low rumble made the bed vibrate.

"Nothing, but everyday she's still alive is a good day. Right?"

"Dude, I'm sorry. I have no idea why she was at the visitors' locker room."

"Man, I wish I had just dropped my gear and left the bus…" Dylan's voice trailed off.

"Stop it, stop now, this is not going to be a repeat of Amy's death. It just can't be. God would not be that cruel." Wes exhaled, his last sentence fraught with untold fear.

"Jon, thanks for coming." I heard the slap of their hands. *What the hell? Are you serious?* In my haze I strained to hear their hushed voices. I'm scared. I can hear the heart monitor picking up speed. *My God Dylan, get away from him!* I wanted to move, protect him, and protect myself. My eyes fluttered, my heart was beating fast and thumping against my sternum. The beep of the heart monitor picked up speed. I wanted to yell, I wanted to tell Dylan the truth. Tell him what happened in the locker room. But I couldn't. So I struggled to stay on the surface. Alarms in the room went off. *I need to protect Dylan.* I finally get one eye to crack open. Alarms were sounding throughout the room. Dylan was staring at me, and all I could see was fear written across his face as he tried to comprehend what was happening. *I'm here Dylan. I'm here.* The room came alive with rushing people and the sounds of clattering equipment. They were shouting and then something cold ran through my vein, and I was gone.

"Seven weeks."

"Really? Wow. What about survivability?" Mike's question was whispered and strained.

"I think at this point, I'd say pretty good; even with all she's been through. But I'd keep this to yourself right now. Maybe she needs to know first. Let her make that decision." The doctor clapped Mike on the shoulder as Mike let out a long exhaled breath.

"Good idea, I'll wait." Mikes voice muffled and faded. The water floated me away.

Have I really been asleep seven weeks? What the hell has happened to Dylan? Did he finish the season? Is he back pitching? Did he make it back to the majors?

A large warm hand covered my right hand and another squeezed the fingers on my left. My fingers were all he could

184

touch, the plaster cast covered my arm from my arm pit to the first joints of my fingers and it was heavy. I could tell when I tried to tighten my muscles.

"Hey, sweetheart, you need to come back now. You've got stuff you've gotta finish out here. There's a whole new world opening up for you. I think you need to share it with someone. So come on open your eyes." Mike was so close I could feel the warmth of his body on my arm, and the brush of his breath on my cheek.

So I did. I forced my eyes open, trying to focus on his face. His face focused and then blurred into a white blob. My forehead wrinkled trying to keep him in my sight.

"Holy Christ!" Mike flew back from the bed. My right hand and arm dropped from his grasp. "Nurse!" he howled. My eyes were too heavy to stay open. They closed, but I could still hear the panic in Mike's voice.

"I swear she opened her eyes and she looked right at me. She. Looked. Right. At. Me." He was so breathy and panicked, I thought maybe he'd have a heart attack. He released a huge pursed lip breath, and I could imagine him rubbing his hand down his white beard.

"Sir. Sir. Calm down. There are a lot of automatic nerve movements. Muscle jerks, eye movement, things like that will happen. But there's still time, and still hope. Hold onto that." The nurse's explanation did nothing for Mike's panic level. He paced the room, and I knew he was watching me. Wanting more, something more. The nurse continued to soothe Mike. I tried to add to their conversation. *I can hear you.* I started to get anxious. I could hear the monitors picking up speed. I needed to get out of here. Since the beeping was a constant, I used it as my life line. I listened to the beeps. As long as I could hear them, I would see Dylan again. So I concentrated on the sounds, until the rest of the room blurred and faded away. Tears made their way down my face and into my ears.

"Do you think she'll remember this?" Jon's voice was small, quiet and concerned.

"God, I hope not." Dylan's voice was so distant. "She walked out into traffic and got smoked by a truck. The fucker damn near killed her. Even though I'd take her any way I could get her, I hope she doesn't remember all the pain, or any of the fear." His sigh ended their conversation.

And a plan started to work itself inside my head.

I was warm. Cocooned in warmth. A heaviness was draped over me. The pressure was reassuring. It felt secure. A warm hand rubbed small circles on my wrist. I felt wonderful. Loved. The machines and the breathing tube seemed distant right then, even though I could still hear them. I felt a heartbeat against my chest, one that didn't match my own. I was afraid to move. Afraid I'd lose the warmth and secure feeling. But, I needed to wake up. There was a soft exhaled breath that warmed my face as I pushed my eyelids up. Everything was still blurred and unfocused but the warmth was coming from a strong man with a chiseled chest with strong arms. His eyes were closed, I thought he was sleeping. My eyes were very heavy and I struggled to keep them open. Absently he stroked my head, which was still wrapped with gauze. I jerked, my muscles moved. Dylan's eyes popped open and I stared into the most beautiful set of blue eyes ever. He was scared, he was afraid to move, afraid I'd slip away if he blinked. My eyes closed slowly, and I forced them back open and tried to focus on his face, so he knew I was there. My muscles jerked again, and I fought against the darkness. I wouldn't let the water swallow me again. I fought to stay there.

Dylan wouldn't blink, wouldn't move, wouldn't talk, wouldn't let go. I knew this, but I needed to protect him. He had to go away. To keep him safe, I had to make him go away.

I furrowed my eyebrows, and tried to concentrate on his beautiful face. The stress was too much, and my eyes closed on their own. A tear formed in my eye and slid down my face. He wiped it away with his thumb, and caressed my cheek where he had removed the wetness.

"Come back, Stacia. Come back." He whispered. Dylan gathered me to his chest. I felt warm, comforted and loved.

I'll come back. I'll make it. But, right now, I have to figure out how to save you.
Since they think I won't remember, that's exactly what I'll do. I just won't remember.

"It's now or never. We take the ventilator off and she either breathes or she doesn't."
Shit! What the hell? How bad does this look? Ok, now or never. Stay awake!

"Ready?" The doctor addressed the room.

"Yep." Mike said.

"Yes. Yes" Chris and Crystal answered together.

"Ok." Emily whispered, her voice barely above a squeak.

"It'll be fine." Dale must have squeezed her because she snuffed.

"Ready." Rob stated, with a confident air.

"Dylan? You ok? She's ready. Really." I don't hear Dylan answer. I hear his feet shuffle and a quick intake of breath,

187

followed by a long exhale. He must have just shook his head, because he never spoke. I forced myself to concentrate.

"Dude, we'll all be right here, we won't leave her." Wesley's reassurance was touching.

Stay awake, stay awake. My new mantra.

Someone cut the twill string, deflated the cuff that held it in my throat, and pulled the tube out of my mouth.

Now. I thought. I took a shallow breath and coughed, the effort was weak and squeaky. *Ow.* My mouth made a perfect 'oh' as I scowled with the discomfort. I took another breath, and coughed again. Gasps and sighs of relief echoed around the room. Dylan dropped to the bed clutched my hand and held it to his face. I opened my eyes, gave a weak smile, and weakly squeezed his hand. This would be the last time I would recognize him before I chose to forget. When I chose to forget what I had done to hurt him. How Jon could hurt him.

Chapter 35

"What do you remember?" Mike grilled me one day in rehab.

"I don't, really." I shook my head slightly. Exasperated, I sighed loudly and fatigue set into my face. I had played mind games, read paragraphs, placed pegs on sticks, exercised my legs and arm until I couldn't stand and sweated. I was tired. I thought my mind worked just fine. But since I had forgotten my accident and much of the three months leading up to it, the doctors had me continuing in physical and cognitive therapy three times a week. Mike was my chauffer. But it was getting old very quickly. The same old questions, on a different day.

"Mike, please stop. The doctor told you I might never remember. Now if you can quiet down, I can finish this and we can go to work." Mike laughed out loud. "Keep it up, and you'll be back to work soon, but not until the doctors tell you, you can!" He leaned back in the chair and watched me stack blocks with my right hand. My hair had started growing back in where it had been shaved to remove the blood clot from my brain. There still wasn't enough to comb, but a soft fuzz now covered my whole head and started hiding the scars. I lifted the heavy plaster cast on my left arm to the table top and used it to hold down the edge of the piece of wood. A snippet of a conversation flowed back into my memory. *Seven weeks. Was I really in the hospital seven weeks?* The pensive look on my face drew Mike's attention.

"What 'cha thinking about?" Mike's voice broke into my thought.

"Just something I think I heard while I was in the hospital." I scowled.

"What?" Mike leaned forward and rested his elbows on the table, looking under my lashes to gage my eyes.

"Mike, if I was in there seven weeks, why is my arm still casted?"

"You weren't there seven weeks. Ah…oh…" Mike sat back hard in his chair and averted his eyes. "Um…Dr. Hobbs will talk to you about that." Mike squirmed in his seat. He dropped his eyes and drummed his fingers on his leg.

"What, Mike?" I asked as I finished stacking the last of the blocks and started fitting formed circles on wooden pegs sticking up off the platform. The games were starting to get old, and I was getting tired. I stopped and stared at him, watching him shift uncomfortably in his chair.

"Damn it, Michael! Spill!" I rubbed my forehead, the constant headache increased with my frustrated yell. Mike wouldn't look at me.

"You weren't asleep seven weeks." Confused I looked at Mike for an answer.

"Come on, Mike. I already have a headache, and I just can't do another math problem right now." I scowled at him. I pushed away from the table and grabbed the crutch leaning in the corner. Mike shot out of his chair, helped me to my feet and stuck the crutch under my arm. I wobbled still unsteady after the doctor pinned and plated my hip back into its socket. I let my mind wander back, and could only imagine how scary I looked with all the tubes, bruises, and broken bones. In addition, the fear that I wouldn't be able to care for myself. Maybe the people rallying around were real friends. Mike was fabulous; he rarely left me during the two and one half weeks I had been home. He worried and fretted like a mother hen. He made sure I got to therapy, had food in my fridge, and even cooked when I was too exhausted to move. He was shocked the day he found out, he was my emergency contact person on my work application. However, he was taking it to the extreme. Now he was just pissing me off by withholding information.

The bruises were fading, the swelling was receding, and I was getting stronger every day. He needed to loosen up.

"I'm the only one who knows, except your doctor." Mike held my arm while I made the slow trek towards the door.

"What the hell Mike, just tell me for God's sake. Don't you think I've suffered enough? This is bullshit!" *Yep, I played the pity card, spill it bud!* I shot him a hurt look. I was frustrated and the headache was getting worse with my worsening mood. Mike stopped. He looked at me as if a huge weight was sitting on his shoulders.

"You're pregnant." The statement came out all breathy and fast. I stumbled, losing my balance. Mike caught my arm and righted me before I fell.

"Oh my God. How the hell did that happen?"

"Well, I assume it happened the old fashioned way, sweetheart. But, if you need me to explain, I am more than willing." Humor edged his comment, and a small smile started to creep out from under his mustache and beard.

"No, I mean, I was on the pill. I haven't missed one." I paled, trying to wrack my brain.

"Well, that's something you need to talk to Dr. Hobbs about. It has something to do with all the antibiotics you were on making the pill ineffective. But the 'seven weeks' you heard was after an ultrasound. Seven weeks pregnant." He seemed proud of himself. My world was slowly disintegrating.

"So how long ago was that?" I was shocked and even more confused. My life was over. At twenty four years old, I could no longer see my future. I was stuck right there, right then, with no future.

"Three weeks ago." Mike whispered.

"Fuck, which means I'm ten weeks along. Two and one half months. Holy Shit!" My face blanked.

Mike laughed, "Since your accident your mouth has no filter! Something you'll need to get a grip on once that baby gets here."

"Shit, Mike, I can't have a baby!"

"Darling, it's no longer your decision. God's hand was at work here. Now all you have to do is be prepared." His smile was genuine, he seemed truly happy smashing my world.

"You're sure no one else knows? Who else was in the hospital that day?" *Oh my God Dylan cannot find out! He would never return to baseball, and I couldn't take his dream, not anymore.* I paled, my breath quickened, and my heart raced. "I've got to sit down, I feel sick." Mike pulled up a chair and helped me sit. He squatted in front of my chair leaning on my crutch, and put his hand on my knee.

"Nobody can find out, Mike, and I mean nobody!" The last word was drawn out and so tight I was sure you could pluck it like a guitar string. I pleaded with my eyes. Tears pricked the corners of my eyes. Mike rubbed my shoulder, his attempt to comfort me.

"Fine, it'll be our secret. I promise, I won't tell a soul. Now, let's get you two out of here."

"Damn it, Mike. Shut the fuck up and take me home!"

Chapter 36

What the hell was I going to do? Dylan could never find out. He'd give up on baseball, and I didn't want him to stay out of obligation. I had worked really hard to make sure Dylan knew I was pulling away. When I woke up, I acted like I didn't remember our activities, or that I had any romantic interest in him at all. When he showed up at my apartment to help out, I played it cool. I acted like he was just a friend nothing more. It broke my heart to watch him insinuating himself into my life.

"I'll stay out here while you take a nap."

"No, Dylan, I can handle this. Go home."

"Stacia, let me help, that's why I am here." He reached for my arm to help me get up. I leaned heavier on my crutch, avoiding his touch.

"I don't need any help, Dylan. I'm fine. Thanks though. Go on, meet up with your team. Mike will be here soon anyway. We're going over copy for the paper. It will be the first time he's let me see anything from work, and I can't wait." I plastered a grin on my face and stood up stretching my back, using my crutch like a balancing bar. Dylan moved forward to help me, held my arm and planned to guide me to my room. I pulled my arm away.

"Goodbye Dylan, I'm fine." I turned and crutched myself to my room. There was an awkwardness with my casted arm, and my limp made him watch me all the way into my room. I slowed when I got inside, and moved in a small circle on my crutch. I gave him a small smile as I closed and locked the door. I heard him exhale loudly. A single tear streaked down my face. I laid my head on the door, listened to him click off the T.V., and to the apartment door as it click closed. Then and only then did I let loose with a flood of tears. Pushing him away so he could fulfill his dream and staying away so Jon would never hurt him. If he ever found out about the baby he'd never follow his dream and would hate me more than he did now. This hurt worse than I thought.

Chapter 37

"Stop it! I'll make it on my own!"

Mike raced around me like a rabbit on cocaine. He opened doors, shoved crutches at me, and handed me anything I reached for. Today he raced around getting me ready for yet another doctor's appointment. This one to see the baby I was carrying. Mike seemed overly excited. I was terrified. Horrified that Dylan would find out, and I would no longer be able to keep him safe from Jon's secret.

"Stacia, come on in. The doctor's ready for you." Mike helped me up, handed me my crutch and tried to follow me in. "He'll do the exam first, then do the ultrasound. That's when 'Daddy' can come in, is that ok with you?" The nurse smiled shyly at Mike and winked. My head snapped towards Mike, he snickered and grinned. His chest jutted out and he was every bit the proud 'father'.

"No, that's fine, he can wait until this is done."

Mike deflated. He dropped his gaze, turned, and returned to a chair across the room. He snatched a magazine briskly off a stand and plopped down, defeated.

I asked the nurse to help me get up on the table, and support my casted arm. I had to have help getting settled onto the table. With my legs up in stirrups, I endured the most nerve wracking exam of my life.

"Well, so far so good." With a pat to my leg the doctor told me to push back onto the table. I struggled, unable to accomplish the task. My leg was still weak and sore, but I was too embarrassed to tell anyone I needed some help. So to avoid a conversation about my ineptness, I sat up and reached for my crutch.

"We'll need to do an ultrasound today. After this little one's rough start, we just want to take a peek at him and make sure everything looks good. We will be watching him closely, with all the medications and surgery you endured, because he went through all that too." My stomach sank a little. Wow, to be the size of a peanut, and survive all the stuff I went through, I worried the baby would be ok.

I felt numb, fearful that this 'look' would show some grotesque looking abolition. What I saw softened me. A round little head, a knobby spine, fingers, toes, and a beating little heart. Mike had snuck into the room when the nurse told him I was having some difficulties scooting up the table.

Then the doctor turned on the sound. The gentle whoosh, whoosh, whoosh made me gasp.

"Wow, listen to that." Mike whispered.
I was quite amazed. I listened to the tiny peanut's heartbeat, and knew I could never tell Dylan. Having a baby would rob him of his future. I couldn't destroy him. This was one heartbeat he'd never hear.

Chapter 38

The summer wore on. At the end of August, the heat had invaded my small apartment. Dylan was stopping less and less and I was restless. I had resorted to throwing a tennis ball at the walls until the neighbors complained to the landlord, and I was threatened with eviction. I needed a diversion. Sitting at home, with only doctor's appointments and therapy was boring. I threw the crutches out, and wanted out of this jail. So, I showered, put on shorts and a nice tee shirt, slipped on some sandals, covered my short hair with a baseball hat and headed out the door.

Keys in hand, I slipped into my car. Freedom! It felt wonderful. I sighed. Content, but still restless. I drove. I took the familiar roads to work and went inside. Mike wasn't behind his desk.

News of my arrival spread like wildfire through the studio and everyone came out to see the 'miracle' standing in the hall. I had reached celebrity status, but not for reasons I would have liked. I was a survivor, someone who beat the odds. I was hugged, caressed, kissed and jostled. After I had greeted nearly all of the staff, I made the excuse I needed a cable from my desk and slipped away from all my well-wishers. I closed my door, and stared around my office. The desktop was clean, the shelving unit straightened and clean. Someone had tidied up. My eyes scanned the office, absorbing it, enjoying the familiar surroundings. Then my eyes fell on my camera tucked into a corner of the shelf. I grabbed it and tried to turn it on, it didn't work. The hatch that held the digital disc was empty. I knew it would be. Jon took it the night he beat me. But, I still wanted to do something familiar. My anger at Jon and how he hurt Dylan started to burn in my mind. I wanted revenge, but not at Dylan's expense. Right now I wanted normal, I wanted to feel good.

I snuck into Mike's office and grabbed the old film camera, stopped at a pharmacy and bought a roll of film. I headed to the baseball field. This might not have been one of my best ideas, but it felt comfortable and provided the diversion I needed. I pulled up to the stadium and parked. I feuded with myself. I should just leave. I didn't want to encourage Dylan. But this felt so right.

I pulled my press pass off my rear view mirror and flashed it to the attendant. The smell of popcorn and dirt invaded my nose. Yes, this was comforting, something normal.

Gingerly, I took the back steps down to the field and got a surprising glimpse of the team. They were in the dugout, middle of the batting order. I stayed behind the concrete wall, behind the fence.

The most natural thing in the world was to put that camera up to my face. Exhilarated and smiling I snapped a picture. This felt so normal and after all I'd endured, and all I was losing, this was all I had.

The click of the film advancement was heard by just one person in the dugout. A beautifully tanned, dark haired pitcher with a chiseled chest and bulging biceps. He came to the fence and leaned his back against the inside of the fence. He looked at me sideways, his smile a response to mine.

"Hello. Are you supposed to be out here?"

"I couldn't stay holed up anymore."

"You're looking great, finally putting a little weight back on."

"You'd put on weight too not being able to move around, and everybody feeding you constantly." I rolled my eyes, but kept the smile on my face. I spied on Dylan from the corner of my eye as I put the camera back up to my face. He exhaled loudly.

"Do you remember this?" He scanned across the field and waited for me to answer.

"Taking pictures?" I asked with true interest, wondering where his line of questioning was leading.

"Yeah, and being here?" He swung his hand in an arch.

"I remember some things, but not much. I know this feels normal. I like it. And this camera feels good in my hands." I scowled, and looked down. I turned over the camera and a smile crept across my face as I remembered other times here at the fence.

"Does this feel normal?" He used his hand to tap the fence, and looked at me out of the corner of his eye.

"You mean standing at the fence?"

"Yes. Does this feel good? Do you remember being here at the fence?"

My face fell, my smile slid off my face and I looked away.

"Do you remember what you and I used to do here at the fence?" he asked. Dropping his eyes to be able to look into mine waiting for realization to bloom.
Dylan's attempt to jog my memory was painful to watch.

"I'm sorry Dylan. This camera is the only thing that feels right. Everything is still fuzzy and out of focus. I just don't remember. Why? What happened here?" I looked around the area with a blank look on my face as if it held no sentimental value to me. My eyes were wide and searching.

"I thought once you'd fallen for me right here at this fence. We spent a lot of time here talking. Does any of that sound familiar?" His right eye was closed against the sun, his left eyed me suspiciously.

I dropped my eyes and shook my head. I couldn't take it anymore. The pain I saw in his eyes was deep. He wanted me to remember. He wanted me to love him. But if I did that, I would only hurt him, or get him hurt. I couldn't do that. I stared at him, blinked, and turned to walk away. If I didn't answer, I couldn't lie. It was what I needed to do, walk away and not look back. I slowly negotiated the stair steps, tears falling at my feet.

Chapter 39

Crystal came to my apartment two days later.

"Listen, I know you're still a little confused about all of us, but the team's getting together after tomorrow's game and I'd like you to come. It will give you a chance to get out of here. Hang out for a while?"

"I'm not so sure, Crystal, but thanks. I still get headaches daily, and Mike's grounded me until the doctors really release me."

I thought back to my outing two days earlier, and my chance meeting with Dylan at the fence. Once Mike caught wind of my outing, and that I had taken his camera, he was pissed. He caught me returning the camera to the studio and I had received my first pit bull mulling. My car keys were confiscated, my car abandoned at the TV station, and Mike chastised me all the way back to my apartment.

"This isn't just about you now, sweetheart! And until all these doctors write you up a clean bill of health, you're keeping your ass at home! And if you can't follow the rules, I'll be moving in until that baby gets here! Do you hear me? You took my camera, drove all over the country side, walked God knows where without your crutches. Wait, where are your crutches?" His own question stopped his tirade. I couldn't lie, but I knew when I answered he wouldn't like what he'd hear. I could only whisper my answer.

"I threw them away." I kept my eyes on my lap, lacing my fingers together, and tapping my thumbs together. Avoiding any eye contact important to keeping my tears at bay.

"Stacia Barnett! What were you thinking? How the hell do you expect…"

And so it went for the seven mile ride home. The longest, slowest ride of my life. And the mulling given by a man who truly cared about me and my little peanut.

"Stacia, we'd all love to see you there."

"I'd love to Crystal, but I can't drive right now, and…" She cut me off before I could continue on my excuse train.

"I'll pick you up, and you just say the word, and I'll bring you home."

I sighed in resignation. My head hurt from arguing my case, and I rubbed my forehead. I had an exasperated look on my face, but she wouldn't relent. Her eyes were bright with excitement.

"Fine, I'll go. Now go home." I agreed to go just to quiet her.

"Oh, you'll have so much fun. Wait and see!" Her excitement should have been contagious, but I wasn't looking forward to seeing Dylan, and partying with all the men that hated me. After thinking about the last couple of months though, I couldn't say for sure any of them really hated me. There were a lot of them that had visited in the hospital, and most of them had checked on me once I was home. Even Jon seem overly concerned, probably because he thought I'd remember what he'd done. I could never take that chance. I could never let him hurt Dylan.
Never.

Chapter 40

Chris and Crystal picked me up at seven, after the afternoon game ended and all the players had had time to shower. I was tired, but couldn't convince Crystal I should just stay home. I plastered a smile on my face, and tried to display as much excitement as the two of them. Watching them touch and smile at each other was painful, they had what I wanted with Dylan. This was probably a bad idea on my part. Seeing Dylan at the fence two days earlier had me in tears for hours. And my heart couldn't take another bashing.

I sat in the back seat of Chris' car and listened to the banter, smiling and adding snippets to their conversation. This was a bad idea. I laid my head against the seat and closed my eyes to gather my jumbled thoughts, and devise an escape if needed. I could always use my accident as an excuse.

We pulled up in front of a beautiful home lit up with flood lights and walkway lamps. A large open front porch with columns was beautifully lit and well landscaped. The pounding rock music filtered out the open windows and silhouettes of people milling about flitted across the window sheers.

"Whose house is this?" I asked. I was admiring the exterior and already dreading the loud music. My increasing headache was due to the encounter I was anticipating with Dylan. Although right now I was blaming it on the music.

"Jon's." Chris answered, as he jumped out of the car and ran to the passenger side to open Crystal's door. He offered her his hand and she glided gracefully from the seat. Chris lifted her hand and softly planted a kiss to her knuckles. A soft giggle floated on the breeze and I watched her throw her hands behind Chris' neck and kiss him hard on the lips. She whispered in his ear and ran her hand softly down his chest. Chris just smiled and stared lovingly into her eyes. Even I had to smile. It was so sweet. He didn't take his arm off her as he reached over and opened the back door.

Chris reached in the open door and offered me his hand. I scooted to the edge of the seat, fear starting to grow in my gut. Not wanting him to see my rising fear, I waved him off.

"I'm fine, this will just take me a minute. I'm a little slow these days." I laughed offhandedly. I slid a little further to the edge. Panic was beginning to get the best of me, and I knew I was getting pale. Chris offered me his hand again, and when I didn't take it, he leaned down to look into the car.

"Are you ok?" His look of concern and furrowed eyebrow met my own.

"I'm fine, the seat's just a little lower than I'm used to, and I need to slide over more. I can do this. I just need a little more time to…." My rambling made him blink and look at Crystal with a silent plea to either shut me up or get me out of the car. He seemed anxious to get to his buddies and my stalling was aggravating him.

"Go on, honey, I've got this." Crystal placed a quick peck to his cheek and Chris stepped back to let us to handle this mini snafu.

"Thanks, Crystal, I just need a minute." I took several deep breaths to tamp down my rising panic. I thought of a multitude of excuses that would have gotten me taken home immediately. Then it hit me. I could possibly find my camera disc. Then I'd have proof. I could save Dylan's future, save his faith, but I would ruin his illusion of his wife's death and his friendship with Jon. Not that I cared about that. Because I was pretty sure Jon would go to jail.

I pushed myself out of the seat and got to my feet with a renewed purpose. I knew I could save Dylan. All I needed was the camera disc.

Chapter 41

The house was filled with loud music and every square inch of floor space covered with people. Crystal gave me a drink, and left me standing in the living room with a host of gyrating dancing fools. I watched them all dancing, the pounding bass making my head pound to the beat. But, I refused to leave until I had a chance to snoop.

"How are you?" A smooth, silky voice whispered to me over my shoulder. I shuddered, the voice sent a shiver cascading down my spine.

"I'm doing great. Thanks for having me."
Jon squared up beside me, watching the crowd of people dance and sing along with the music. I winced with every bass beat and put my hand to my head. Softly rubbing my temple.

"Sound bothering you?" His eyes skimmed my face, his eyes narrowed as he tried to read me. I did my best not to be nervous, or give him any indication I remembered anything. His concern seemed genuine, but I remembered his mantra of 'friends close, enemies closer'.

"It's a little loud in here." I admitted. I looked at him, imploring him to find me some relief.

"Let's go sit out by the pool." Jon took my arm and I forced myself to relax. I smiled weakly, still wincing as the stereo pounded.

"This is a nice place." I commented nonchalantly.

"Thanks." Jon answered, still leading me out the sliding glass door. The pool area was filled with people too, and a radio was playing in the background, the beat less imposing, but still present.

"Here have a seat." Jon offered me a chair pretty close to the main action poolside.

"What are you drinking?" Jon's smiling face appeared in front of me as he placed both hands on the arms of the chair he had seated me in. I smiled back as sweetly as possible, making my shoulders relax. I tilted my head.

"Tonic water."

"Want another?" Jon was being too kind. '*Enemies closer*', whirled through my mind. I couldn't let on I was really nervous around him. I couldn't let on that I remembered what he'd done to me, and I planned on finding the disc and destroying his business, when I found it.

"I'd love one, Thank You." I smiled again as sweetly as I could, and kept my eyes on him as he disappeared into the house. I rested my head in my hand and closed my eyes, shutting out the light and trying to stop my pounding head. A hand rubbed my shoulder. I jerked to attention.

"Jesus, are you okay?" Dylan's concerned voice made me melt.

"I'm fine, just a headache. There's a lot more noise here than I wasn't expecting. But it's quieter out here. I'll be fine, Thank you." Dylan kept rubbing my shoulder and even though I loved the feeling, I had to pull away and act as if I didn't remember all his past gentle ministrations. Our past sexual encounters tumbled through my memory. It was the hardest thing I had to do, but I had to do it. I slid away from his caress.

"Jon went to get me some water." I said flatly. I looked up at Dylan blankly. My eyes wide with wonder. Dylan's look was full of longing.

"What is it Dylan?" I knew as soon as the question left my mouth, I was going to regret any answer he gave back.

"I…I just…miss you." Dylan's eyes went watery.

"How can you miss me? I'm right here." I chortled. Dylan dropped his eyes. Pain flitted across his face, then a small smile tipped the edge of his mouth and he slowly lifted his eyes. His beautiful baby blues glimmered.

"Do you remember the eight buttons?"

"Eight buttons? What buttons? On my camera?" I looked up at Dylan through my lashes, a confused look plastered on my face. "I don't think there are eight buttons on my camera." I stated as a matter-of-fact.

"No, on my shirt." His voice lowered to a hum. His eyes softened and he sought some type of recognition in my face.

"Um, Dylan? That's a tee shirt. You don't have any buttons on that shirt. I scanned the front of his shirt imagining what lay beneath it. My hands itched to touch him, feel his warmth, rub his muscles, and kiss his chest. Knowing that if I gave him any hint I remembered, it would only get him hurt; I smiled at him quickly changing it from seductive to amused in a flash. Dylan's face fell.

"Keep thinking about it, Stac." He reached for my hand just as Jon returned.

"Here you are." I reached up with both hands and smiled broadly at Jon.

"Thank You." I took the bottle of water, and struggled to twist the top off. I exhaled loudly and tried again, failing to pop the top. Jon reached over, snatched the bottle, twisted off the top and handed it back all without taking his eyes off the pool, and never breaking conversation with Dylan. He turned his eyes towards me only after I had taken the bottle back.

"You look a little tired." His statement was said flatly and with a glint of amusement in his eyes.

"I'm fine really. Just this headache. I'll rest later, right now I want to enjoy the activity."

Players and friends chit-chatted with me all night, stopping by on their way to refill their drinks, or to grab towels from a rack by the pool. I was able to relax a little, but kept my poker face on and kept my fear in check all evening. Jon and Dylan talked baseball beside me. I yawned. My eyes were heavy and their rumbling voices lulled me. My eyes flittered shut for just a second before my head fell forward, and I was asleep. Dylan reached out and took my drink from my hand.

Jon spoke in what could be considered little less than a whisper.

"Does she remember anything?"

"No, dude. She just looks at me like I've grown horns. She won't even let me touch her." Dylan sighed.

"Did the doctors say she'd remember?"

"Maybe in time, but they told me not to push it. But damn, Jon, this is fucking hard. I want her to remember."

"Maybe its better she doesn't." Jon said honestly.

"For who, Jon? Her or me?" I could hear the pain in his voice. I heard him swallow loudly.

"Look, it's her way to protect herself, protect her mind. File away the pain, so it won't hurt again."

"But, it's killing me." I heard a loud exhale of air, and his hands rake through his hair.

"Dude, let it go. Really, it's better that way."

"Yeah, maybe it is better."

The two men moved on to talk about baseball, and coaching. I listened contently for a few minutes with my eyes still closed.

I took a deep breath, pretending to wake up. I blinked and smiled sleepily at the two men sitting next to me. I absently rubbed my headache at my temple and I yawned.

"Sorry about that." I said as I stretched and yawned again. Two faces smiled back, one happy to see me awake, the other weary.

"That's ok." Jon looked at me sideways, a small smile creased his lips.

"Yeah, it's fine. You're still recovering." Dylan leaned forward as if to touch me. I leaned back to avoid his touch. I could see the hurt in his face. I turned my attention to Jon.

"I think I need the 'little girls' room, excuse me for a few minutes." I struggled to get up and both men jumped to their feet.

"Let me help." Dylan stuck out his hand.

"Here." Jon scooped under my arm intending to help me up. I winced as my broken elbow was lifted in his attempt. My facial grimace was witnessed by just one of the men. Dylan's face fell, as he stared me in the eyes, waiting for me to say something.

"Really, guys, I can do this. Back up." I patted Jon's hand softly to get him to let go. With a set jaw, I pushed my way from the chair, knowing I needed to get away. I stood getting my leg underneath me before letting go of the chair with my good arm. The pain played across my face. Dylan looked at me, my pain reflected in his eyes.

I headed towards the house my heart breaking. As the sliding glass door opened the thump of the music hit me. Instinctively, I rubbed my head. The headache had reappeared, brought on by the pain I saw in Dylan's eyes. I staggered a little, tears pinched at the corners of my eyes.

"Please, let me help you." Dylan appeared at my right elbow. His face was full of pain at watching me struggle to make my way to the house. My mind told me to decline his offer, my heart wanted me to lean into him, and accept all he was offering. My heart wasn't going to win. I knew this to be true.

"No, I'm fine Dylan." Seeing an opportunity, I turned to Jon. "Would it be ok if I took a few minutes in a quiet room? I need to get this headache under control, and I am exhausted." My eyes pleaded with Jon for some respite. He sighed, probably trying to think of a way to keep me under his watchful eye. He softened.

"Come on, I'll let you rest in the spare room." He placed his hand on the small of my back, all my muscles tensed. I forced myself to relax and not show him I was nervous. I moved my hands over my ears to block the thundering bass from the stereo, acting like the tension in my back was from anticipating the impending beat of the music.

"I'm sorry." I shouted, as Jon lead me through the room filled with dancing drunks. Included in the mix were Chris and Crystal.

"What have you got to be sorry about?" His eyes searched mine, looking for a hint of understanding or maybe some recognition that I had remembered.

"I'm ruining your party. I never should have allowed Crystal to talk me into this. It's just too soon. And I am overly tired. I'm sorry you've had to baby sit me tonight. You should be spending time with your teammates. I'm just sorry."

He led me to a set of steps. I stopped and looked up at the daunting set of carpeted stairs. My face fell. I knew I could make it, but if Jon was allowing me to use his spare room, more than likely the disc wasn't there. I looked beseechingly at Jon.

"Got a closer room?" An office or somewhere I can just close the door, and maybe some aspirin? I'll just sit a few minutes and get this pounding headache under control." The tears in my eyes from earlier rose to the surface again, and this time I let a few trickle down my cheeks.

"Use my office." He led me to a small room behind the stairs and down a short hall. He held the handle and said, "Just a minute." He tried to scoot in front of me, but I pushed my body against his back as he opened the door, not giving him any space. I kept my ears covered by my hands until he pushed the door closed; making sure he saw my hands as I slowly dropped them from my head. Continuing the ruse that I didn't hear his request for me to wait.

"Thank You Jon, I am so sorry for putting a damper on your night." I sat on a loveseat positioned in front of a long dark wooden desk. I rubbed my head with my hand and watched Jon from the corner of my eye. I watched him closely as he scanned the room, noting where his eyes lingered the longest. I knew the disc was close. He hesitated to leave the room with me there. I needed a diversion.

"Is there water close by?" I asked as I dramatically dropped my head to the sofa back, and rubbed my forehead, acting as if I just couldn't take the pain one more second.

"I'll get a glass, be right back." He looked directly at his desk, and scanned the top where his computer lay plugged into the electrical outlet. He then turned to look at me. I sighed, and covered my eyes with my arm, and let a frown slide on to my face.

Jon left the room, softly clicking the door closed. I leaned forward scanning the room looking for the areas his eyes had floated to earlier. I saw piles of papers and books on a shelf behind the desk. The wooden desk held the computer, a small lamp and another pile of papers.

The door latch turned, and I laid my head back again, and covered my eyes with my arm. Jon slipped in with a glass of water, and a bottle of aspirin.

"Here, Stacia, I brought some aspirin." Jon lowered his voice, and when I didn't respond right away, he touched my arm. I lowered my arm revealing new tears. I had worked hard to press my arm into my eyes to cause the new set of tears as I contemplated how to retrieve my disc.

"Thank You, Jon. You are too kind." I took the glass as he opened the bottle and poured two pills into my hand. I swallowed the pills, hoping and praying they wouldn't hurt my little peanut. "Join me a minute." I moved over a little and Jon slipped onto the sofa. I used every ounce of mind control to relax and settle in next to the man who planned to harm me.

"I am sorry Jon. I didn't mean to be such a drag. You don't have to stay in here with me, but I appreciate all your concern and caring." I patted his arm and calculatingly slipped my hand into the crook of his arm. I gave him my most endearing smile and intentionally put my head on his shoulder. I closed my eyes and rubbed my head, and snuggled in closer. All the while conveying a security to him that I indeed had forgotten my past; all the time keeping my enemy closer. It was the hardest damn thing I had ever done.

Chapter 42

A soft knock came to the door, and Jon called out to the person on the other side. The door opened slowly and a sliver of light cascaded across the floor. A broad form filled the light and I knew without looking Dylan had come to see me. I knew before I ever looked up, I could feel him, smell him, craved him. I slowly rolled my head off of Jon's shoulder, and blinked at the crest fallen face of my true heart's desire. I hurt deeply knowing I was leaving him in the dark, and my heart was scattering. But I was protecting him.

"Jon. Dale and Glen are leaving. They wanted to talk to you before they leave." Dylan dropped his eyes as I slipped my hand out from under Jon's arm. His eyes stayed fixed on the gesture as Jon started to unfold from the couch.

"I'll be back in a few minutes." Jon placed my hand back on the sofa. His exaggerated pat of my hand was absorbed by Dylan's eyes. Pain drifted across Dylan's face, and furrowed his eyebrows.

"Take your time, go say goodbye. I just need the quiet for a little bit." I reached out and grabbed Jon's elbow. He looked at me with wide eyes. Quietly I said, "I really do appreciate everything you've done Jon." I dramatically closed my eyes and put my arm over my head. The headache was real, the pain I felt was real. Probably brought on by my broken heart.

"Go, I'm fine. I'll be out in a few minutes. As soon as the aspirin's kick in." My eyes searched Jon's face, then Dylan's, pleading to be left alone. Silently asking for time to search Jon's office. I covered my face with my arm, stealing glances at the two men who are contemplating leaving me alone in this room. I settled myself further into the sofa and sighed. The two men looked at each other, and together slowly exited the room.

I heard the door click and sat up straight and looked around. The desk was maybe six steps from the coach, but if I crossed in front of the lamp light, outside they would know what I was doing by the shadow I cast across the windows. *Think, think!*

I crawled off the couch and slid towards the windows. I crept along the floor and slithered my way between the wall and the desk. I opened up the top drawer and felt around. Papers, pens, and a ruler. I continued to dig without finding any camera discs. My hands were sweating and my breathing was fast and heavy. I was nervous, if I got caught, both Dylan and I would be in danger. I opened the second drawer, this one I could see the inside edge, and I felt around hoping my fingers found the small flat rectangular disc. Nothing. The third drawer was file folders, I quickly scanned them, figuring this hiding spot was improbable. Back to the top drawer. I sat up a little making sure no shadows fell outside. I carefully lifted the tray that held the pens and pencils. Bingo! A square flat disc touched my fingertips. I plucked it out of the drawer. I couldn't tell if it was my disc, but I pocketed it. Then I spotted the computer, its external drive attached, and there in the small SD slot was another disc. I snatched it, and pocketed it. I was on borrowed time. I needed to move before they returned. I felt around the second drawer under some papers coming up with yet another disc. I shoved it deep into my pants pocket and started to reexamine the second drawer, and came up with yet another disc. This one the right color and shape to the one I had in my camera. I pocketed it too. My breaths were coming fast as I worked my way around Jon's desk. Panic was setting in as I figured I had three discs too many in my possession, and that at any minute I could be caught in the middle of my deception. I started to search the first drawer again. As long as I was searching, I'd take them all. As I crawled around to the back of

215

the desk, I heard laughter in the hall. I pushed the drawers closed, and crawled as fast as I could to the couch. I had almost made it when the door handle rattled. I flew as fast as I could to the sofa and threw myself up as the door opened about one inch. I settled as quickly as I could, threw my arm over my face and slumped onto the arm rest. Jon swung the door open wide just as I had settled and assumed a position of sleep and forced myself to relax. I used every ounce of energy to calm my thundering heart, and held my breath, letting small amounts of air escape my burning lungs in an attempt to calm myself. I was sure Jon could see my heart beat through my thin tee shirt. Dylan slipped in behind him.

"I think she fell asleep again." Dylan whispered as Jon took a step towards the sofa.

"Yeah, I think you're right." Jon squatted down and looked at my face. I was grateful the dim light of the lamp wasn't enough to illuminate the room, hopefully he wouldn't see my flushed face or be able to see my rapid breathing. The pulse in my neck jumped at a wild pace. I took a deep breath and sighed. My lungs had been screaming for air. I stretched dramatically and blinked at the closeness of Jon's face.

"Are you better?" Jon brushed my arm with a flat hard palm. The connection made me shiver. I knew I was in danger, I needed to play this as cool as possible. I took another deep breath, and pushed myself up on one elbow.

"I am better." I stated with amiability. I gave Jon a shy smile, and took his offered hand to help me up off the couch. "Let's go join everybody else."

Chapter 43

Crystal was toast. I shook my head at her overly exaggerated attempts at dancing, and her normally quiet voice rising above the beat of the music. Chris was laughing and smiling at her antics and thoroughly enjoying her present state. He kept pulling her into his side, and groping her. I stood in the living room, still forcing myself to remain calm while my insides were a quivering mass of nerves.

"I think they've had a little too much fun here." Dylan's voice slid into my ear like silk. I smiled, tipped my tonic water bottle back to my lips and kept my eyes focused on Crystal and Chris.

"I think so too, and those two are my ride." I tipped my bottle towards the two overly intoxicated people writhing in the middle of the living room. I laughed out loud, as Chris did his best to keep Crystal in an upright position, after he dipped her backwards for a kiss. The two were sloppy and clumsy. Dylan watched with humor in his eyes, and glanced at me sideways.

"You might need another ride." He said, his amusement at their dance floor antics barely contained.

"Yep, probably. I think Jon should take their keys now, and send them upstairs before they end up with permanent injuries." I sipped my bottle again and smiled as the two started a horribly mismatched dirty dance, their beers sloshing out of the tops of their bottles.

"I'll make sure you get home." Dylan cocked his head to the side waiting for me to give him the answer he longed to hear. I dropped my eyes and sighed. I would need a ride, but I worried about him pushing me, and the inevitable pain I would feel. I pulled up short, and took a deep breath to fortify myself.

"That will be great. Thanks Dylan."
He took off to find Jon and put an end to the floor show being put on by my two friends. When they returned the couple was not quite ready to give up. The two men ended up dancing with Chris and Crystal, singing at the top of their lungs and laughing. They finally wrestled the car keys away from Chris and convinced him a night in Jon's spare room was the only way to get his keys back in the morning. My heart softened at the lengths the men went too to keep each other safe.

"That was so sweet." I said to both men as they returned from depositing their friends in a bedroom. I absently touched the discs I had stashed, refusing to show any anxiety or nervousness. My insides were a mess, but I refused to let anything show. Knowing if I had pushed to go home earlier, I would have raised suspicion, I stayed for just enough time to indicate I was comfortable around Jon. I yawned.

"This has been a busy day for you." Dylan tipped his water to his lips and took a long slurp. I smiled, he was obviously tired after his game and the party.

"Yes it has, but I've had so much fun." I intentionally stepped into Jon's chest. "Thank You." I slipped my right arm around his waist, and gave him a quick hug. His hand slid down my back and I tensed, an instinctive reaction to his touch. But the fear of him finding the discs was foremost in my mind. My breath kicked up a hitch and I forced myself to sigh in an attempt to show contentment and not nervousness. "I had a great time, thank you again for inviting me." I gave him one last squeeze and let go.

"I'm ready." I smiled so sweetly at Dylan, I saw his heart melt. He handed his water to Jon, clapped him on the back, and shook his hand in one movement.

"I'll see you on Saturday, Jon. Have a good night." The two separated, and Dylan placed his hand in the small of my back to lead me out to his car. A tingle ran down my spine, my body responded immediately to his touch. A small gasp escaped my lips, and Dylan's head snapped in my direction, absorbing my reaction. He wasted no time in ushering me to his car. My nerves played havoc on my brain. I was almost home free. I absently touched the discs again. I was being lowered into the car when Jon came running out to the curb. I went into full panic mode. I pushed Dylan out of the way, slammed my door, and locked it. I was breathing heavy and shaking. Fear registered on my face. Dylan's shocked face looked at me through the glass window. 'Let's go.' I mouthed. He laid his arm lazily over the door frame covering the window with his body and turned to meet Jon's eyes. I was hyperventilating, and holding my stomach to keep from getting physically ill in Dylan's car. I stared straight ahead not meeting Jon's eyes as he talked to Dylan outside the car. *Please, please, please get in.* I pleaded in my head. The two men talked for just a few seconds, and Dylan shook Jon's hand again. I jumped when Jon rapped his knuckles on the window and waved to me. I couldn't even fake a smile. I was past the point where I could have even looked out the window, I was shaking so badly. My heart kicked in my chest thundering on my breastbone. It felt like I was getting trampled by a herd of horses. I gasped for air. The lack of oxygen had my ears ringing. Dylan started around the front of the car keeping his eyes locked on my face as he slipped to the driver's door.

"What the hell was that about? Are you okay? You look physically ill!" Dylan's eyes were wide, searching my face for an answer. I couldn't slow my breathing, the panic was overwhelming. I shook like a leaf in a fall wind storm.

"I…I…have to tell you something." I stuttered and stammered, clutching my chest with an open palm, comforting myself with the small circle I rubbed. My brow was covered with a sheen of sweat. I wiped it with my forearm gathering every ounce of courage I could. I swallowed repeatedly, trying to clear the lump of bile sitting in my throat. I blew out a stale breath of air and took a deep one, hoping to steel myself against the pain I was about to dispense.

"I wasn't hit by a truck." I exhaled hoping I had made my point, my mind raced as I thought he'd understand.

"What do you mean? I was there. I watched it. It was the worse fucking night of my life!" His eyes dropped and a frown creased his forehead. He swallowed past the lump in his own throat, and sighed. He dropped his head to his backs of his hands as he held the steering wheel. My thoughts were jumbled, racing inside my head. Ping-ponging between happiness and straight terror. *Worse night of his life?* Had that night replaced the worse in his life when compared to the loss of his wife and baby?

"It's not what happened first."

"What do you mean, 'it didn't happen first'?" His voice was escalating. Fear pinched his voice into a squeak at the end of his sentence. He lifted his head off his hands, and twisted his hands on the wheel.

"Jon was there the night I ran into traffic." There I'd said it, it should make sense now, and I looked across the seat. Dylan's eyes were wide, searching for understanding.

"Stacia, *I* was there. No one else. I came for you after the game. Wes had gone to the stadium and he said you went to the visitors' locker room. Do you remember going there?

"I followed Jon." Fear was taking over my emotions again, tears started streaming down my face.

"Jon wasn't there honey, it was *me*. I took longer on the bus, and you were coming to *me*…"

"I followed Jon into the visitor's locker room. He met a man there. Jon said they'd lost five thousand dollars of product. I took pictures. When he caught me, he beat the shit out of me. He was going to hurt you Dylan, I was scared." I was consumed with sobs.

Dylan took a deep breath beside me. His eyes widened, and a furrow started on his forehead and continued down his face until his eyes were small slits of doubt.

"Stacia, I'm not sure you're remembering all the facts the way it happened. Wes drove you home from…."

"Westerville." I interjected.

"Yes, and you weren't feeling well because…."

"I had a stomach surgery." I added. I stared at him, no amount of reason crossing his features.

"Yes, and when you got back to the stadium…."

"I took my camera and followed Jon."

"But, he wasn't there!"

"Yes he was, Dylan!" My voice hitched an octave.

"Stacia, he was on the bus with me."

"He was there, I know he was! I followed him."

"I think you've put a lot of old memories together and are trying to make sense out of things people have told you. Honey, none of that make sense." He sat back hard against his seat and partially turned to face me in his seat. The look on his face was one of pity.

"He hurt Amy!" I yelled. I wasn't sure now myself if I had really lost my mind or not. My breath hitched in my chest, and tears careened down my face. Sobs and gasps ratcheted from my chest. Dylan was in denial. I was desperately trying to make him understand. Dylan was silent. He tried to make sense of my outburst. When he looked at me, anger careened across his face.

"Now that's just fucking crazy!" Dylan smashed the keys into the cars' ignition, slapping his hands loudly onto the steering wheel. He slammed the car into reverse and flew out of Jon's driveway. My head jerked forward almost touching the dashboard.

"Dylan!" I screamed. He was pissed, shaking with anger as he tore down the small side street at twice the speed limit. I grabbed the door handle and tried to protect my wounded left arm. My eyes were wide in fear.

"Stop, Dylan, stop! You're right, I don't know what happened. I was just telling you what I *thought* I remembered. Please stop, you're scaring me!" I was screaming. Terrified, I gripped the console and tried to calm him.

"You're right. What I *think* I remember, just can't be true."

"Yeah, you're remembering wrong! There's no way in hell Jon would *ever* hurt Amy. He loved her! He would never do anything to hurt her. You're wrong!" His fury fueled him. He drove faster down the main drag of the street, his chest heaving with anger. He slowed for a corner, and I took the opportunity to open the door. He slammed on the brakes as my feet hit pavement, sending me flying into the door jamb.

"Fuck! Dylan!" I struggled to right myself, and get out of the car. I wheeled on Dylan. "Are you crazy? Fucking go home!" I screamed. "I was wrong! I really don't remember anything! I was trying to make it make sense!" I stood by the open car door, screaming at the top of my lungs, "I'm sorry, I can't be sure what's real, and what's not. You're right, I guess, he'd never hurt anyone!" I was pissed, sarcasm dripped off my tongue. I stood on the sidewalk as he tore off. His demons haunting his vehicle, attacking him. All because of me.

I watched his car as he sped towards the stop sign, praying he'd make it home safely. Suddenly he veered and turned left, back into the sub development. He was headed back to Jon's house. A ribbon of fear raced down my spine. I needed to leave.

It was late, not a single vehicle drove down the desolate road. My cell phone and purse were at home. I patted the discs hidden in my pockets and knew what I needed to do. I walked the abandoned back streets of our little town, painstakingly making my way to my apartment. I had two things to collect, and then I would need to disappear. I was doing the one thing sure to devastate Dylan. I would use my pictures to hurt someone on the team, and it was going to be him.

Chapter 44

"I quit." I stood in front of Mike, I threw the discs and my computer down on his desk, spun on my heels and headed for the door. Mike launched from his chair, and barely missed grabbing me by my arm.

"Whoa, whoa. What's this all about? You can't quit on me!"

"Mike, I can't do this anymore." I sighed. "Take my computer, look at the discs, do with it what you want. I'm out of here. I will call you when I get settled."

"Settled where? What are you doing? Running? From what? I didn't take you for a quitter!"

Tears burned behind my eyes, my head buzzed with them, threatening to spill down my face.

"You were right. He's gone. I can't stay here. Look at the stuff in my files, you do with it what you want. I am going to leave town for a couple of days, I just need a vacation." I turned to leave, the pit bull stunned into silence.

I was lying, I was leaving, maybe for good. Too scared of the fallout I was creating by giving all my stuff to Mike. I was afraid of the pain my pictures were going to cause Dylan. I never reviewed the discs or computer. I knew I couldn't bear it.

No ties. I left everything in my apartment, my clothes, my phone, my pictures, everything. I took just essentials, my car keys, clothes I could get in my back seat, and I left a note for the landlord. Thank God my bills were paid, and I had pocket money. I drove south, running from life. Scared it would catch me, scared I had ruined Dylan's. Scared for the peanut.

The news article appeared in the paper three weeks after I left town, complete with pictures. I only knew because, I checked in at an internet café in South Carolina. I changed hotels frequently, and applied for a job at another small town newspaper as a freelance photographer. I refused to give specifics of my last job, and used Riley as my first name. Using Dylan's last name reminded me daily of who I had hurt. A camera was all I needed to be able to submit local event pictures, and I picked up one at a pawn shop outside of town. One month later, I found myself at a high school football game. I snapped pictures of dirt, shoes and mid-air catches and spectacular tackles. I submitted them to the paper. They ran the next day. I collected my check the following Friday. The receptionist had a slip of yellow telephone message paper attached to the envelope. It said simply.

'Call me. Mike'
I took the note, and thanked the receptionist, knowing I wouldn't call.
The next week, I submitted pictures of a local farmer's market. Another yellow slip waited for me.

'Come home. Mike'
A week later, I submitted more football pictures and covered a high school soccer game. Another yellow piece of paper waited for me.

'Now, or I'm coming there. Mike' I asked the receptionist when the last message had been delivered. I wasn't afraid of the pit bull, I just didn't want to know what I had done to Dylan.

"The day before yesterday, I think, Riley. He gets kind of gruff on the phone. Insisting he needs to talk to you."

"He doesn't need to talk to me. Don't tell him how to find m…" The door to the building closed with a bang.

"You weren't hard to find." Mike's ruff voice drew me up short. My eyes widened. I stared at the receptionist my eyes begging for her help.

"I just viewed the newspaper's pictures, and I knew." His voice immediately softened. "It's time you came home, sweetheart."

"I can't Mike, I hurt Dylan and I ruined Jon's life." The tears sprung to my eyes.

"Jon's gonna get what he deserves. There are a couple pictures on your disc of him beating you in the locker room. You looked terrified, your face was smashed into a table top. Bleeding. Killed me to look at that." He dropped his eyes and shook his head, obviously deeply affected by what he saw. "When I found it, I turned everything over to the police. They're working on a case, but Jon's been arrested for intent to sell drugs. There were pictures of his selling drugs at a motel on there too. Now you need to file a report for the physical abuse. The candid pictures from your computer showed Jon with some low level drug dealers in town. The police are using those to get to the suppliers. If you wanted a big story, you got it. It's just too bad your name's not on it."

"What about Dylan?" I was afraid to ask, but I needed to know. I was sure he would never speak to me again. I had done the one thing he asked me not to do. I had ruined his friendships and his world with my pictures.

"I haven't given him a thing. He's upset, who wouldn't be? He knows what Jon did, and also knows what happened in the past. The night he left you on the side of the road, Dylan confronted Jon about your allegation that he was involved with his wife's death. Jon denied it all until your pictures showed up at the police station. Dylan was asked to go in to the police department because there were so many pictures of him on the discs. He's seen the evidence on your computer and camera; the police showed it to him. I think he's put together the pieces, and the story it shows isn't pretty. You know it'd be hard to

226

find out your best friend was really some dick who beat your girlfriend, and hid the fact he sold drugs that helped kill your wife. He asks about you, I think he even looked, but I didn't even know where you were until I saw your pictures in this local paper. But he's gone home for Thanksgiving and will be leaving for baseball camp in Florida soon. I think he'd like to talk to you, but I won't let that happen if you don't want it. But, it's time to come home."

"I can't Mike, I left a note with the landlord to get rid of everything, and rent out my apartment. I have nothing to go 'home' to." I dropped my eyes. Mike sighed, and reached out to pat my shoulder.

"You're apartment is there. I must have called that landlord every day until I found you. I paid your rent, hoping you'd come home. I've also got a job transfer for you. Upstairs to the sound room, if you want it.
But, it's time to stop running. Come home."

"So, Dylan's gone." A statement I knew. The truth churned and tightened in my gut. It roiled my stomach, and blurred my eyes. He was gone, just like Mike had predicted. What was left of my heart burned wildly in my chest, and was finally smothered by my falling tears.

Chapter 45

It was good to be back at the station. My new office was a sound room on the second floor of the TV station. Glass windows, and in full view of the hall, and stairs. The holiday's had come and gone and January was fast approaching. I thought back through the past couple of months. The changes in my body, my life, my circle of friends all felt new and intriguing, but it did nothing to fill the emptiness left when Dylan returned to baseball, or the pain I felt when I thought of how I had used a camera to ruin his life. Dylan hadn't even tried to contact me. It wouldn't have mattered anyway, I had nothing to say that would fix the hurt, and there wasn't enough glue to fix my heart.

The commotion in the hall caught my attention and I raised my eyes off my computer screen. Dread filled me. My glassed-in office afforded me no privacy. My office door flew open wide and Dylan stepped in rapidly. Deliberately he squared his shoulders, his curly, mid collar length hair flowing and tousled. The sunlight lit up his auburn highlights in his medium brown colored hair. His appearance was commanding. His stare bore holes into my head. I could see his biceps twitch under his linen shirt. His short-sleeved button down was rolled over the bulging biceps. I remember why now; his shirts were too tight on his upper arms, he had the potential to rip the seams if he didn't roll them up. His muscular chest heaved under his shirt. His waistline was trim and I knew that under that button down shirt sat a washboard abdomen. He narrowed his piercing blue eyes. He was obviously trying to regain his composure, or he'd just run a marathon.

Although I knew why he was really here.

I stood up, instinctively guarding my territory, and crossed my arms across my waist protectively. Trying to give the illusion, I was in control. I walked to the front of my desk to stop his pursuit. I lifted my head and looked him squarely in the eyes, leaned back on the desk front and tried my best to look confident and unruffled.

Ashley stepped in right behind Dylan stumbling and stammering.

"I tried, Stacia, he made it past security and up the back stairs before we could stop him. Security's on their way."

As calmly as I could, I said, "Thank You Ashley, security won't be necessary." I waved my hand dismissively. She stood stoically in the doorway, her protective nature was endearing.

"I'll be fine, just make sure security knows to stop running so no one needs CPR." I feigned a smile, my feeble attempt at humor failing miserably. The crack in my voice gave away my rising fear and panic. Ashley's eyes never left mine, as she slowly backed out and closed the door. The click resonated across the room and hit me in my core. I sucked in a huge breath, and tried to hold it. I was shaking. I needed to regain my control.

I could see security personnel flying out of the stairwell door. The look on their faces was like watching a Laurel and Hardy comedy. Eyes darting wildly, heads turning in all directions. Somehow, I knew they never would have stopped him if he made it past them. I just had not figured his visit would happen so soon after the article appeared in the paper. I could feel my heartbeat in my ears. My face was hot and flushed. My breathing was heavy and rapid; I was prepared for a fight.

"Why didn't you tell me? I would never have let you drive me off if I had known."

He seethed. His voice hissed through his teeth.

"You didn't want to know!" I retorted, "You believed him, I get that, he was your best friend. You made your choices, mine were made for me."

Adrenaline surged through my veins. I couldn't peel my eyes off him. My heart beat furiously against my chest and could be seen through my silk shirt. My breathing came in small shallow bursts. And I strained to swallow the lump in my throat.

"I never meant to hurt you." he slowly spit from his mouth. A small muscle on his jaw jumped sideways. His eyes narrowed, and he looked at me through small slits. His anger was visceral and the tension in the air felt as heavy and wet as a London fog.

I gasped for air, my breaths never quite deep enough to keep me from getting dizzy and lightheaded. I stood in front of my desk beginning to feel woozy. I grabbed at the edge of my desk, and looked for better footing before my knees buckled underneath me. My fear glued me in place. I had never seen Dylan this mad before. I had seen a rainbow of personalities, but this type of anger and hurt was deep. It cut me to my core.

Dan and Gary from security waited right outside my glass enclosure shooting pensive looks through the windows. Pacing, waiting for the clue they needed to break down the door and forcibly remove Dylan from my office. Dan held his radio in one hand and a cell phone in the other. Gary's eyes never left me. He watched my every move. The waiting game had begun.

Dylan's chest rose and fell rapidly.

"You lied to me!" His shouting brought frightened faces to my glassed enclosure. "Tell me something, how did you think

this was going to end? Did you think I'd just walk away? Did you think work was my only goal? Did you need to tear me apart in the process? When did you remember? Because it would kill me to know that you never forgot." A defeated look ran across his face and his eyes looked watery, some of the anger was dissipating but was still a present undercurrent. "Stacia, honey, I never thought I'd fall head over heels, crazy in love with you. Please. I will love you until I take my last breath, until the day God takes me off this earth. I will *never* leave you. *Please*, talk to me; tell me you feel the same. Tell me you love me."

I tried to take a deep breath. My knuckles were blanched white and throbbing under my grasp. I tried to regain my composure.

"No, Dylan, I can't." My response croaked from my throat, my eyes filled with tears, but I refused to let them slide down my face. I shook from my unshed tears. I squared my shoulders, looked through my window, and nodded to Gary. My door opened. Dylan left willingly, but he didn't stop staring at me. Begging me to reconsider with his eyes. The door closed and when the lock clicked; I jumped, feeling I had made the biggest mistake of my life. I never forgot, I will always remember.

"Wait!" I screamed as I lunged for the door, flinging it open in a wide arch. It banged against the frame, making the windows shake and the artificial Christmas tree outside the door rattle in its stand. Dan and Gary were guiding Dylan towards the exit. Dylan's head hung down, his shoulders rolled forward. He dug his heels in and twisted away from our fearless security force. He faced me, his eyes begging me to explain. I took the deepest breath I could, still feeling lightheaded.

"I never planned to hurt you. I was wrong to even take those pictures in the first place. But, I used the pictures I took to expose the truth." I looked at Dylan willing him to understand. He looked away, and took a deep breath. "Dylan, please." I wanted to reach out and cup his face, and force him to look at me. "Jon was selling drugs, and he sold them to kids, to people who hurt themselves, people who hurt other people. To the driver who killed Amy, and that was six years ago. So he's been doing this for a long time. How many other people has he hurt?" I sigh and step up close to his chest. His sweat, and pure male smell invade my nose and I automatically take a deep breath, and close my eyes. "I am only worried about one of those people he hurt. You. He destroyed your whole life, and now with what I've done, I'm destroying it again. I'm sorry. I know I've said it a lot in the past, but I really mean it. I just wanted you…all those times we were together, I just wanted you."

"Wait. What? …in the *past*? Oh my God." Dylan's face paled, he rubbed his hand through his hair, then down his face trying to absorb the idea banging around in his head.

"You never forgot." His eyes met mine and anger flashed across his beautiful face again.

"YOU NEVER FORGOT?" he screamed. Gary stepped between us, put his hands on Dylan's chest and shot me a look to 'back up'. I did. This was not going to end easily or quietly. My hands crossed my stomach again and my shirt pulled tightly, my 'peanut' bump became very visible. Dylan's eyes glued themselves to my stomach as I quickly smoothed my shirt down letting it hang free to try and hide my belly.

"What's…what is…when did….? Oh my God!" He pressed out breathlessly. He was so pale he started to shake again, this time I didn't think anger was his motivation.

"Get him a chair Dan!" I yelled as I watched all the color drain from him. His breaths became so shallow he looked close to passing out. I leapt forward and grabbed his arm guiding him into Ashley's chair. He threw his head forward into his hands. I kneeled in front of him caressing his arms, feeling the glistening sweat cooling his skin. Enjoying the familiar feel of his muscles. Unknowingly, a small moan escaped my lips, and my thighs tingled as I remembered all our interludes. He dropped his hands between his knees, recovering just enough not to need to hold his head up. He cocked his head, squinted one eye, looking into my face.

"Were you going to tell me?" The look on his face was pained and devastated.
I just stared at him without answering him. Tears tickled my eyes, and I bit my lip.

"I can't hurt you anymore." The pain in his face is overwhelming. I just can't bear it. My heart can't stand it. "No, I didn't plan on telling you. You didn't ask for this. I'll deal with it, I'm fine, really." I began building the wall around what was left of my heart.

"Jesus…I didn't know." Tears rimmed his eyes. He threw his head back taking a deep breath, then blew it out through his pursed lips. He closed his eyes. I wanted to crawl up into his lap, and take away all his pain. He didn't look back at me, he was struggling to gain his sanity; to get some control of this situation.

"I'm sorry…I really am. But, we'll be fine. Goodbye Dylan." Watching him is too hard. I turn and start back into my office. Dan and Gary help Dylan out of the chair and lead him to the elevator. I don't look back, the tears I have barely contained roll down my face, splashing on the desk like raindrops in the middle of a hurricane. I am shattered as I sink into my chair, unconsciously rubbing my small belly bump. I put my head on my desk and bawl, not caring who was watching through my glass cage.

~~*~~

It takes me three weeks to pull myself together enough to actually work a full day at work without crying or getting physically ill. Mike starts to get worried, he called the doctor and went in to speak to him by himself. I refuse to go to any additional appointments, since I am now seeing the doctor every two weeks. It's what you do in your last two months of pregnancy. I should be excited, I should be preparing to bring a baby home. And all I can do, is think about was Dylan. What I took from him, that he'd never see his baby, how I had ruined him.

Chris and Crystal call or visit daily. Chris told me the story of the night Dylan left me at the side of the road. He returned to Jon's house after most of the team had left, and Chris and Crystal were safely tucked into the extra bedroom. Brian had ended up sleeping on a vacant couch. Others were still loitering around the pool. Dylan burst into the house while Jon was cleaning up the kitchen and emptying half-finished bottles of beer. Brian says Dylan's yelling could have raised the dead. Brian said Dylan was furious when he confronted Jon. A fight ensued, where Dylan threw the first punch. Jon used the only weapon he had and hit Dylan with a bottle. It broke, but the shards fell helplessly to the floor. Brian jumped over the back of the couch at the sound, and Rob flew in from the pool area. The two friends threw punches and wrestled on the floor until

Dylan had Jon pinned to the linoleum. He pounded Jon until they were pulled apart by the remaining team members.

I wasn't proud of myself. If I had never said anything, the team would still be supporting each other and not crumbing before my eyes. Chris tells me they don't blame me, but I can't help feeling I caused the collapse of this talented group of men. If I just hadn't given Mike my pictures and computer, this would never have come to light. I feel so guilty, I wanted Dylan to give up his whole life for me and ended up ruining it. I tried to take the one thing that gave him peace, his baseball career.

Crystal tells me Dylan asks about me and the baby frequently, and that I need to call him. Whenever he calls directly, I let it ring to voicemail. He never leaves a message, but occasionally I can hear him sigh or wait to see if I pick up. I just can't hurt him anymore. I have never recovered from the pained look I saw on his face the last day in my office. I had messed up relationships my whole life, this one was no different.

Chapter 46

"Come on, let us take you out for lunch." Crystal crooned to me as I wasted another day lying on the couch.

"No, I don't want to go anywhere. I'm so fat." My belly has swollen and the baby rolls around inside like an alien. As if conjured, my stomach rolls and a flutter tickles me across my belly button. Crystal leans over and puts her hand on the lump that forms to the left of my naval. She playfully pushes it and the baby rolls again to make an appearance on the other side. She keeps her hand on my belly and the baby kicks at her intrusion. She leans over, her mouth close to her hand.

"Come on peanut, let's go get a bite to eat." she whispers. My belly jerks and rolls under her hand. Crystal breaks into a huge smile. "I think she wants lunch!!"

"She? What if it's a he?" I smile and crook my neck to look into her face.

"I want a girl! Bows, ribbons, dresses, and *priss*. Someone to keep us grounded, and give us an edge over these men."

"She probably won't like baseball you know." I laugh at my friend's logic. We have just spent three hours converting my office into a nursery. Chris is cursing at the crib, and Mike is cursing at Chris. Dale and Rob are almost done working on the dresser. Pieces of it were spread all over the living room floor, and the two tall men were crawling around looking for lettered parts for hours. Emily had asked a hundred times if the curtain was straight, and folded all the baby clothes we had washed earlier. I had good friends. No. I had great friends. It was still sad that I was missing the one person I really wanted here. Dylan.

"We're heading out to Hitter's." Rob announced. He looked defeated, the dresser wasn't easy to assemble, and the guys look like they need more than one beer to ease their pain.

"Come with us." Chris' tone is almost begging.

"We'll set you up and you can take it easy." Dale's palms rested heavily on his hips.

"Come on baby girl." Mike smiles. He likes this. He likes that I am fat, slow and pretty much miserable. He smiles under his beard and I can tell he is getting tired of fighting with the crib, and Chris needs a break from the pit bull.

"I think we can finish this later." I struggle to sit up, bouncing like a beach ball on the waves of a choppy lake. "Crap!" The room erupts in laughter. I still guard my left arm, and I have never regained its full use. My hair has grown to a respectable length, and I keep it trimmed in a longer bob cut. I have long healed physically from my ordeal, and am slowly getting my heart back into check. I think about Dylan daily, and often wonder how he is faring in Florida. Oh, the team keeps me updated. The Astros have called him, and he is moving back to the major league. His dreams were being realized. Chris said he has started classes again on line, and plans to finish his degree in criminal law, and then pursue a law degree. I am proud of him. He is on track, he is going to make it, even if it is without me. Without us.

"Lunch sounds good. We're outta here." I grab onto Dale and Chris' hands and stand up, rubbing my hand protectively down my belly. The apartment erupts in a flurry of activity. Every man heads towards the door, all rushing for their well-earned beers. The girls grab purses and sweaters and followed them. I stand for a few minutes in the quiet room taking in the chaos, and boxes spread on the floor. I miss him, I really miss him. A sad tear pricks the corner of my eye. I take a deep breath to keep it there. These people can't watch me cry again. I am spending time gathering my crumbled heart and these friends are my salvation. The door squeaks as it opened.

"Hey, sweetheart, everybody's waiting."

"I'm on my way, Mike, just getting my keys." I slip my license into my pocket, laughing at my inability to get it to slide in easily over my expanding butt. I turn and follow him down the steps. Cars and trucks are filled with all the people who had just filled my small apartment.

Laughter and shouts of glee float on the breeze. I am loved, and this baby is loved. As long as they are here, I am going to be all right. I will find all the pieces of my heart. And I guess the way to start collecting them is to go back to where I started.

"Hey Mike?" I look at him, lifting my chin in defiance, and take a shaky breath, blowing it out through my nose.

"Yeah, darling?"

I take another deep breath, cock my head, gather all my nerve and ask, "Can I get a camera back?" A huge smile creases his face and he runs his hand down his face and tugs on his beard.

"Think you're ready for it?" His eyes furrow a little while holding a sparkle that he knew I wanted to see.

"Yeah, I need it, it's the one place I want to be, what I need to do to move on." And I will, I will find the pieces of my heart all over town, and put them back together.

Epilogue

Laboring for seventeen hours has not been fun. I make Mike stay out in the waiting room. He is just too doting, and concerned. But he keeps coming in and checking on progress, always pressing his hand into mine, or giving a chaste kiss to my sweaty forehead. Women have done this for millions of years, and this birth will be no different. Nothing special. Crystal has been a wonderful labor coach, although I am pretty sure that by the time she watches this scenario unfold, she may never have kids of her own. I am exhausted, and pretty sure I have not been the kindest person to everybody who comes into my room. In fact, if the truth be known, I haven't been nice to anyone since Dylan left for spring camp in January.

"Well, it looks like this little gal isn't planning on making her debut anytime too soon." The doctor pats my leg and at this point I don't care if I cover up my naked ass or not. "You're only dilated to five centimeters and only fifty percent effaced. This could take several hours yet."

"Great!" My sarcasm is dripping off my tongue. I haven't slept since I woke up twenty nine hours ago and my labor started after dinner at Chris and Crystal's house. I just thank God my water waited to break in their driveway.

Another contraction starts and I take to concentrating on the spot on the wall behind the doctors head.

"I know you don't want this, but I'm thinking we may have to use the Pitocin to get things moving. When you get too tired you're ineffective and...."

"No." I state as a way to cut him off.

"With the rough start...."

"You keep saying that, but 'No'."

"Do you want to think about that epidural so...?"

239

"No."

"Pain medication would at least.... "

"No." I glare at the doctor, and give him a look of total disgust. It's a standoff, we stare at each other. The doctor's arms cross over his chest. He sighs in resignation, shakes his head, and heads towards the door.

Alone for a minute, I close my eyes and rub my belly. I don't want to do anything else to hurt this baby, including more medication. Mike thinks I am using the pain as a form of self-punishment. And maybe after all the pain I have caused Dylan, I *am* using this to punish myself. I do deserve it in a perverse way.

Mike sneaks back into the room. I think Crystal's had enough. I stare at him as I ride the crest of another contraction, and exhale loudly, blowing off enough air to send birthday candles flying off a cake. He looks at me with a look of disdain tinged with concern and fear.

"What? Mike." I glare at him, pissed he's taking sides with the doctor.

"I just think that…"

"Out Mike!"

"Sweetheart, you're getting tired, and this isn't good for either one of you."

"Mike shut up or get ...Ahhh!" Another contraction starts. The tightening starts above my belly button and pulls across both hips. I take a deep breath and look back to the spot on the wall to concentrate. I inhale and exhale through the crest and concentrate as the contraction starts to loosen, the pressure below is tolerable, but just barely. Mike gets a concerned look on his face as I ride the contraction to the end. I close my eyes for just a second. I am tired, but women have been doing this for millions of years. Right?

A nurse enters my room and takes my blood pressure. It's higher than it was before, and my pulse is racing. She adjusts the monitors and runs a paper strip to see the effectiveness of my contractions, and the baby's heartbeat.

"It looks like he's getting tired too. His heart rate is lower than before, but I am sure it's a temporary thing. We'll let the doctor know." She takes off with the little slip of paper, and exits my room quickly. I think to myself, she has no idea I think this baby is a girl, and how disappointed Crystal will be if it is a boy.

Another contraction starts right after she leaves the room. I take my deep breath, and look back to my concentration spot on the wall. My mind drifts. A small smile tips the corners of my mouth as I think of exactly how I ended up here. I think of the night I seduced Dylan, and his eight buttons, and the hotel, and our last encounter that ended our civility. A tear forms in my eye and it makes a slow decent down my face. Mike sighs, reaches over, squeezes my hand, and uses his thumb to wipe away the tear.

"I'm fine Mike, really. You can go back out."

"Not gonna happen sweetheart. But I've about had enough of your martyrdom. You need to take that medicine the doctor's talking about and get that baby born."

"Out, Mike!!" I yell at him as another contraction starts to build. The tightening starts around my belly button, and pulls straight down to my vagina. Hard.

"Ow. Ow. Damn it Michael, I…" I struggle to regain the metered control I had earlier. I'm breathing heavy, blowing out breath after breath. "Something's happening now!" I look at Mike, proud of myself for sticking to my guns and not giving into the badgering I was taking from the doctor, Crystal, and Mike.

The nurse comes in seconds later.

"She says 'something's happening now'." Mike parroted my earlier comment. I shot him a look of disgust. His sarcasm wasn't wasted on me.

"Mike, do you want to leave?" I growled. The next contraction hit hard and fast. No build up, no warning. I gasped at the pain as it seared straight to my insides. I strained to gain some control over it. Without any ceremony, the nurse snapped a glove on her hand and lifted the sheet.

"Well something is happening, but it's not what you think." She pulled her hand out from under the sheet, it was full of blood. She reached over and smashed a button on the wall, I heard buzzing down the hall.

"Shit!" I mouthed. I had pushed this natural delivery thing too far.

"Stacia, we need to move now!" The room exploded with activity. Within seconds, I was being paraded down the hallway on a bed headed towards surgery. Mike was running next to the bed, barely keeping up.

Crystal's horrified face appeared at the waiting room door.

"No more choices, darling. This baby's coming now." He huffed and puffed as he ran to keep up. "I'll see you in a few minutes." Mike said as the nurse dragged him off the bed by his elbow.

A cesarean section was not what I had planned. Tears stream down my face.

~~***~~

I am numb from my waist down. A cloth screen covers my chest. This is the best I have felt in two days. My arms are strapped out to my sides, and I can't move except to wiggle my

242

fingers. The surgery door opens and someone clad in blue scrubs walks in. I can see that they are covered with a hat, facial mask, surgery scrubs and paper booties. The nurse ushers the blue man toward the head of the bed. I can only see the man's eyes. The broad shoulders pulling at the cloth. His biceps rippling under his rolled sleeves.

"Ready?" he asks.

"Where have you been?" I ask.

"Flight out of Tampa took longer than I expected after the news conference, and reviewing some crazy pregnant woman's pictures for the press conference took forever." He rolled his eyes. "You know what? That women flew down to Florida, snapped a bunch of pictures and submitted them to some major magazine and wrote a huge story for them. I had to read it and then I had to follow up with some interviews." He paused and sighed loudly. "You know, the life of a baseball star, busy, busy, busy." His teasing voice insinuate he likes my pictures and my article, and it has gotten him a lot of publicity.

"You almost missed the party." I sulk. Sparking blue eyes beam back; excitement and glee edging them.

"Well, I'm here now, so let's just see if you can badger and manipulate anyone in here. Mike and Crystal say you put on quite a performance earlier." He glances around the surgery suite, a smile shines in his eyes.

"Good grief, Dylan, I waited as long as I could. Chris called your coaches last night when this all started.

"I tried to get here, honey, as fast as I could. I just can't stay away from you, I love you. Being away at spring training is killing me. All I want is to be home with you."

I sigh. He is finally here, I don't need to wait any longer.

"Let's have our baby, Stacia. I'm not going anywhere." Dylan kisses my forehead, and slides his hands down my arms. His firm biceps resting against mine. He absently twisted the ring on my left hand. The one he placed there on my last visit to Florida. Our beach wedding was beautiful, a loose white dress, and a linen shirt with rolled sleeves. The sun, surf and our witnesses; his team. He presses his forehead into my cheek. "I love you." he whispers into my ear. He isn't leaving, and I know it.

~~~***~~~

I yawn, my eyes heavy and blurry with exhaustion.

"Go ahead. Take him out to see Mike and Wesley. They're probably having a fit by now. Crystal's already called Chris, and will soon be pushing her way back in here. Rob and Dale will call the rest of the team. And you need to call your Mom and Dad again. Sara has already called. She's coming down in a week." I yawn again, trying to blink away my fatigue.

"Oh, babe, he's beautiful. Look at all of his dark hair and I think his eyes are going to be blue. Just like mine."

Dylan coos and talks to the baby. The baby squeaks and stretches in Dylan's arms. He softly strokes the baby's hand and smoothes his hair. A small wrinkled forehead and yawn are his reward as the baby settles back into his father's arms. Dylan unwraps his blanket and rewraps him as he counts toes and fingers and inspects every square inch of him. The tiny baby in his arms squeaks again as Dylan coos to him again and tucks him up under his chin. By the time he comes back with our son, I am asleep. Blissfully exhausted and thoroughly elated. I am in love with both of my boys, and them with me. And we will be together, in all the candid shot pictures I can take. The only candid's I will ever take again.

Acknowledgments:
I have so many people to thank. First to Barb Vanderdonck at Flower Hospital, thanks for the challenge! I did it! And thank you for all the encouragement along the way, and the blank pieces of paper. If you hadn't told me I could do it, I never would have tried! To my co-workers there, I love that fact that not one of you said 'give up' even when I wanted to. Thank You.

To Beth Sikorski, Thank you for the *fantastic* cover and the time you spent with me when I had computer issues and for calming my frustrations as I worked through this book.

Gabe? What can I say? In the next book, I may have to kill you off! But you always encouraged me. Thanks.

Eric. I may have used your middle name and with as often as you've talked about it, I hope you will read it someday. Even if you do embarrass easily.

Wesley at our local restaurant. Thank you for being so positive. Your enthusiasm the night we talked meant a lot to me. And yes, I put you in the book!

To all the random people I dropped the prologue to for their review. Thank you too! If not for all of you, I never would have tried to finish this project.

To all of you who asked what was next?

Brick and Mortar 2015
An accident forces Brecken Bristow to face the possibility of losing her cattle farm. Even with her second job, she may not be able to save it. When Caiden Carter steps in, Will he help her save it, or force her to give up her dream?

Oil and Water 2015
Colton Carter had endured a horrible oil rig accident and is headed to Colorado on a forced 'vacation' when his truck blows Reagan an avid runner off the road. Can two damaged people help either heal?

Codes and Sirens 2016
Chase Carter's relationship with his girlfriend heads south and leads to their break up. Caught in the middle? Lindy's three year old son, Charlie. Can Charlie help the two adults in his life realize that their competitiveness needs to be tempered so they can be a team to raise him?